NO SELL DEA]

A Tale of Cambodia

NO SELL DEAD

A Tale of Cambodia

*

James Jennings

molecular press
geneva

ISBN 978-2-9700376-5-1

Text typesetting and inner design
by Gerry Cambridge
gerry.cambridge@btinternet.com

Set in Baskerville 10 Pro and 120 Pro

For David

Prologue

H E LANDED IN NEWARK, NEW JERSEY, almost three thousand miles from his target. He stayed there for two nights, holed up in a travellers' inn near the airport. He needed to adjust his bearings, to make his acquaintance with the cold sun on the sidewalks and the smell of the local marshlands. Something told him to stalk his man gradually, as a jackal would a beast twice its size.

When he felt less shy of the country, able to imitate the careless walk of others in the street, he boarded a bus at the Seven-Eleven stop and began the long westward journey. Pittsburgh, Cleveland, Toledo, then Chicago. From Chicago he caught a train to Minneapolis, deliberately off-route, with a two-day stop in Eau Claire just because he liked the French name. Take your time, he thought, throw dust across your tracks and let this vast geography do its work. Breathe in the mountains, the shining lakes, the scent of scalded Greyhound tyre. The land is huge and generous; it will absorb you as one of its own.

Sometimes other travellers approached him on the bus. He was visiting relatives on the West Coast, he said. That was enough. The other people were glad of a chance to talk about themselves. In Sioux Falls, a big woman from Guangzhou asked him to get off the bus with her. She had a restaurant called Great Wall and he could be an assistant stir-fryer. They could marry if he liked. She could see it was his first time in Falls because he didn't know what to do about the wind. Clench against it or bend into it or just unzip and pretend it wasn't there. And like so many of the new Asians in those days, he had half the horrors of the world written across his eyes.

In Sioux Falls he bought a pair of Zeiss high precision binoculars and a Glock 17 handgun. He packed them deep in his rucksack and journeyed on, watching the alien names roll by. Woonsocket, Pukwana, Kadoka, Belle Fourche. Other people's buildings and burnings; other people's histories. Not his. When he awoke the pneumatic brakes were puffing and wheezing in the coach station: he was in Denver. He found a motel on Powhaton Road. Sunshine was on the way said the lady on the Rise Again news. Good folks should feel the love burning in their hearts, because fine weather was just around the corner. Praise be. He tuned the dial to a news channel. After a long battle, Rock Hudson had finally been carried off by AIDS. There was an airfield somewhere nearby, with military planes coming and going. He switched off the radio. Lying on the bed, listening to the distant rumbling, he remembered the beautiful scraping noise of the fighters as they floated into the air. The Dassault Mystères, lifting off from Pochentong.

A night in the motel, then back on the road, through Colorado, through Utah, and into California. California. Excitement; the anticipation that locked his throat. And because he felt the fear rising through his calves, gripping his insides, he took a slow train to Bakersfield, and did absolutely nothing there for a day just to let the adrenalin subside. To make his peace with the country. He was a nobody, a rock in the landscape, a rook on a wire. Identify yourself as a man with a purpose, and the whole world sees it at once.

The following day he was in Long Beach. Long Beach, California. Khmer territory.

He locked his gaze on a dead-straight avenue called East Anaheim Street. Named by German settlers, the home by the Santa Ana River. He saw a few signs for *tacos* and *mariscos*, *panaderías* and *pastelerías*, little businesses owned by men and women who had been there for longer than his warring tribe ever had. But crowding out these few Hispanic enterprises, there was a string of discount stores, jewellers, hairdressers, beauty salons, medical clinics, coin-op laundries, party supply stores and seafood carry-outs, all of them adorned with names from his country, emblazoned with the script of his home. He felt immediately cramped, back in the damp New Jersey inn, freshly arrived. When he moved into the Royal Splendora Motel, a brick box with a white façade and a skinny eucalyptus at the front, the woman at the desk took one look at his eyes and spoke to him in his language.

[8]

It was going to be hard to blend into the crowd. There was no crowd to blend into. He had imagined a city, with bars and alleyways and high-rises, something like Bangkok but richer and cleaner. But this was not an Asian city. Not one bit. This was a district from nowhere, row upon row of plaster-coated cubes, a street that never curved to left or right, simply stretching into more suburbia. Occasionally there were people on the sidewalk, and some of them were speaking the language. Most stayed in their cars. Behind the Anaheim commercial strip there were perpendicular residential lanes, each plotted with little houses and patches of lawn, the lanes themselves dissected by more lanes.

One day the woman in the motel asked him if he was looking for work. Because if he was there was a wedding consultancy in Gladiola Avenue. They wanted a driver. No, he said, immediately timid. He was just visiting relatives. Where do they live? Central, he said, central downtown LA. She gave him a searching smile. The day after, he got her to put a call through to the wedding firm. And of course the place was called Chenda Matrimonial Services, so there would be no cultural acclimatization needed there. The job was to drive large fluffy wedding dresses to local clients who wanted to try on something for the big day. And then bring it back, and take it back again when it was adjusted. The clients were all from his country too, except for a few Mexicans dotted around who wanted pink gowns for their teenager's *quinceañera*. The driving job was good. He could scope the entire township; see who lived where and who was shit rich and who was dirt poor, and all this through the windscreen of a company Ford van. Some of the families were finding it hard, if the scabbed window frames and messy back yards were anything to go by, but others were doing just fine, spacious mansions with white clapperboard frontages and porticoes like downsized Louisiana mansions. A few of these people had done very nicely for themselves. And when he turned the van down Ernestine Drive and stopped opposite number 7625, he saw that his target had done as well as the best of them. Better, even.

Someone approached his van from the sloping lawn of the mansion. His car had Gladiola Avenue written on it — was he heading

[9]

for the centre by any chance? And this person asked his favour in the national language, in Khmer, as if it was the most natural thing in the world. He was the odd-job boy, he told him, who came to trim the grass and water the camellia trees and rake over the mulch. He was dark-skinned, this fifty year-old mulch-boy, and by the sound of it he was from Takeo. They drove down. The man told him a few things and when he dropped him off in East Anaheim Avenue, he offered him another ride for the following day. No worries, there was a delivery to do two streets away. No trouble at all. And after they had started to feel at ease with each other, he began to find out more.

One day he took a hired car with shaded windscreens. He drove up to Ernestine, parked at a safe distance and deployed his binoculars, watching Nary, the wife and the children as they came and went. He logged their habits and schedules. In the following week, when the house was empty, he broke into the carport. That was when he saw that the Glock would not be necessary. Nary had something else that would do just fine.

It was not hard to complete the picture. The woman behind the desk in the Royal Splendora knew everything about everybody. As the Khmers always do. Yes, Nary. The man on Ernestine Drive. He had a successful dealership: Japanese luxury cars. His wife was also Khmer; there were two daughters and one son. He was well known in the émigré community; a popular figure at the community hall, glad to pay for the singers who came to croon the old village songs. But a man you didn't want to cross. Yes, like everybody else, a dark past, but what do you expect? Everybody has a past. Why are we all here if we don't have a past? In the motel bar he heard two men who were talking about Nary. His other commercial interest. Porn. He had shares in a production company. Nary obviously knew the entire Cambodian community, including the ones who were short of money, and he liked to set up job interviews for some of the teenagers. Which is what an émigré community godfather might be expected to do, help the newcomers get into their stride, lend a helping hand to the families still wet with the milk of the motherland. When they got to the studios, these girls thought they were auditioning to become starlets. Which you could say they were, but they hadn't been warned about what they had to do to pass.

"Apparently your boss has a thing for the skin flicks?" he commented.

"In the old days, it was the real thing" chuckled the mulch-raker. "You didn't need a video screen back in 77." He said Nary watched movies on the VCR player in his car. When he killed the engine in the carport, he would always spend a quiet moment on his own before coming out. Sometimes he would call his son into the garage to show him how it went. You know. Educate him in the ways of life.

The man chose his day. Over on the other side of town, he found a hunting supplier and bought two 120-gram ballistic tip rounds. He went to a pharmacy and bought a pair of elbow-length latex gloves.

*

One evening he drives up the lane, following the big man's car at a respectful distance. He watches as the car mounts the slope and a light goes on in the carport. He parks the Ford fifty yards from the house and pulls on the gloves. He waits for three minutes, steps smartly from the vehicle, walks up the slope. The tilting carport door is half open. He slips in behind the big SUV. It is a warm evening and the driver's window is rolled down. Nary is there, unbuttoned, his groin an inflatable toy beginning to rise, while the bodies of big Caucasian men and little Cambodian women pump and jerk on the video screen. When he sees the intruder Nary is quick to react: he stretches fast for the glove compartment. Before he can extract whatever he has in there, the man punches a tidy hole through his hand with the Glock. Nary is shocked motionless, and begins to dribble. On the screen the copulating bodies continue their work.

Nary lifts his head. "You."

"Expecting somebody else?"

"Please. Please." He begins to weep with the pain in his hand, then starts to shudder, suddenly resigned to what is coming, knowing there is no possible means of escape.

The intruder turns to the wall, grasps the old Mannlicher Schönauer hunting carbine and lifts it carefully off its bracket. Nary sobs. He loads a ballistic-tip bullet and holds the barrel about a foot away from his head. He tightens on the trigger, feels the rifle lunge in his hands, and sees Nary's head pitch sideways at a ridiculous angle. He has not quite decapitated him. A squirt of blood jerks upwards from the neck, then drips down again from the car roof.

He places the rifle back on its wall mount, removes the surgical gloves, and steps casually down the slope.

PART I

Yangon, Myanmar

I

IT WAS AN ODD PLACE TO BUILD a hotel. It was called The Charleston and the Burmese taxi drivers pronounced it as if it were the Charles Town. Two separate words. *Char Tau.* The building was set back from Kandawgyi Lake. The lake — green by day and black by night — was a place where people gathered for walks and gentle entertainment. It had swings and slides, places to buy snacks, and benches to sit and admire the water and the fountains. Once night had fallen, the outer pavement accommodated the odd strolling couple and a few skinny hookers, lounging against the stout acacia trunks. Dogs adopted leonine positions in the headlights, removing themselves at the last second, forcing the traffic to slow to a crawl.

The Charleston was typical of its kind, built in the days when government hotels were under no pressure to excel. Well-worked without being downright shabby, it had started its life with five stars and still claimed the same status. Travel sites gave it two and a half. It had an anaemic arm-chaired lobby, a craft shop with a bored attendant dressed in the costume of one of the hill tribes, and a breakfast selection designed to please Chinese tour groups. Who knows — the hotel may well have been chosen by Vann for precisely those characteristics. An inconspicuous place for people who were happy not to be noticed.

When Lucas got out from his taxi he was saluted by a porter. He went in to the lobby and waited for Vann to appear. His friend was running late. An attendant loomed so he sat in a raffia arm-chair that creaked under him. He ordered sparkling water, which came with potato crisps. He was watched from a distance by a security man, dressed in beret, epaulettes and corps boots, with scarred cheekbones and irregular teeth. The Myanmar Times on the glass table headlined with an article about the new Yangon stock exchange, which seemed to have got off to a slow start.

To his right was a window where money could be changed, and beside the money changer's was a banner, supported on two aluminium legs, that read:

Myanmar Welcomes the IV EURO-ASEAN International Humanitarian Law Symposium.

Below the writing were the emblems of various humanitarian organisations and regional development banks. Lucas was trying to recognise them in the low-lit gloom when Vann appeared.

"Lucas. Do forgive me. How nice to see you! I seem to be experiencing an attack of dizziness."

"Hey! Good to see you Dermott. It's been a while. Take your time. Dizzy? It'll be the food. I've been a bit... unstable too."

"I think I must have eaten something. I was having a shower and suddenly this terrible nausea hit me."

"Might also be the jetlag kicking in."

"It's so rude of me. Nice to see you. How was your flight?"

"It was fine."

"Oh. Yes. Good."

Lucas Bellwether had a career behind him as an international criminal lawyer. Not such a long career, but long enough to have set himself up in London's world of consultants and experts who get invited to international legal gatherings. Dermott Vann was a senior conference interpreter. This was not the first time that the two friends had met for dinner during a global congress.

"I was just thinking. This is an odd place to put a hotel. Not many eating places anywhere near. There is a road up to the left where apparently you get to a sushi bar. If you keep going for a couple of kilometres."

"I see. Yes. Lucas, we both live in the UK and we both talk of kilometres."

What on earth was the matter with Vann? He didn't look so good. The clothing, yes, well, the clothing was alright. The clothing was

[16]

typical Vann, the calculatedly Graham-Greenish effect of double-pleated tropical wool trousers, impeccably pressed short-sleeved cream shirt and tortoise-shell spectacles. Vann always sported his own retro chic. Did he know any quiet Americans? people would quip. As a rule, he enjoyed his friends' teasing, often replying that a sharp intelligence deserved exclusive clothes to go with it. Or some such rejoinder. He had a handsome face that had softened with his fifty-plus years. Born to mixed parents, it was the European strain that had prevailed in his physiognomy, leaving a few Cambodian flourishes — the unobtrusive nose, a full upper lip — to embellish his mother's delicate French features.

Vann muttered something in his native Khmer. Sartorial chic was definitely not what he was radiating right now. Not this evening. It seemed that the man had left his suavity behind when he stepped out his hotel room. He was giving off something more akin to distress. His skin was sallow against the orange couch upholstery.

"Vann, are you sure you are alright? Look. I'm tired too. We don't have to go out."

"No. Come on. I've been looking forward to this."

They got up, Vann insisting on signing for Lucas' Swiss water. The concierge asked if they needed a taxi. Vann declared he would rather walk. They marched downhill from the reception portico to the lakeside road.

"Is that a bench there?"

Vann needed a rest. They sat down as the cars drove by. Each time the resident dog was picked out in the headlights, it moved sulkily from the centre of the road. As soon as the car passed, it resumed its position.

Then — without warning — Vann gave a brusque cackle, his mouth dropped open, and his head lunged forward. He toppled from the bench and landed on the pavement. In a sudden movement, he arched his back violently, pushing his head and feet backwards, and then straightened before twice repeating the same violent movement. His shirt rubbed hard against the wet concrete and tore. Lucas looked around him, distraught. A young woman with long ginger hair and vermilion lipstick stared in horror from behind an acacia tree. He ran back to the hotel and called for a medic. The hotel had a nurse on the staff, but she had already gone to bed, and by the time she arrived it was too late.

II

Deputy Township Police Commander Captain Win Maw Oo was giving the report a final read-through. It was not an easy thing to write. The right tone had to be struck. On the one hand it was important to conclude that the incident qualified for an investigation by Special Branch. It was a matter of course in circumstances involving the death of a foreigner for Special Branch to become involved. On the other hand, this initial report would carry his signature and his text should suggest a township that was well policed under a competent deputy who knew what was what. The Township Commander was retiring from his post in only six months. There were many advantages that came with the top post. If you excelled yourself in a difficult law enforcement situation you could be rewarded. He might even be able to send Moh-Moh to university in Singapore. Such a bright girl. So much promise. If only her mother could see her now. Singapore, safe and orderly, would be just right for her.

He had interrogated the Englishman who was the companion of the deceased man. Mr Bellwether was his name. The man had been reticent at first, as people always were, but when he engaged him a bit he had been forthcoming. The man was a lawyer, the international sort that you find in United Nations tribunals. He had worked in Cambodia and before that in Africa, in places where people had lost touch with their humanity and turned to axes and machetes to solve their problems. He had a friendly face, a bit like a family dog, and seemed quite sympathetic for a Westerner, not stuffed to the nines with prejudice as these people so often were. At one point in the conversation the Englishman had asked him if he thought there was foul play.

"Nothing can be discarded at this stage Mr Bellwether."

"It's just so appalling. Might anybody have had a grudge against my friend?"

"You never know. You simply never know. People can take offence. It is important not to offend people."

The incident occurred on the eve of the opening ceremony of the EURO-ASEAN International Humanitarian Law Symposium, a gathering of the highest importance. The victim was a self-employed translator from the United Kingdom who had been hired to perform real-time translation at the congress in the Cambodian, French and English languages (the Cambodians being represented at ministerial level). This is generally deemed a strenuous task requiring strong mental powers and high concentration. The deceased landed at Yangon Mingalardon on morning, 10.35, of Friday 21st of the present month. Time was spent at Charleston Hotel recuperating from fatigue (known as jet-lag). In the afternoon the subject visited the Bogyoke Ze (known by visitors as Scott Market). He travelled by taxi according to the hotel porter. He purchased a few small souvenirs (sandalwood scented combs). Nothing suspicious was reported by parties interviewed in Bogyoke Ze. In the evening he had a rendez-vous with Mr Bellwether.

The Captain ran his hand through his hair, his fingers a rake, aligning the strands across his scalp.

"Kindly describe your impressions of Mr Vann on the Friday night."

"Yes" said the Englishman. "Very strange I would say. He was unwell. Fighting to maintain his equilibrium. Not at all the charming person Dermott Vann can be."

"How long have you known Mr Vann?"

"Not so long. We were first together in Belgrade for that Red Cross thing ... oh, off and on for about three years I would say. Acquainted with, if you see what I mean. But we got on well. I don't know how many people can say they actually know Vann. Or knew, if you prefer, Officer."

Win Maw Oo took his pencil and tapped the wooden name-plate on his desk. Deputy Township Commander. He smiled feebly and ran his fingers across his hair again. "Let me ask you about Mr Vann's origins. I believe he was descended from a Cambodian father and a French mother."

"I believe so, yes."

"Half Khmer. Franco-Khmer, perhaps I should say. Now you, Mr Bellwether, you have a Cambodian wife do you not?"

Lucas was not prepared for this.

"Er, yes, that is correct. Well yes, sort of. We are, how can I put it… estranged now."

"I see. A brief idyll, then. And what would you say was the cause of your estrangement with this woman?"

Again, the question was unexpected.

"Er…well, all things considered, I suppose we didn't really see eye to eye on a number of things."

"Marriages can be difficult, Mr Bellwether. Tell me. How did she react to your work at the Khmer Rouge Tribunal? If my records are correct, that is where you were employed at the time. You were doing research into abuses that had happened in her country. Not everybody would feel comfortable with that."

"No, you are right Captain. She was not particularly comfortable with that."

He had loved his research into human rights abuses, he explained. The entire trial was about intent: had these Khmer Rouge chieftains really intended to kill a quarter of the population or did the slaughter simply escape their control? To this day opinion was still divided. Only last week…

"I see. You certainly sound very taken with it all, Mr Bellwether."

But his wife, no. His wife had seen no need to dig up the past. No need at all. The past was a black pit as far as Sovany was concerned, and it should be put behind them. Lucas had been hired to climb into the pit with his spade and start digging. Not a good start for marital harmony.

"Mmm" said Captain Win Maw Oo. "It sounds like what you might call a conflict of interest. And am I to take it that your marriage just fizzled out after that?"

"Sort of. Yes."

[21]

It was a story without much originality, as he had discovered when he started going to bars after work to chew the fat with other expatriates. In fact, the pattern was cruelly commonplace.

"The point that strikes me, Mr Bellwether, in this somewhat dismal saga of yours, is that you are still married to a Cambodian woman. In this country at least, it would be considered that she had legitimate grievances against you. I am faced with the strange case of a man who appears to know Cambodia well, who has been paid handsomely to research its history, who has entered into matrimony with a Cambodian woman, who comes to this country, Myanmar, Burma, call it what you will, who dines with a Cambodian man with whom he is acquainted, sits with him in a not very salubrious spot, and witnesses him dying a sudden and violent death. What do you expect me to make of it?"

"With all respect, Captain, you will decide what to make of it, not me. All I can say is that Dermott Vann was the finest, kindest, most helpful and good-natured man you could ever hope to meet. His death is a tragedy."

"You are not a run-of-the-mill kind of fellow, Mr Bellwether. But that is not a crime. In and of itself, it is not a crime. Well. I think that just about covers it. We have your details if we need to be in touch. Just sign the sheet here. Thank you for assisting us. And — er — we are deeply sorry that such an incident should occur while you are visiting our country. Deeply sorry."

A medical report is currently being established. All of the standard required procedures have been scrupulously followed. The medical investigation into the causes of death will be established shortly. It is not to be discounted that the combined effects of travel fatigue, extreme mental strain, severe climate conditions to which the victim, who resided in Great Britain, was not accustomed, and some form of food poisoning may have generated a unique set of circumstances resulting in a life stoppage such as cardiac arrest. Such incidents have occurred before within the purview of this Deputy Township Commander and have been handled with due dispatch. If, however, the medical report reveals an instance that might be considered as intoxication, more precisely wilful intoxication, it is the opinion of this Deputy Township

Commander that the matter should be referred immediately to Special Branch.

Signed and dated. Deputy Township Commander Captain Win Maw Oo.

The Deputy Commander stepped outside the police station, a breezeblock building that the British had dumped there in 1931, crowned by a dish antenna splattered with pigeon excrement. It was 6 pm; he watched as the sergeant crashed the sliding barriers into place and locked the gates.

An antiquated tree stood on the street corner, the paving stones dislodged at wild angles by its ancient roots. It had seen things, that tree. It had seen a lot. Maybe it had been there in the days of King Thibaw, when Burma had been ruled by a dynasty that worshipped albino elephants. The huge trunk was knotted with tendrils. The local people had suspended ribbons and strings from its dusty bark and wooden shrines containing little human effigies were nailed into the tree: animist scenes of nativity and death. In the lower branches, a busy community of crows had gathered for an evening cackle. A gang of myna birds was fretting anxiously on a higher branch, and from higher still the bats were detaching themselves, one by one, flitting off to murder insects in the eventide. Everything had its place. This was his Yangon, and he loved it as it was. Why change all this, for goodness sake? It was essential that he protected Moh-Moh from all the new, progressive forces.

Loosening his leather belt, he sat down at a low pavement table, and without needing to give an order, someone poured him a cup of warm milky tea. Through the gaps in the trees he could just make out the red brick of the law courts building, a large Victorian edifice, still in use today. The British may have had their faults, but they also had their ideas properly worked out. They understood the need for strong institutions to defend the deeper stability of the universe.

He would not let Constable Maung turn into a problem. He was fresh and he was headstrong, and you could forgive him that. What was less forgivable was his poor sense of deference. The young policeman did not have hierarchy in his bones, and some-how he was going to have to learn some respect for his superiors even if he had it cracked into him. The Captain had given him the benefit of the doubt. Other young recruits came to him with degrees in engineering or administration. Michael Maung had applied with a degree in botany from Sittwe University! Plants! It was hardly a qualification that was going to get you somewhere in life, anywhere at all, and least of all in defending public order. Maung ought to be damn glad he had a job as a rank-and-file policeman and start saluting his superior officers and speaking only when spoken to. But, he repeated to himself, as the warm tea began to flow through his upper body, he was not going to let Maung turn into a problem.

"Ready when you are, Sir."

Sergeant Myint Tin Tin pulled up alongside the pavement in the navy blue Toyota pick-up truck. Two policemen sat upright on the back benches clutching automatic rifles, their bony faces lost in their oversized helmets. The Deputy Commander downed the remainder of his tea, fumbled with his pockets and was told it was on the house, it was a pleasure. He climbed in beside Myint Tin Tin who kicked the truck into gear with a rattle of diesel and steered up the Kbar Aye Pagoda road, cutting right at the top of the hill and then hard left into Thayawaddy Lane.

The senior police officer collected his thoughts. That English-man. Some unexplained coincidences, but probably not going to lead to anything conclusive. He seemed rather an amateur, especially in matters of the heart. How can you justify marrying someone and then simply throwing in the towel? Absurd. And very unkind to the unfortunate wife. And as for that that poor Khmer translator! The Cambodians had their own ways with people. Oh yes, we have had our difficulties here in Burma, no doubt about it, but nothing on a par with Cambodia. You did not want to mess with Cambodians when they had a grievance. No you did not. What could that unfortunate man have done to deserve his fate? It must have been deliberate. Nobody died on a dirty pavement in a great paroxysm of pain unless somebody else meant them to. The doctor reported that he had never seen anything like it in twenty years of practice.

The Captain turned to face the great bulk seated next to him.

"Anything new on the dead foreigner, Sergeant?"

"No Sir. Should have the medical report in tomorrow. Then we'll see."

"Got any thoughts about this case?"

"Don't like it Sir. Not really our remit is it? We need to call in the heavy brigade."

"I think you're right, Sergeant."

"Pick up at seven a.m. tomorrow, Sir?"

"Seven a.m. tomorrow, Sergeant."

The house was down a thin alleyway, behind a wall circled with razor wire. It was a modest enough place, a three-bedroom bungalow with damp-stained walls. What might have been a garden was a layer of cement, thus allowing the police truck the room it needed to turn. The windows were fretted with light metalwork, the rust showing through the paint. A necessary precaution against intruders. It wasn't much to shout about, this house, but it was in Bahan Township, a stone's throw from Golden Valley where those mindless foreigners were prepared to pay any amount, literally any amount, for property. All those United Nations envoys who had lectured them for years about human rights and were now renting luxury villas off people on the sanctions list! Go tell that to my poor dead wife, God rest her soul. And if this house was shabby on the outside, don't forget he had only paid fifteen thousand dollars for it when he bought it in 1986, and now it was worth twenty times that amount. More. Besides, behind the cracked tiles and the green monsoon stains, there lived a jewel, a rare and precious stone.

Right on cue, Moh-Moh appeared at the door, head cocked to one side, smiling sweetly.

"Hello father. You must be tired. Let me pour you a Wincarnis."

III

Sambath is attending a drinks party at the Japanese Embassy, gracing it with his fluid, impeccably sociable presence. The guest list is a select picking of Asian diplomats and high-ranking experts attending the big EURO-ASEAN human rights congress, along with a few European Ambassadors and a selection of the more promising First Secretaries. He has endured several conversations now about his country, Cambodia, all of which have taken an entirely predictable route towards tactful inquiries about the trial of war criminals in Phnom Penh. What were the Prime Minister's intentions, in his informed judgement? Was there any strategy for closure, now that the leaders had been sentenced? Did he think that the judges would be indicting any more middle-ranking suspects? Had he met the new investigator personally? An able man, by all accounts. He has answered the questions diplomatically, courteously and evasively.

Now he is beginning to get bored. It is time for some entertainment of a lighter kind. That Burmese waitress serving at the drinks table, for example. Might she not be good for a little fun? Their eyes had already collided several times.

Sambath is wearing an elegant suit of charcoal tropical cotton and a Vietnamese silk tie. His hair is oiled, and he is tall enough, when he lights a cigarette, to blow the smoke over people's heads. He has easy good looks: a quick, conspiratorial smile and a playful glance that says there is enjoyment to be had.

The Burmese waitress is delighted with all of this, thrilled to realise that of all the important people milling around the room, one of the most handsome men seems to be making a pass at her. Her! She adjusts her blue silk *yin hpone* blouse, part of a uniform that she looks good in but is dying to take off because it is tight and scratchy, and when you are pouring drinks at that rate, too hot as well. Of course she cannot agree to go for a drink with him after the party. There is cleaning up to do and she is expected at home. She giggles his suggestions away. Are you mad? But

Sambath was never a man to take no for an answer and within forty-five minutes, all the while maintaining strictly conventional conversations with serious people, he has returned four times to her table on the pretext of needing another whisky, and she has finally capitulated and agreed to meet him at the Tiger Lilly bar at 10.30 pm. There is a curfew at 11 pm, and half an hour is not going to hurt anybody, is it? Her name is Rosie Phyu and she is a true Burmese, in contrast to the other three waitresses, who are all from the Karen minority. She is a good foot taller than those dumpy Karen girls too, and in Sambath's eyes, a million miles prettier. Pretty? Untamed; unrepentant. Pleasing by not attempting to do so. That is what he likes.

He takes his leave of his Japanese hosts, and drives the big Lexus himself. That too is part of his particular individualism: all the guests have drivers, and more than one powdered spouse won-ders at the daring of this man who breaks such an elementary rule. He gets to the Tiger Lilly before the girl, experiences a pulse of distaste at the graffiti wall-motifs and the young crowd dancing there and decides he will fill her with as much drink as he can, and then get her out quickly. When she appears on the staircase she is wearing a loose, emerald-green top which sparkles in the probing spotlights. Her arms are long and her face is young and carefree. She wants to drink Red Bull so he presses through the bar throng and orders her one, along with two Jägermeister shots. He persuades her to try the German con-coction, which she has never come across before. She tries her best to enjoy it, and holding the glass to her mouth he makes her swallow it faster than she wants. He pours most of his drink into her glass. It's revolting stuff after all; you can't expect him to drink that. Before she knows it she is in the SUV and they are driving to his hotel, and she is laughing at his jokes about the curfew, tumbling unsteadily on to his arm as he drives. Eleven pm! What is this country? *My country!* she answers, dissolving in a fit of giggles. The room is large and the bed is, to her unprac-tised eye, huge. The curtains have silk tassels and the kind of gold trimmings it would take her auntie a whole day to sew. He offers her another drink and feeling wildly proud with the suc-cess of her conquest — did she not conquer him? — she accepts a double Drambuie with ice and when, a little bit later, he starts to unbutton the green top she does not try to stop him.

She lies naked on the bed but he does not approach her. She props her head on her elbow, smiles through her lipstick, and looks puzzled.

"Come" she tells him.

He replies that he has never seen anybody so beautiful in all his life, and he is not used to such beauty. This is something really special for him, he explains, and if she does not mind, he will just look at her for a while. Rosie Phyu is flattered by this, although she is not sure what this man is really after. But she enjoys the knowledge that his eyes are on her body and she is quite ready to be admired. She stretches across the large bed, on her back, arms and legs extended outwards, then turns on to her stomach and lets her hair tumble across her face before gathering herself on her knees, rump upwards. Sambath watches her, and makes no move. Eventually he lights a cigarette.

"Let me pour you another drink."

"Thank you. My darling."

Rosie's English does not go far, but it goes far enough. She turns, kneeling to face him, her hair not quite long enough to cover her small breasts. He passes her the fresh whisky. That is when a wave of nausea hits her and suddenly she can hold herself upright no longer. She topples sideways, a kneeling penitent that has lost its centre of gravity. She tries to coordinate her movements, a jumble of hip and pubis and arms and hair, a doll that has been wrongly manipulated by a spiteful child.

"Sambath I need water now please."

"Water? It's water you want, is it, bitch?"

His tone is abruptly hard and suddenly she is scared. Sambath rises, approaches the bed and grabs a fistful of her hair. He drags her, screaming, into the bathroom. He thrusts her head into the toilet bowl and presses the flush, shoving her head hard into the gush of water.

[28]

"Is that enough water for you?"

Rosie flails her arms and tries to yell but opening her mouth is a bad idea and water quickly fills it. Her head is yanked from the toilet and she spits and pukes and lies on the tiled floor like a dying fish, flicking her limbs, then she vomits a large amount of water and brown alcohol and moves her head to the side.

"Better now?" he asks.

Her only wish is to be out of there. To survive. To stay alive. This man is a maniac. She crawls out of the bathroom, and retrieves a heap of her clothes. He follows her, rips the clothing from her hand — it is all so tiny, this underwear, this rubbish outfit — and rolls it into a ball. He opens the bedroom door and hurls the clothing down the corridor. There is a stream of saliva down her chest and she has started to shiver. He takes her hand and propels her skinny body through the door, then closes it heavily and sets the security lock.

"I'm sure you don't mind dressing outside. I need to catch some sleep. Busy day tomorrow."

Within ten minutes he is asleep.

IV

Once again, Myanmar Police Constable Michael Maung explains that he is from Rakhine State.

"Where do the Rakhine people live?" asks Police Constable Hoo Tin Maw, lighting a Red Ruby, tapping the lighter on the table, fretting with the flint. Hoo Tin Maw was always fidgeting. A jittery young man, thought Michael. But a nice enough guy.

"Have you ever looked at a map of Myanmar? Do you know your country? We live by the sea. North West."

"Oh". A pause. Hoo Tin Maw works his thumb on the lighter, which flashes sparks. "And what do you do there?"

What do we do? They are so odd, these Burmans. "My family originally came from Bangladesh. We are Roman Catholic. Not Buddhist like you."

"Why do you say you are Roman, Michael? You studied so much. I wish I had had a chance to study." Hoo Tin Maw has become a policeman through his father's connections.

The Deputy Township Commander is away for the afternoon. The two men sit smoking in a side-room at the station. They are dressed in uniform: grey shirts with epaulettes and badges, dark blue trousers tucked into high leather boots, and soft blue forage caps. The walls of the police station are a soiled spearmint green. Across the ceiling runs a single neon strip, dimly illuminating a stack of well-used riot shields and grey helmets piled neatly in the corner.

"I studied botany. Plants."

"What an odd thing to choose. Here take another Ruby."

"Did the chief get the medical report on the foreigner?"

"Sure. It's in his desk."

"Interesting. Why did he tell you and not me?"

"He doesn't trust you."

"I think he's right. I want to read that report. It's all about poisoning."

"Michael, be careful. You know he's got his eye on you."

"Do you know where he keeps the key?"

"No. Yes. The Sergeant keeps it in his locker."

"Wait here. That way you have seen nothing."

"Michael you are an arsehole! This is a serious disciplinary breach. Don't do it!"

"Light a Ruby for me."

Police Constable Michael Maung is a tall man. He strides into the corridor, past the chief's office, goes through the back door into the rusty-roofed shed where the team's lockers are ranged alongside the red and white road-block barriers, the coils of razor wire, the washing line of towels and underwear, finds the Sergeant's locker. He locates the desk key on a hook inside the metal door, returns with it to the chief's office, unlocks the central drawer and extracts a yellow manila envelope, photocopies its contents on the machine next to the fresh water stoop— four pages — and then returns the envelope and key to their original places.

"Easy as pie. And you, Constable Hoo Tin Maw, you didn't see a thing."

"You will get screwed for this. Screwed to the middle of, of... of deep fuck."

"Come on brother. Let's cycle down Shukhinthar Road and pick up some pirate money changers."

*

Maung was reading.

Michael Maung lived in a room in one of the older parts of east-central Yangon, near the Bogyoki Stadium. He had been lent the room by his uncle, with whom he shared the apartment along with Auntie Lilly and the two girls, in exchange for some help with teaching the kids. The building was one of several damp-stained blocks squeezed alongside each other in a tight little lane. From the kitchen you could see straight into the kitchen of the next block and smell their curry. The place had a gloomy stairwell with dirty concrete steps splashed with red betel-spit, and two half-wild dogs that slept just inside the main entrance. Straight outside the front entrance was a heavy-duty Korean-made generator which the janitor spent a lot of time cleaning, as if it were his car. The generator roared into life at least once a day for at least two hours, its diesel fumes blending with the curry odours. The city was chronically under-powered; the government awarded most of the power cuts to the poorer parts of the city.

Michael had to strain to read the small print in the reference books. The overhead light was watery and dim. His uncle's apartment was originally a large room with a kitchen and a washing area. Now the three separate rooms were wooden enclosures, each built around a bed and table. The plywood walls did not reach beyond shoulder-height, and that way the one ceiling strip-light could light all three cubicles at once. It was also not too bright for the two girls when Auntie Lilly unfurled their mosquito nets and kissed them goodnight. Usually the children refused to sleep until Michael had told them a story. This evening he had said he would tell them a story about Jesus walking on the road to Emmaus, and Aye-Aye put her foot down. She did not want another story about Jesus. So he told them a Kachin story about how the different races were given their homes, and how God built a house on the mountain, and a dancing floor on the plain, and when he had finished his work he called the people together and told them that he was going back to his great palace, and the people begged him to remain, for without him they would be helpless, and he said no, he must go, but he did agree to give the wild boar his tusks, and the hornbill its plumage. "I want a hornbill" whispered Aye-Aye before falling asleep.

It was a good enough place, and Michael felt at home there.

Back to work. The literature was not copious, but the few books were detailed. There was the standard *Botanica of the Union of Myanmar*, a 700-page compilation of the expertise available in a country that had always taken an interest in its own flora. There was William Lauderdale's 1924 *Flowering Shrubs of the Uplands of Southern Asia*, a work that was more eclectic in nature but extremely thorough in areas where the great British botanist's curiosity had been whetted, and beautifully illustrated with Lauderdale's own watercolour prints. Finally, there was what he liked to call his secret weapon, the heavy volume written in the Rakhine language by Mun Tin Aye, *Trees and Berries of South-East Asia*. Mun Tin Aye was a Sittwe man, and although his work was barely read outside the State of Rakhine, Michael found it often equalled the *Botanica* in detail and on some points surpassed it. All of these were books that he had acquired in second-hand sales during his university days. The Lauderdale, unfortunately, was an artful photocopy. The real thing would have been quite beyond his means.

He took from his table the envelope containing the four pages of the photocopied forensic report and concentrated on the key paragraphs. A full post-mortem examination of the subject had been performed. The evidence would suggest that the subject was healthy prior to death. There was no evidence of previous significant impairment to or degradation of principal cardiac/ respiratory/digestive functions. It was considered unlikely that the subject had died of natural causes such as massive cardiac arrest or stroke. It was noted that the subject had experienced severe muscle spasms according to the evidence of the witness present at the time. The witness had described the arching dorsal movements of the subject prior to death. The report respectfully suggested that such convulsions could be symptomatic of strychnine poisoning. Strychnine ingestion caused violent convulsions and a sudden rise in blood pressure due to the stimulation of the spinal cord motor ganglia, strychnine poisoning fatalities being normally due to asphyxia from respiratory arrest. On the basis of that conjecture, laboratory tests had been conducted on the urine, blood and gastric aspirate of the subject. The tests were negative, however, since no traces of $C_{21}H_{22}O_2N_2$ were found in the body fluids. There were however minor traces of a crystalline alkaloid similar to that derived from the *nux vomica* but of an unidentified type. The report concluded that death by ingestion of lethal substances was a possibility that was not to be entirely discounted but could not be conclusively proven either. A different and possible cause of the acute muscular contractions observed on the subject (arching and tonic spasms) was tetanus, for which such symptoms were typical. However, the subject displayed no evidence of a wound or non-intact skin through which the bacterium might have entered, and moreover, he had in his possession vaccination documents indicating that his tetanus prophylaxis was in order. Finally, the subject had no history of epileptic seizure.

I see, thought Michael. So they are sitting on the fence. Passing the problem on to someone else. He removed his glasses, used his shirt to dry the perspiration on the bridge of his nose, wiped the lenses with a different part of the shirt, and continued reading.

Most of the report was occupied with administrative details: the time of death, the dates and times when the body was received at the Yangon City Forensic Facility, the names and qualifications of the physicians who had performed the examination, the arrangements for officially placing the deceased within the custodianship of his country of legal residence, namely Great Britain, and sundry references for samples taken and stored in the facility.

Michael Maung was no expert on violent death and its symptoms. He was not a physician or a pathologist. He had read that the lethal dose to humans of strychnine was between 30 and 120 mg. You could breathe it in, as a vapour, or take it intravenously. The report had referred to *nux vomica*. In his *Botanica*, he looked up *Nux vomica* within the genus *Strychnos*. A tree, present in India and in South-East Asia. The tree had small white flowers with an unpleasant smell. Its fruit was like an apple which turned orange when it ripened, and contained a white jelly holding five seeds. The seeds were shaped like flattened discs and were very hard. They were odourless but had a very bitter taste. In very low doses *Nux vomica* was traditionally used as a gastric tonic in dyspepsia and for other medical applications. Some claimed it had aphrodisiac properties. The bark of the tree contained brucine, which was also deadly.

Michael opened the pages of his Lauderdale. The British

botanist, it seemed, had little to add to the information given in the Myanmar *Botanica*, apart from his water colours of both the delicate white flowers of the *Nux vomica* and the seeds as they appeared when dried — dark little discs, almost like some kind of coinage. Interestingly, however, Lauderdale commented that the tree was one of a number of different *Strychnos* species, without actually going on to list the others. Indeed, thought Michael. So. Our *Nux vomica* has cousins. And might one therefore postulate that there was indeed a fatal intoxication, even if not by the alkaloid of the *Nux vomica*, but by something similar, from within the family? He turned to his trusted *Trees and Berries of South-East Asia*, his Mun Tin Aye. Flipping through the pages to the references under *Strychnos*, he was delighted to find that Mun Tin Aye had been considerably more meticulous in detailing the other species. To begin with there was *Strychnos toxifera*, which yielded curare, used as a deadly poison by the natives of Guiana. There was *S. Ignatii* found in the Philippines (a Jesuit poison?), there was *S. innocua* which was eaten in Africa, as harmlessly as its name suggested, there was another *Strychnos* used to make arrow poison in Java, and there was *S. Cardamemsis*, very rare, very toxic, native to the Cardamom mountains of Cambodia.

Uncle Richard knocked on his door. "Don't stay up too late now my boy. There is work for us all tomorrow. We are going to bed. Your aunt has ironed your tunic. God bless you."

"Please thank her Uncle. Have a good night. God bless you too."

Aunt Lilly, sliding into bed in the adjoining room, could hear everything he was saying. There was no need for Uncle Richard to pass on the message. But it was good to pretend, to observe the conventions of privacy.

"This highly toxic white crystalline alkaloid can easily be hidden in any foods or drinks that have a bitter taste. It can also be ingested if vaporised in spray form" he read. How fascinating. So if no traces of *Nux vomica* had been found in the victim's body fluids, and yet he exhibited symptoms of such poisoning, might he not have been poisoned by one of the other species? That he had been felled by jungle curare or Javan arrow-poison seemed a little romantic and far-fetched. The African version, meanwhile, was supposed to be harmless. Okay. What did that leave? A species of poison from the Philippines, with a Jesuit ring to it, and something from Cambodia, named after the Cardamom Mountains where it was occasionally found.

In a deliberate act of over-simplification, he asked himself: Who might want to kill an Englishman named Dermott Vann? A Filipino or a Cambodian?

Uncle Richard had begun to snore; a low, regular growl. It was time to turn in. Michael deliberately thumped the big books shut, and the man next door stirred and turned on his rump. The growling ceased. Perfect. Time to go to bed myself now. A Filipino or a Cambodian? A Cambodian or a Filipino? Stripping to his underpants, he climbed into his bed. Quickly his thoughts abandoned the subject of trees and poisons, and turned to imaginings of his girlfriend. He pulled the pillow towards him and held it tight against his body. His very secret lover. His Moh-Moh.

V

They were sitting on the farthest part of the lakeside, their backs to the Saudi embassy building. The dusk was gathering and people had come out for an evening stroll along the path. There were quite a few older people, walking in that strange jerky way that suggested they were on an exercise routine. Not many of them got as far as the corner where the couple were. The lake was very still, fringed with boggy water foliage, and there were intermittent plops and splashes as the aquatic rodents dived and swam. Little fish-hunting birds plunged beneath the dark surface and then emerged a full minute later dozens of yards from where they had started. On the far side was a golf driving range, powerfully illuminated against the darkening sky, where wealthy Burmese came to hit their balls into the lake.

"They send boys to dive and find them" said Michael.

"*Dá geh là?*" whispered Moh-Moh. Really?

"Really."

Michael pulled the parasol closer. Like so many Burmese lovers who lived with their respective families, places for them to do their courting were in short supply. Lake Inya was a favourite venue for many a young couple seeking some intimacy together, although the privacy was limited here too. The golden rule was to avoid being seen by anybody who knew them, and for this each had brought a large parasol which they held together, tilted almost horizontally, as if they were sitting in the back of a tent.

Moh-Moh brushed the fringe from her eyes. Her hair was long, tinted chestnut brown, in gentle defiance of her father's injunctions, with the darker roots showing in the way that was fashionable. Her complexion was pale, as befitted the daughter of a senior police officer who spent most of her time indoors. She had soft, deer-like eyes which drooped when she was pensive and came alive when she smiled. A single rose was clipped in her hair. She had chosen the flower to match the red of her lipstick. On each cheek there were carefully painted dabs of amber sandalwood paste. Moh-Moh was wearing traditional clothes, as most Burmese girls did when they went outside. She had an upper tunic, cream-coloured, buttoned tight down the front to emphasise her small chest, and a tight ankle-length *htamein* skirt. Not a local design, the cotton *htamein* was midnight blue with a weft overlay in waving black curves. A Rakhine pattern, just to please him. Her police constable from a faraway land.

Michael wore a less strident *pasoe* sarong of browns and blues, and a chequered shirt. He had a handsome angular face on which the eyebrows and mouth both moved in a happy unison. She liked the way that cheerfulness came naturally to him. His skin was much darker than hers, partly because he had inherited it that way, and partly because he had spent half of his twenty-six years at the beaches around Sittwe and Ngapali. It was a hot evening, and he perspired slightly. Someone in one of the houses behind them was playing an old Aye Chan May favourite, and Moh-Moh started to hum along to the sugary melody. It was more than the man could take, and he leaned to place a lingering kiss just below her right ear. She smells of cinnamon, he thought, and sunshine, and flowers.

"No! Michael! Somebody will see us!"

"Oh! How long must we go on like this?" He smiled.

"Just be patient. Imagine if I can go to Singapore. Then you will come and see me and we will be free to do everything we want."

"I don't have a passport."

"I will help you get one. It's not hard if you know the right people."

"And what will we do when we get to Singapore, my pretty butterfly?"

"We will do this." She darted her pink tongue from between the lipstick and licked his mouth from one end to the other. She giggled, and then pursed her lips, the insolence lighting up her oval face.

"Moh-Moh I have something serious to ask."

"Not now." She gave him a fuller, longer kiss.

"You are such a hypocrite."

She let her hand drift across his clothing. "You are my big, long, tall, strong and a little bit standing-up policeman."

"Just say yes and then we will forget all about it."

"Yes. Oooh yes!" she mocked.

"I want you to tell me about yesterday."

"Oh Michael it's so boring. Not now."

"It's important. A man has died. Maybe poisoned."

Moh-Moh drew back. What was all this talk of poison and dying at a time like this? Michael could be *so* tasteless. "Why do we have to talk about this?" A moorhen squeaked nearby and another replied with a clipped little peep. "Why?"

"Just bear with me. I need to know what you told the English lady in Café 99."

Now half sulking at her boyfriend's new sincerity, Moh-Moh simply said "She was a nice lady. I quite liked her."

"What did you tell her my butterfly?"

"All those things. The things you said."

"Tell me now. Exactly. In English."

Moh-Moh adopted a slow, half-mocking monotone. "I say: Please to understand. The seed of the tree is not the only one. There is one in Cambodia called Strychno Cardamom and here is one of its seeds for you to kindly take. Do not overlook."

"Very good. And did you give the text? About toxicity?"

"Of course! What do you take me for?"

She punched him in the stomach and chest and he grabbed her arms and kissed her on the cheeks. Then she ran her hands through his curly hair and down his cheek.

"You are so dark my love. I can't believe it. You are a Bengali who has been toasted on a fire."

"And you are white like snow. Put out my fire."

VI

The pool at the Irrawaddy Luxor Hotel is roughly kidney-shaped. It is flanked by two towers. There is a part of the kidney that catches the powerful afternoon sun and a lobe that remains shaded by Tower B. Sambath likes to keep himself to the shade. He has no wish to tan his body, like the Western tourists, and he is by nature somebody who avoids the more searching light.

Sambath listens to the ice cubes in his double Chivas, enjoying the pings and clicks as cold fights with warm. He has every reason to be feeling satisfied. The conference went well and he has achieved what he set out to. The various meetings he had set up for the days following the big event have turned out to be reasonably productive. There was a lot of work to do, and these Burmese are unbelievably greedy, always asking for sweeteners, but now the job is done. He can go home content. This place is a good way behind his native Cambodia, but people's instincts are in the right place. They respond to the same kind of promptings.

He has not yet decided how he will reward Thirith. He knows he will have to do so. His sister has kept an eye on the information passing through about delegates and attendees and all the sundry staff of the human rights symposium, including the people flying all the way from London to do their simultaneous translation or whatever it was they did. Sambath sips his whisky, barely kissing the glass with his lips. Thank you, Thirith. And here in Myanmar too. So near yet so wonderfully, so deliciously far. Safely here in Asia, with all the systems and assumptions that Asia offers, and yet a million miles from Cambodia, away from the fingers that might point to any connection with the old days. Myanmar. Such a fashionable venue, such a perfect diversion; such an ideal red herring.

After all those years. How very pleased his dear father would be.

Sambath is used to travelling with his government's delegation when they grace high-level conferences. It helps. You can see who is who. Who sits next to who, and who whispers in whose ear. The diplomatic immunity makes it much easier to get business done. You can also keep an eye on who is saying what about Cambodia. Like that English lawyer who spoke about the compensation for the victims of the Khmer Rouge, or *reparations* as they call it. Nothing that has not been said before, mind you. Sambath likes to keep a watch on the international human rights crowd. Mark them down. Especially if they are friends of Vann.

And in addition to all that patriotic homework, you can use these occasions to relax as well, to stretch your legs, to indulge yourself in the pleasures that are on offer when you are away from home. Like that pale blonde girl over there for example. The tall one sipping her mojito and nibbling at a club sandwich. Her second mojito actually. And reading her paperback novel so avidly. There is something so *European* about buying a story book and then actually reading it. He has noticed her already. Marked her down. Last night she ate alone by the pool. Sambath likes tall, blonde Europeans. Why wouldn't he? Khmer women are so small.

Sambath watches carefully as the woman rises, walks to the edge of the pool, meditates for a second, and makes a deep dive, holding her breath until the last second, rising in a triumphant gasp for air. She swims four more lengths before pulling herself confidently up the ladder, flicking drips across the tiles as she ruffles the water from her hair. She towels her body, squats down on her recliner, and reaches for her book. The dusk is growing. She will not read for long. Underwater illuminations flood the pool. A swallow flits across the water, hunting for moths, the azure light catching the undersides of its wings. Slipping his feet into a pair of suede loafers, Sambath buttons his navy blue shirt and approaches.

"Good evening. I see you are a strong swimmer."

"Oh... er thank you."

"My name is Sambath."

She raises her head awkwardly towards the man who is standing in front of her, extending his hand. The blue lighting in the pool has lit one side of his face, the other is dark. A smooth complexion, an easy smile.

"Olivia". She holds out a hand — the other is clasping the towel across her chest.

"Well Olivia, I was going to say, I couldn't help seeing you dining alone last night by the pool, and I would hate to think you had the same plan for tonight. I'm just visiting Yangon as well. Perhaps you might let me take you somewhere for a bite of dinner?" He catches sight of the title of her book: *Fifty Shades of Grey*.

"Oh no, that's not necessary" she replies firmly. "I mean, I've never met you. We don't know each other."

"Precisely. And that is the way it will stay. Unless of course you consent to share a little dinner. It's only eating. People do it all the time."

"Yes, I'm sure they do. But…" Olivia pauses. She looks upwards at Tower A and lifts a corner of the towel, dabbing a tiny reservoir of water that has collected on an eyebrow. She is flying home tomorrow. "Well. I suppose I could just fit in an early dinner."

"What a pleasure that would be. Shall I see you in the lobby at 7.30?"

Sambath watches as she piles her poolside junk into a tote bag and deposits her towel with the attendant. Much nicer legs than that silly Burmese girl, he thinks. So incredibly white.

VII

Folly. Pure folly.

Olivia looked out of her hotel window. Beyond tower A, the sun was setting over Inya lake. Far below, the crowds were out for the evening, strolling and milling beneath the huge trees that seemed to be a hallmark of this country. So many trees. It was as if the city had been carved out of a jungle. Well, don't be silly, Olivia, it has. There seemed to be as much fig, acacia and banyan as there was building. The residences themselves seemed to be scrappy, stained things, built without love and left to the mercy of the annual rains.

She had accepted a dinner invitation with an unknown man. For Christ's sake. A wild and foolish thing to do in a country that was far from anywhere. What did people take her for? Some kind of good-time girl?

Calm down, Olivia, said the voice in her head. Don't you think you deserve a bit of the lighter kind of distraction? After all you have been through? Oh, and shoulders back please, Olivia Trelawney, tummy in. It's only a dinner date.

Yes headmistress.

When Olivia Trelawney had married Wystan Green, bespoke art connoisseur, she had taken a step downwards in personal nomenclature.

The Trelawneys were fine Cornish folk, stout of heart and not given to being pushed around. John Trelawney, her father, was a Falmouth man. (He always said he was a descendent of Sir John Trelawny, the royalist chief who had been held in the Tower of London and who occasioned the famous Song of the Western Men. She took that one with the pinch of sea-salt it deserved). But there was no doubt that Dad, erstwhile trawlerman, was made of stern stuff. From the moment she married Wystan, however, she had become Mrs Green. Not surprisingly, her friends all called her Olive Green, and somehow the joke had stuck. Resistance was futile. So here she was, Olive Green, née Trelawney, a self-employed précis-writer at the service of the United Nations and its multiple spawnings, living south of the river Thames, and currently employed on a consultancy to Myanmar to write a report on the sudden and mysterious death of a linguist colleague. Nobody else had volunteered to go. So she had.

She selected a pale blue cotton dress with three-quarter sleeves. Anything longer on the sleeve, and she would keel over in the heat. Anything shorter, she would be suggesting some kind of availability. Am I really doing this? Am I really having these thoughts?

You could say there was a reason for her being here. For volunteering to do the report, that is. You could say her restlessness had a history to it.

Travel had been severely curtailed that winter, as had most of life's normal pleasures. It's only stage II. That had been the motto for the cold months. She had said it so many times that she no longer knew if she was saying it to Wystan or herself. Only stage II, Wystan, and stage II was a million miles from stage IV. Stage IV was the worst, and by that time, well, the devil was out there marauding around the body, barging its way into tissues and organs like nobody's business. Stage III was already a good step down from IV. Partial colectomy was the name of the game and yes, the knife was in there, and you had to chop off those vile lymph nodes and then get a good dose of chemo to batten down the hatches of the colon wall. Lay them low with Folfox. Look Wystan, we are not getting into a panic about this. No dear, of course we are not. The tiny quiver on Wystan's finger as he turned the page of his novel. The barely perceptible movement of his mouth as he read, the lines newly drawn around his eyes. They had grown old that winter. Grown old together, become hunched geriatrics sitting by the heater, drinking hot chocolate and watching My Fair Lady and other family classics on Sunday afternoons. It had rained, slow, English, unstoppable rain. The Morfeld Centre had been marvellous. No dear, you can't beat them. Lovely people. Tremendous. Really tremendous my love. Olivia knew that Wystan hated their guts, and he hated their guts because they took such a free hand in inspecting, slicing, and bombarding his. Olivia had needed to be quite stern with him, quite Trelawney. It was touch and go whether he didn't want a blanket on his knees for the Sunday film. What next? A Zimmer frame? "*Why can't a woman be more like a man?*" roared Rex Harrison. "*Men are so decent, such regular chaps.*"

"You're not exactly regular, are you Wystan?"

"Not exactly love." A tear welling in his left eye.

"Oh *love*. I was only joking. Come on. It's going to be okay. It's only stage II. How many times do I have to tell you?"

Olivia examined herself in the bathroom mirror at the Irrawaddy Luxor, pressing fingers to the flesh of her cheeks, inspecting the very pores. True, when you thought about your husband's cancer, you tended to look at your own body rather more closely. A definite need to keep everything under review. She counted the freckles on each of her breasts. Three more on the right. Tonight, she declared to the face, we are going to look good. We deserve this, you and I.

Stage II was okay. Stage II was do-able. Yes, we had partial colectomy. Yes, we have had to do adjuvant chemotherapy. F-5U and the combinations. Why did these drugs all sound like fighter planes? Russian F-5U engages with Ukrainian Folfox in the skies above Kiev!!! And yes, it had been a bit of a bumpy ride, but yes, dammit, we had pulled through. So stand by fore and aft, HMS Wystan, we are casting anchor and returning to the high seas. And now spring had come, and Wystan's dark winter of color-ectal discontent was over, because he had just been for his last scheduled check-up and Professor Dreyfus had given him the 99% all-clear and told him he didn't want to see him for another six months! Yes! And Wystan, true to form, had hopped on the first train from Victoria and gone to celebrate with his mummy down in Hampshire.

Olivia applied a toner to her face. She then drew her eyebrows with the tiny Bobbi Brown pencil she had picked up in Qatar duty-free. My God, what would Wystan think if he saw me pampering myself like this?

Olivia's beauty was not the brash kind. She was more a person of temperament, of character, and that is what tended to shine through when the prettier faces had run out of things to say. Olivia was not talkative. She liked to hold her cards in reserve, let people misread her if they wished, and trump them in her own sweet time. Among the exotic birds of the professional language menagerie, she was something of a starling, but she could sing her song when she wanted. She was quietly respected for her understanding of languages, especially the Russian, which she had doggedly mastered after fifteen months at the University of Novosibirsk, a snow-blasted town where the skinny girls all dreamed of becoming models in Tokyo and New York and the men only wanted to show her how much alcohol they could absorb without killing themselves. She survived; she was not a Trelawney for nothing. In appearance she dressed with modest chic, displaying that same inverted pride that made her hesitant in conversation. She had an angular frame and a sporty figure and was not against wearing jogging shoes in town if it meant that your feet would be more comfortable. But the shoe was chosen with care, always carrying a discrete flash of style. Her hair was pale and looped itself prettily at the tips, a gift from her very curly-haired mother. She had strong, blue-grey eyes, and wore a pair of designer glasses that she barely needed. They were a vanity, and most of the time she kept them lodged in her hair. And when the titanium frames sat on her nose, they suited it well — a pretty nose, let's admit it, with pepperings of freckles and perfect proportions. Olivia travelled widely. Her skills were prized — not merely the confident mastery of Russian, but also the temperament that fitted quietly into the team, did not seek to rock the boat, and never needed to hear an instruction twice.

When the face was ready to her satisfaction, Olivia crossed the room and slid open the window. A blast of heat and noise bowled into the room. She could see the blue amoeba of the swimming pool. The man was gone from his place. What did he say his name was? Sinbad?

Three weeks ago, Olivia had woken feeling benignly happy. Happy, of course, because Wystan had got better. Benign to the

[47]

point of deciding that she would, after all, go to the meeting of the Global Federation of Professional Linguists. The GFPL. As a rule, she tended to send in her voting proxy and give the gatherings a wide berth; they were just too boring. The interpreting chapter tended to lord it over the translators and précis-writers, as if their business was more important. The translators tended to bunker down and…Now come along, Olive Green, no sour grapes. And no harm in showing a bit of support to the professional federation just once in a while, and since the meeting was being held quite literally just down the road, within half an hour's walking distance, then why not? And since, as everyone knew by then, something rather dramatic had happened recently in Myanmar, she was anxious to catch up on the news.

There had been a decent turn-out. Perhaps she wasn't the only one wanting to hear about skulduggery in Myanmar. There were faces she was familiar with from her UN circuit, but a good many others she barely knew, people who served corporate markets where different languages were prized. The room, rented off a Methodist church, was not as dispiriting as she had feared. Up on the high table, presiding, was the European president, a French woman from Nice named Claudia Pons. Pons was an interpreter. She was flanked by the secretary, Raymond Osprey, a translator from Southampton. There were greetings and hugs. Olive found a place towards the back, pulled out her Samsung and checked for news of her husband in Hampshire — nothing — and waited for Pons to bang the gavel, which she duly did.

The meeting proceeded. The President immediately explained for the benefit of colleagues who were behind on the news that Dermott Vann, a UK-based interpreter, had died of unknown causes while servicing the EURO-ASEAN Humanitarian Law Symposium in Yangon, Myanmar, exactly one week ago. The police in Myanmar were still trying to establish the cause of death. It would be unwise to speculate until they had more facts.

"Now I suggest that Mr Osprey read out the resolution. Raymond please."

The GFPL declared itself appalled at the sudden and random

loss of an esteemed colleague; expressed its outrage; was anxious to obtain further facts from professional sources; conveyed condolences to the family and loved ones; and urged the national police authorities to inform the GFPL Secretariat of the cause of death as soon as such facts were available. They resolved to send a GFPL member to conduct a fact-finding mission in the country concerned with a view to compiling a report on all aspects of the tragedy.

Pons had called for a volunteer and the only hand raised in the room had been Olivia's. So here, not three weeks later, she was. In Rangoon, or Yangon if you prefer, in the Republic of the Union of Myanmar.

She closed the window. The heat was making her perspire. Upending her bottle of Versace Vanitas, she anointed herself across the chest like a Portuguese woman leaving a cathedral, shouldered her handbag, and let the door clunk shut behind her.

Ready for you, Sinbad the Sailor.

PART II

London, UK

LUCAS BELLWETHER HEARD THE PERCOLATOR gargle and gave the gas knob a quick flick. He poured a small, strong cup of coffee. A brisk breeze was racing across Eel Brook Common; people were returning from the Sainsbury's on Fulham Road laden with shopping bags, their anorak hoods squashed against their faces and their dogs' hair blown madly backwards. It was mid-June. From his flat he looked across the main road to the grassy triangle where, two months earlier, daffodils had blossomed. A late frost had momentarily freeze-dried the remains of their stalks, making their patch of long grass look greener than the rest of the common. From his top-floor flat he could see the roofs of the buses as they barged up the New King's Road. The toast catapulted upwards in the old Rowenta and he delved in the fridge for the thick-cut marmalade.

Breakfast was coffee, toast and marmalade, accompanied by an avocado half with olive oil and salt. Lucas, a strong-shouldered man, pulled the cord of his towelling robe tighter around his boxy frame. His physique was compact, suggesting to those who didn't know him that he might have had a busy time in the army before settling down. Basra? Helmand? He also looked as if he was probably good at rugby, which tended to endear him to the kind of English woman who likes that sort of punchiness. His fair wavy hair, still wet from the shower, was beginning to exhibit a few strands of grey, but it was the right kind of greying, the sort that suggested you had travelled widely and done much. Lucas had, though not as a soldier.

Bellwether I, as he had been known at prep school to distinguish him from Bellwether II, his (perhaps more discerning) brother Duncan, had studied law. Lucas was not one of the high-flyers and after getting his qualification his mother had pulled strings with the family in Brazil. The firm that took him for his training contract was a manufacturer of automotive components. When he finally qualified for the Bar he took off for an adventure safari to celebrate. Rwanda was the destination. The idea was to observe rare gorillas in their mountain habitat, and generally have a good time. Lucas experienced a few moments of emotion at the stunning beauty of the land, while remaining solidly indifferent to the primates. More importantly, he met Muteteli the dainty one (as the name translates), also known as Philomène (hereinafter Philo), who opened his eyes to her country's history and in particular the genocide that had occurred there six years earlier. The affair with Philo did not last, but the episode served him well. It cleared his mind, told him what he really wanted to do with his life, and where, more or less, he wanted to do it. He decided he would become a kind of humanitarian, not the courageous sort that helps desperate people in refugee camps, but a man of the law. A man who would practice law in places where law was not systematically practised; a man who would bring judicial fairness to places where that notion was not common currency. You could say it was a peculiarly English calling, although Lucas would not have taken the suggestion kindly. He was not off to build red-brick law courts in the far-flung reaches of Empire! He was, on the other hand, deeply enthused by the idea of international criminal law and the opportunities created, after the statute of International Criminal Court came into force, for the arm of the law to reach into places where once it could not go.

He decided to work in Africa, and naturally enough for someone with English and Brazilian parents, attempted to play his Portuguese-speaking card. It did not get him far. There were no international criminal tribunals in Angola or Mozambique, or even in Guinea Bissau. There was, however, one getting started in Sierra Leone, and when Lucas applied as a junior prosecutor at the end of 2004, he was called for interview at the United Nations in New York and hired on an initial contract of one year.

The Special Court for Sierra Leone had the jurisdiction to try war crimes committed during the recent ten-year civil war. Its remit covered murder, extermination, enslavement, deportation, imprisonment, torture, rape, sexual slavery, and more. He began as a case manager, sifting through pages of testimony, lining up witnesses, rehearsing arguments, helping to structure the prosecution's game plan. He was bullish, hardworking and enthusiastic. After his contract was renewed for a second year, he was allowed to plead in court, duelling across the chamber with the international lawyers working for the defense. Lucas began to find his voice and feel happy about his vocation. When Charles Taylor, the grizzled old warlord, was finally apprehended, he was airlifted to the Netherlands to be tried. Things were too volatile back in Freetown. Lucas joined the team preparing the prosecution case in The Hague, harnessing his skills to the task of trying the biggest gangster of them all. But The Hague is not the same as Freetown, and after one year, the soggy climate and the pickled food got the better of Lucas Bellwether. He applied for a transfer to Arusha, in Tanzania, where the perpetrators of the Rwandan genocide were being held to account before a team of international judges. This time, he lent his skills and his increasing eloquence to the defense bench. It was always good to be versatile. After the Netherlands, Lucas felt alive once more in the sandy streets of Arusha. He improved his French, which was useful because, among the staff members working for the court registrar, he found his old friend Philo.

The dormant embers exploded back into life. Philo, no longer dainty, had become tall and lovely. She had eyes that could knock a man down in the street. It was a highly charged affair, and for Lucas it became his main reason for living. But as the months went by he began to receive comments about his appearance in court. He was unshaven, he looked slaked-out and his performances were becoming sloppy. Twice in the last month the prosecution had picked apart his ill-prepared arguments. These setbacks were happening at the same time as Philo was piling on the pressure to marry her or leave her free to entertain other admirers. After many sleepless nights, he decided to call it quits with the woman and the job before it was too late for his reputation to recover, handed in his resignation letter and went back to London.

Back home, his parents gave him a warm welcome. Duncan had opened an agency in Islington selling specialised travel tours to Brazil, so he was never far. But Lucas — this was the return of the prodigal son! Back from salving the woes of the world, and ready finally to settle down. There was much celebration, Sunday roasts, talk of barrister work in the English courts, getting a rung on that property ladder, meeting a nice girl. The nice girl, retorted Lucas, could wait. He was completely spent after the last Nice Girl.

"He looks *esgotado* the poor darling" said his mother.

"Don't worry dear. Feed him some broccoli. He'll be right as rain in no time."

The property ladder was more fun, and assisted by his little brother, Lucas enjoyed the hunt that eventually led to the flat on Eel Brook Common, right at the top of a pretty brick house with wisteria clinging to its New Kings Road facade. There was a large bedroom, a kitchen that extended into the living room, and an open patio at the back that looked on to the neighbour's buddleia trees. For the young ladies of Fulham, the rugged, well-travelled, fair-haired lawyer who seemed to be throwing no end of bubbly summer parties on his patio was just too good to be true. The one who finally got to share the Savoie bed with him was called Jemima. In reality, however, it *was* too good to be true. Lucas had been hit harder by his relationship with Philomène than he fully realised, and furthermore he had become a man with serious purposes in life, and a suitable marriage was not one of them. One day, when Jemima, armed with a tape measure, announced her intention to start measuring up for pelmets, he told her he wanted to break it off.

Jemima, humiliated, rolled her tape into a ball and slammed the door. Lucas poured himself a hefty single-malt, clonked an iceberg in it and breathed a long sigh of relief. What a fool he was! What a mistake all that had been! That very evening he was checking the UN website for criminal tribunal vacancies. Freetown, Kigali, Arusha, nothing doing. The Hague, which had become a huge Yugoslavia judging factory, *nee dank u*. He heated a can of Campbell's creamy chicken mushroom, ripped open a Sainsbury's wholemeal, and continued scanning the job sites. And in due course, late at night, with the soup bowl unwashed in the kitchen and the whisky bottle seriously depleted, he found something. Call for international candidatures for researcher officers in the Extraordinary Chambers in the Courts of Cambodia, Phnom Penh. Lucas started reading, his curiosity piqued. The Khmer Rouge Tribunal in Cambodia was seeking a research officer with proven experience of international criminal trials to assist the existing prosecution team by conducting research on questions relating to the historical aspects of the period when the country was known as Democratic Kampuchea. Well, that was quite a UN mouthful, but what it meant in essence was stepping out of the courtroom, into a backroom scenario. Exploring everything there was to know about the history of Cambodia during the Cold War that might help build a prosecution case. The job-hunter was immediately drawn to the idea of the discreet, meticulous role.

Two months to the day after seeing the announcement, Lucas — to his mother's despair and his father's exasperation — was on a Vietnam Airways flight to Phnom Penh, his face buried in a book called *Pol Pot: The History of a Nightmare*.

The more he read, the more Cambodian episode seemed to be different to the others. For a start, the trials were taking place more than three decades after the events. Pol Pot and the Khmer Rouge had instituted Democratic Kampuchea in April 1975, and the regime had collapsed when the Vietnamese invaded in January 1979. This was not a time in recent memory, unlike the civil war in Sierra Leone or the slaughter in Rwanda. The need for verifiable historical fact was commensurately greater. Lucas quickly patched together a grasp of the basic history.

In 1970, with the war raging in next-door Vietnam, the United States had backed a coup in Cambodia. A general named Lon Nol assumed power and instituted a republic. That meant the nation was dispossessed of its king, the charismatic Sihanouk. The dethroned king called for a popular uprising and threw in his lot with the burgeoning guerrilla movement which he dubbed the

[57]

Red Khmers or "Khmers Rouges". These people were trained in the jungle under their leader Pol Pot. They were armed by the Chinese, and driven by a peculiar brand of Maoist fundamentalism. Year by year, the jungle fighters closed in on the towns which filled with refugees. The Khmer Rouge finally broke into Phnom Penh on 25 April 1975, two weeks before Saigon fell to Ho Chi Minh's armies.

The next day the people of Phnom Penh were told to leave their homes and walk into the countryside. Many hundreds died, unable to sustain the shock of a gruelling march in the hottest month of the year. People belonging to the old administration were rounded up and executed. The remainder were put to work in rice fields and labour camps. The country was re-named Democratic Kampuchea. The national currency was declared worthless. Monks were disrobed and religion was banned. Family relations were proscribed. Love was illegal. The Year Zero had begun.

Over the next three years, roughly two million people died. Many collapsed from exhaustion in the rice paddies and the salt fields. Others were simply executed for failing to meet work targets or asking for more food. The erstwhile city-dwellers were always considered the greatest enemy of the new agrarian society. To own a pair of spectacles, or have hands that were not calloused by manual work, was to risk immediate execution. Punishments were often barbaric. There were also widespread purges as the revolution, gripped with paranoia, consumed itself from within. Hundreds of thousands were eliminated. People were sent to be re-educated, a code word for detention and torture culminating in a feigned confession. The purpose of the confessions was to incriminate others to feed a never-ending spiral of arrests. After confessing, the victims were trucked off to burial grounds to be dispatched.

After three years and nine months the Vietnamese invaded and the regime collapsed.

II

Lucas' time in Cambodia, working as a researcher for the Khmer Rouge trials, lasted a total of thirty-eight months. Over that time he had been able to set aside enough of his salary to establish himself as a self-employed expert once he had returned to London. He became affiliated to a group of humanitarian lawyers known as Burden of Proof, which had offices in London's Inns of Court and in Washington, DC.

The phone gave him a start. "Hello, Lucas Bellwether?"

"Becky."

Rebecca Mayne ran a one-person secretarial service for Burden of Proof. She took the calls, talked to the clients, explained what the lawyers did and what they charged for it, kept a log of each person's availability. She wasn't too expensive and she was extremely efficient.

At that moment the bell rang. He opened the front door. Duncan and Rowena.

"Wow. Duncan. Ro. Come in! How's things? I'm just clearing the breakfast! Give me two seconds. I'm on a call."

Lucas returned to the phone. "Sorry Becky. Little brother just walked in." Duncan gave a knowing wobble of his shoulders. He was a good ten inches taller than Lucas.

"Okay, so this is to address a gathering called The International Criminal Law Round Table. They want you to speak on Joint Criminal Enterprise and how it is illuminated by the Cambodian case. I thought it would be straight up your street that one, Mr Bellwether."

"Straight up indeed. Have you got dates?"

"First week in September."

"Ok. Place?"

"Place? Phnom Penh. Cambodia."

"Cambodia? Really? Tell them I am available!"

"Don't get excited. Unconfirmed so far, my dear. I'll keep you posted. Expert has confirmed interest and availability. Ta-ra then."

She hung up.

"Sorry guys" said Lucas. "Make yourselves comfortable! Coffee?"

"I'd kill for a fruit juice" said Ro.

They talked about the business — his brother's — and how the patterns were changing. Nobody wanted to go and laze on Copacabana beach any more, he said. But the eco-tourism was upbeat. Jungle trails, butterfly reserves, local organic meals. You needed more and more reliable people on the ground to keep the wheels running smoothly. Duncan was going to make a three-week trip to Brazil to check up on the guides and the circuits. Terrific said his brother. And what about Ro, you're not leaving her behind I trust?"

"It's a long flight" said Rowena, glancing at her husband. "I'd rather not take any risks at this juncture."

"You'd rather not...What do you mean? I don't believe it! Are you telling me...?"

"We wanted you to be the first to know, Lucas."

"I can't believe it. Congratulations!"

Without knowing quite why, Lucas was moved to tears. He clasped Rowena and then Duncan in a tight hug. Why did he deserve to be the first to know? Why should he, whose marriage was a ridiculous mess, be the first to know of this baby? It made no sense. They were such *good* people, these two. Lucas loved his brother deeply, more deeply than he could understand. Tall Duncan, so like Dad, so profoundly good-natured, the thinning hair and the red pullover, the ready smile, the man who sought the positive in all things.

"This is simply wonderful. We have to celebrate. Imagine what Mum and Dad are going to say."

"Chuffed, I daresay" laughed Rowena.

Lucas popped a bottle of pink Catalan bubbly that someone had left in the fridge. They toasted, spoke of good times. Lucas was unaccountably happy. After their toasting, the trio strolled into Fulham, heads cocked against the wind, and settled into a lunch of Spanish tapas. Later Lucas saw them to the tube and walked gaily home.

When Rebecca Mayne called some days later, he naturally hoped it would be to confirm the Cambodia speaking engagement. No such luck; the organiser was still waiting for budget clearance. She was calling about something else: it had come to her attention that a memorial gathering was being held for the interpreter, Dermott Vann, in a hotel in North London. She was aware that he had been a friend of Lucas. She had no idea if the tone would be religious or social, but all who had known Dermott Vann were warmly invited.

Ever since Vann had breathed his last on a dirty, cracked pavement in Rangoon, Lucas had felt a strong wish to talk to somebody, somebody from Vann's family, about being there at the final moments. But he did not know his friend's family and there had been nobody to talk to. In fact, the more he thought about it — and God knows, the pair had talked into the small hours in cities around the world — the more he realised that he knew precious little about his friend. It was the least he could do to go to the memorial gathering.

III

The hotel, near Finsbury Park, was the kind that you could find anywhere in London. Brick walls painted with magnolia gloss, reproductions of anodyne horticultural watercolours, institutional carpeting that had seen better days, staff from Croatia. But there was a discernible warmth to the gathering. The room was nicely prepared with fresh flowers and there was an enlarged photo of a laughing and very sartorial Vann standing in a Manhattan avenue about ten years earlier. Some of the throng, as he later discovered, were Sussex folk who had made the journey to London, some were professional interpreters from the London scene. He recognised an elderly colleague of Vann's, Dawn Heck-Montalembert, wearing a Chanel ensemble and pigeon-blood lipstick, blowing plumes of smoke. There were also several Asian family groups, including well turned-out children. The Asian families had an old-fashioned look: they seemed to be shy, restrained people. Becky Mayne was standing in a corner, talking animatedly to somebody he did not recognise. Near the drinks table, he saw a tall Asian woman holding an orange juice, pretending to enjoy the flower arrangements. Lucas decided to take a gamble.

"*Suorseday.*"

"*Suorseday.*"

"Lucas Bellwether. I was a good friend of Dermott."

"*Bong jeh phiasaa kh'mai te?*"

"Only very badly. I was living in your country for a couple of years."

"How do you know it's my country?"

She was probably in her early fifties. She had a thin face, carefully made up, with a pronounced jawbone and artfully piled hair; one piece was a fringe, another a central sweep swirling around the base of an elaborate bun. She wore a black silk dress with a laced frontage. Her head was raised and her eyes were fixed on the portrait of Vann.

"So you knew our Tepp?"

"Tepp?"

"We never called him Dermott you know. That was something he invented for the English. If you are acquainted with Cambodia you will know we all have many names."

She smiled and as she did so lines sprang across the edges of her eyes.

"My name is Elise Vann. I am from the family. He was my brother. My very loyal brother." She nodded slowly, as if to emphasise the *very loyal*, and tears quickly collected in her eyes.

They shook hands. "Tell me" said Lucas "are your family all in the UK?"

She sighed, as if fatigued by social small-talk. "One or two are here. Some over in California. And some still in Phnom Penh of course. Everywhere. Paris too. There is a big Cambodian diaspora."

"Yes, I know that. Let me say it was always a pleasure spending time with your brother. He was a distinguished man, and always very attentive to other people. It's... er, a dreadful loss."

"Yes."

"Actually, do you think, Elise, I could give you my card? I hope to be in Cambodia in September. If there are any family there who were close to Dermott, I would love to visit them to pay my respects. As one who knew him as a friend."

"I see."

At that moment Becky Mayne came rushing up to him and told him that there and then he had to make a speech. Sorry about zero notice. It had been decided by the group over there. There was to be a speech by a friend and then one from an uncle of the family. The friend was him. Somebody started tapping a champagne glass. Lucas pulled out his wallet, extracted a business card, pressed it into Elise Vann's hand, turned, smiled at the expectant party, and spoke. By the time he had finished five minutes later, Elise was nowhere to be seen.

*

"Well I thought you absolved yourself quite honourably there, young man."

"Thanks. It's what we're trained to do I suppose."

"It is indeed." Dawn took a meditative pull on her Dunhill. "Nevertheless, some do it better than others."

The gathering had broken up and people had gone their separate ways. Becky had befriended Dawn, the conference interpreter woman, and they had gone for a cup of Earl Grey in an artsy tea-shop somewhere down the road. Lucas purchased several pretty tins of tea. Always useful as gifts, he claimed. Dawn needed to smoke. So they sat outside, which was a pleasure in the warm summer's evening. Conversation turned to how the death had affected the rest of the interpreting profession. It must have come as quite a shock. Dawn explained that a report had been commissioned and a conference linguist had been sent to Burma — or whatever they called it nowadays — to write it.

"What does the report say?" asked Lucas.

"Well, do you see... It says that she talked to a very helpful police officer, and ... she writes this up at some length, well, the helpful policeman ends up having no final conclusion on it at all! She requested to see the corpse and was not allowed. Oh, and she acquired evidence from a source which she is not prepared to reveal that it may have been deliberate intoxication. That's the long and the short of it. You mark my words" intoned Dawn, her patrician syllables rising to a more dramatic pitch "she's put the fear of God into me with that poisoning idea. I can hardly look at my tea without wondering what it might have in it. Arsenic? Rat poison? I mean fortunately the whole experience belongs to Asia and shall, I trust, remain within that corner of the world. They really are a most inscrutable lot. Poor old Vanny. He wouldn't hurt a fly."

Vanny.

"Does the report discuss motive?"

"Not directly. I think she's leaving that to the Burmese police. But she suggests we need to be on the look-out. Someone who has a grudge against interpreters, do you see. Though I can't possibly see why. I remember a long time ago, Addis Ababa it was…"

Dawn embarked on a story of a long-forgotten conference. Lucas allowed his mind to wander.

More than ever, Lucas wanted to be in Cambodia, to find out more about this man he had befriended without ever really knowing him. Make no mistake, this was not a Myanmar affair, it was a Cambodian one. That much he could sense. So, while he waited for confirmation of his speaking engagement, the impending trip to Phnom Penh was assuming grander proportions in his imagination, as if he were going on a pilgrimage to the tomb of some visionary. "Trip" was not an appropriate word; it was a *voyage* in the proper sense of the world, a journey to unknown territory. There would also have to be a travelogue, a daily journal of his wanderings. After all, he had, by sheer force of circumstance, become the custodian of Vann's memory: his credential to that office was unassailable. Had he not been with Vann at the moment of his death? That should be interpreted as a privilege. But privileges always entailed duties. His was an obligation to discover more. It seemed to him that he could not let a sleeping dog lie. It would amount to a kind of moral idleness.

Dawn's saga was far from finished. Becky was nodding dutifully. Lucas was drowsy from the cheap wine. His mind drifted further.

He was back in Phnom Penh, several years before. How many years ago? Two? Three? A century. A night in June. His wife had prepared the evening meal. They ate on the balcony beneath an electric lamp. The traffic was honking in the street below and a mosquito coil was infusing the air with its sharp scent. At each

[65]

of the two places, Sovany had laid a table napkin with a wooden ring.

"What is this?" he had asked.

"It's a table napkin. It's the western way" she replied with a smile.

"The western way?"

"I thought it would please you."

With Sovany, meals were a litmus test for acceptance of the tremendous differences that defined their union. Most things required patience, concessions, understanding, compromise. There was nothing strange in that, and both knew that with enough affection, enough love, such things could be overcome. The dietary regime had been particularly problematic. He was definitely not taken with the Khmer cuisine; she had little time for meat and two veg. Going out to restaurants was a ritual that she knew was meant to flatter her but which only succeeded in puzzling her. Eating out was also, in her view, a tremendous waste of money. She was a former catering manager, after all. She knew how much the true cost of food was multiplied by the time it was served on a plate. Even in a cheap restaurant. And Lucas liked to take her to expensive places. His wife could not see the point of choosing your food from a menu; you picked your morsels once the different dishes were served on the table, not before. Anyway, there was one principal food, and that was rice; the rest was entertainment for the palate, no more. Gradually Lucas had come to adopt a When in Rome attitude. He was in her country. He would behave as she wanted. They ate Cambodian meals at home. It took a considerable effort on his part.

So when Sovany laid napkins with rings, something inside him was deeply moved. She had been to buy them, obviously, in a high-end boutique somewhere and was making a demonstration of her readiness to reciprocate, to accommodate his tastes. She must have taken somebody's advice and made her choice with care. He said how touched he was, rose from his place and kissed her fondly. It was important to her that her gift, and its weighty significance, be appreciated, Lucas could see that, and he was not going to let her down. He made great play of removing the pretty linen napkin from his wooden ring and placing it across his lap. She imitated his movements. Her face, frank as a stick-drawing in sand, registered deep pleasure. She had made a move in his direction to show her love for him, and his heart was warmed. Tears would have added melodrama, and he was determined to avoid that, but he would have been well capable of crying if he had not restrained his emotions.

She put a helping of rice in his plate.

But the emotions stifling him were not so simple. There was a bigger battle resounding in his chest. The napkins were *wrong*. Simply *wrong*. Lucas could not conceive of himself using table napkins. It was a leap too far. It was that little jut of rock that suddenly crumbles when the chasm seemed successfully negotiated, leaving the climber swinging from a rope a hundred feet below. Sovany had made an unwitting mistake. A harmless error, a mistake of gigantic proportions. And as he examined the polished wooden ring, its subdued shine collecting the lamp's light, the earth's crust fractured before him and he toppled into oblivion. He knew for certain that he and Sovany would never, ever reconcile their differences enough to be together, to be one. The ring had magical powers. Or perhaps the powers belonged to the woman. With piercing accuracy, Sovany had illuminated a place that was supposed to be invisible.

He was appalled by the precision of the realisation. Instantly he felt cruel, uncaring and unfeeling, and immediately he tried to disguise it. That evening he treated her with great gentleness, wrapping her naked body as she stepped from the shower, enveloping her in tenderness, and making love to her with great care, holding her like a bird that had tumbled from a nest and needed to be returned to it with the least damage.

But Sovany was not a fledgling missing her nest. She was a woman of strength who was happy to put her childhood behind her. She was a woman who would have been ready to become a mother if only her husband could come to terms with the idea.

"And so..." continued Dawn, warming to her theme and tapping him on the arm for emphasis "once the minister from Senegal finally understood that he was *allowed* to speak French, that was precisely when his microphone broke down! Chaos! The chairman was almost in tears, you mark my words..."

PART III

Phnom Penh, Cambodia

I

Travel Journal of Lucas Bellwether

Phnom Penh, Cambodia. 8 September

Hotel on 19th street. Standard PP boutique offering. Mattress ok but carpeting has damp aroma. View over red tin roofs. Thin walls. You can hear the TV in the next room. I called downstairs in the middle of the night to get him to turn it down. Then he started coughing. An Asian cough, loud and dry. In Asia clearing your bronchial tubes is blessed with noble entitlement. Every 40 seconds, for half an hour. It is funny how little it takes to want to strangle somebody.

There is a rather attractive pottery bowl on the bedside table. Might buy a set for London if reception will tell me where they got them.

The Criminal Law Round Table has been ok so far. Seen a few old faces from before. There are the itinerant windbags trying to find important things to say, jumbled in with others who have interesting points to make. (I class myself among the latter). Jens from ICC is here and we had a good evening catching up in the new restaurant that has replaced Rahu. A Senegalese guy (prosecutor) called Dieulouard is here to talk about the trial of Hissène Habré in Dakar. Four investigating judges. An Argentine forensic anthropology team doing exhumations. The courts of one country (Senegal) prosecute the former Head of State of another (Chad) for human rights abuses. This must be the first time this has ever happened. Like France putting Tony Blair on trial in a court in Poitiers. Exciting! Habré went bananas on the first day of the trial, yelling about the injustice of it all. Echoes of our own dear Ieng Thirith, cursing the Belgian prosecutor to the seventh circle of hell. Must get Dieulouard into a nice restaurant so he can tell us more.

Round Table ends tomorrow.

Phnom Penh is still lovely Phnom Penh. Went for a walk along Riverside early this morning. Down by the Chaktomuk theatre, the light was like tinsel. People had gathered along the water, merchants of coconuts, pomegranates and lotus flowers, pushers of carts with sodas and mineral water, fortune tellers shuffling decks of cards, straggles of snotty children. They were there because it was congenial, it was near the Royal Palace, and it was where people came to buy their flowers for the shrine. They were there too for the light, which the river radiates — an incandescent blue. This too is why all these people have chosen this spot. The confluence is blessed.

As the sun rose and the traffic thickened I cut across to FCC for a coffee and a scan for emails. Good coffee; waitress half asleep. There was an email from Elise in London, Vann's sister.

"Dear Mr Bellwether,

I hope you have been doing well since we last met at my brother's commemoration gathering. I was touched by the speech you made on that occasion and would like to thank you for your words. You will understand that it was rather trying for me to be present with all those people and I hope I will be forgiven for making an early departure. Since then I have had time to consider your request for the contact details of my family in Cambodia. Perhaps you are in Cambodia already — I believe you said you would be there in September. There is a lady, rather elderly by now, who helped bring us all up, who lives at no 64 in Street 398. Her name is Makara. She will be able to tell you about when we were all younger (she speaks French, I assume you do as well). She will help you if you are patient with her, and you might find a way to thank her as she is always short of funds.

Sincere regards, Elise Vann."

This was perfect. And unexpected. Thank you Elise. I had rather given up hope on that source. My next port of call is now clearly mapped out. A telephone number might have helped but a name and address is a start.

12 September

Saw the lady called Makara this morning. Dropped in on her at 10.30 — it seemed a reasonable hour. A nice old 1950s house, divided into flats, worn fleur-de-lys tiling, steep stairways, a little terrace shaded by a fan palm admitting long blades of morning light. Strange toblerone geometry — triangular ventilation shafts.

My mission took a bit of explaining at the 3rd floor: *Je m'appèle Lucas, je suis un ami de Vann Tepp et voilà... sa soeur Elise m'a encouragé de venir...* This old lady wasn't used to people turning up on the doorstep and sounding off in bad French. Elderly, tall, rather powdery figure. A lot of pride apparent in the way she looked at me. When she eventually clicked about who I was and what I wanted, became quite affable; ushered me in, made tea and spoke in educated, old-fashioned French.

Bizarre thing this evening. I have changed hotels to a little guesthouse near the Psa Chas. Market as smelly as ever. The room is cheaper than the hotel. No pool but nice simple room, view goes up across the roofs towards the Japanese Friendship Bridge. Anyway, the same pottery bowl has appeared on the table. The same one. Only this time there is an odd little pottery disc in it as a kind of decorative feature. I *must* ask where these bowls come from. The room was very quiet. I slept fine apart from the *kdao kdao* man in the street selling his savouries at 6 am. Rose early and took a walk along the river. People waving their arms in mass exercise routines, the early light playing on the water. Barges chugging their way downstream to be fed by dredgers. Breakfast of chicken soup with banana flowers. Back to see Madame Makara for a second visit this morning.

Makara was probably rather beautiful when she was young. A high forehead and well-drawn lips. Cheekbones like ivory billiard balls. Her fingers are very thin and carry many rings which I could imagine switching from one finger to the next like a counting game for a child. She talked about her curtains, apologetically. It really was time she had them changed. (She was right.) The sofa too, while she was at it. It ran out of bounce a long time ago. On the shelf were a couple of photos of children taken at a beach. There was also a family group with a father with swimming trunks and brilliantine hair and a mother displaying an absent-minded, lost look.

We talked for about three hours, then she got tired. I left her in her sunken armchair and went down into the street, where the air was fresher. There is no air conditioning in her little apartment and the ceiling fan was not really up to the task. Promised to drop by again. I walked all the way up Pasteur and by the time I got to the bistro I was drenched with the heat. I sat down, ordered a cold Angkor beer, and contemplated the story that Makara had told me. Roughly, this is what I have understood so far:

There were three children. Tepp was the eldest, followed by Chanty, followed by Vuthy. These were the names by which the Cambodian father knew his children. Their mother, who was from France, called them Marcel, Elise and Sophy. This dual naming system, said Makara, was not a problem in the family. Their father was a Cambodian man who had an army job that was something to do with commissaries and supplies. He had been born into the comfortable end of Cambodian society and was quite well connected. He met his wife at a social gathering of officers that took place at the time of independence, in the mid-fifties. She was accompanying a French delegation from St Cyr that had come over to Cambodia to provide training to the army officers of the new country. Makara did not know exactly how or why the young Odette was included in the delegation but the fact is that she was and she met First Lieutenant Vann Ang at a cocktail reception at the French Embassy and the two of them fell in love. They were married in Phnom Penh in 1956 and Tepp was born in 1957. It was a happy union. The two girls were born in 1958 and 1960. Odette was not a strong woman and childbearing did not really suit her gentle constitution. That was partly why Makara got roped in to help. Aged in her late twenties, she was the widow of an artillery colonel who had died in an accident on the firing range. She needed somewhere to live, and she gradually joined the family, part half-sister to Odette, part surrogate mother to the children, for all a confidante. Makara became family; where they went, she went too.

In those days Phnom Penh was a quiet, leisurely city. The wide avenues saw little traffic; the occasional Ami 8 or Renault 4L chugging alongside American saloons sold off by the US Embassy. The houses were white and clean and fountains adorned the parks. The elite enjoyed a contented life and the serving man knew his place. For the Vann family some of the happiest times were spent away from the city at Kep-sur-Mer, as Kep used to be called, where Ang built a Corbusier-ish villa that looked out onto white sandy beaches and the Gulf of Thailand beyond. The children always loved the seaside. It was where they found themselves and grew into teenagers, socialized with other Franco-Khmer families, held hands with their classmates from the Lycée Descartes for the very first time, and had their hearts broken. When Elise saw her fourteen year-old paramour Jean-Sébastien kissing a local girl behind the breakwater, she didn't know whether she was more outraged in sentiment or in social rank. *Une pute Khmère!* The old lady could still remember Elise's outraged expletives. It was to Makara that they came with their troubles. On her shoulders they wept. Lovely Sophy/Vuthy was her biggest worry, always launching herself in the deep end with the boys, losing her virginity earlier than either of her two elder siblings, her nights a series of no-holds-barred trysts as the Asian moon slipped deep into the ocean. Tepp, or Marcel if you prefer, was very much a Daddy's boy, thrilled to be helping with the fitting-out of the Kep villa, keen to learn the secrets of army life and to talk the military jargon. The boy had his admirers among the *collègiennes*, but he tended to keep them at arm's length. Why go dancing in the Club Zodiac when you could be learning to strip a M1 Garand rifle? Elise was the one who was closest to her mother. She sensed what the others did not: that her mother was an outsider, that she missed France more than she dared say, that she often felt alone. It was the moral solitude of the exile compounded by the physical loneliness of a woman whose husband was often caught up with military duties. In the summertime merriment of Kampot crabs and white wine, the dark sea smashing against the rocks, I imagine Elise saw something in her mother's candlelit glance, a premonition of the nightmare to come.

By the time the seventies were in full swing and Johnny Hally-day was singing *Je t'aime, Je t'aime, Je t'aime*, Cambodia was at war. With itself. Prince Sihanouk was removed from the throne in a coup. A General called Lon Nol took charge of the country. We were all appalled, sighed Makara, when Sihanouk was de-throned. *Consternés!* But what could you do? Vietnamese troops were stirring up trouble in the north, spreading Ho Chi Min's ideology, and in the Eastern part of the country there was a home-grown communist rebellion by a bunch of lunatic Marxists called the Khmer Rouge. Lon Nol fought back, and the children saw less and less of their father, who by now had been promoted to a Colonel or some such rank and had duties to perform on the front line. Odette was gripped with anxiety. She knew other women who had lost their husbands in the fighting. It was a crazy war. Lon Nol was a stargazing nutcase who told his troops that if they wore the right lucky charms, the enemy bullets would not hurt them. The government soldiers threw themselves into action with great bravado and were quickly cut down. Vann Ang was too wise to listen to Lon Nol's nonsense, and despite Odette's fears he managed to return unscathed.

The children continued with their schooling, moving up from *collège* to *lycée*, while the nervous city filled with refugees from the hinterland. The new Cambodiana Hotel became a base for the fugitives who camped out in the unfinished rooms and turned the swimming pool into an open cesspit. Odette helped organise school fundraisers to buy food for them, and she and Elise (now aged 16) were constantly ferrying provisions and medicines down to the Cambodiana by tuk-tuk or bicycle. Elise...the wiser sister, forced to mature at a faster rate than Odette would have wanted. By early 1975 artillery shells were exploding in the streets; the sight of corpses had become commonplace. More and more people flooded into the city from all over the country, desperate to escape the unstoppable advance of the Khmer Rouge. By April the enemy had pitched camp on the other side of the Mekong, from where the guns continued to shell the streets. People who could afford to leave made their escape plans. Lon Nol flew out to exile in Hawaii in one of the last Dakotas to lift off from Pochentong airport. Colonel Vann Ang instructed his family that as soon as the Khmer Rouge reached the gates of Phnom Penh, wherever they were and whatever they were doing, they were to go immediately to the French Embassy. On 17 April 1975, the Khmer Rouge entered the city in triumph. The children did as they were told, and Makara and Odette followed, hauling the last suitcases. Their father entered the embassy the following day after burning his uniform and ditching his Garand in the nearest sewer.

Then as now, the French Embassy occupied a large estate at the top of Boulevard Monivong, and for a while life continued almost normally. Consul Jean Dyrac was in charge, an able man who had been tortured by the Gestapo thirty years earlier and who knew a serious crisis when he saw one. People poured into the embassy grounds and by the time there were 1000 people inside, the two gendarmes at the gate were told to admit only those with foreign passports. The French doctors evacuated Calmette Hospital and set up a clinic in the grounds. For the time being, there was enough rice to go round. The general hygiene of the surroundings worsened, however, with people defecating behind every available bush. Tepp was inseparable from his father, helping with manual tasks, hefting rice sacks, digging latrines. Elise stuck with her mother, doing her best to boost her flagging morale. Sophy sat under a tree and wept. Her latest Cambodian boyfriend was nowhere to be seen. She had lost touch with him completely. The Khmer Rouge had told everybody to pack enough belongings for a few days. Everybody was to leave the city on foot because, so the story went, there was a strong likelihood that the US Air Force would bomb the city. Columns of people shuffled past the embassy gates every day, heading out to the countryside in the hottest month of the year, not yet knowing they were the expendable manpower for the new agrarian revolution. Some collapsed and died at the roadside.

[77]

The crunch came when the local KR official (Nhem) told Dyrac that only foreigners were to remain in the embassy and all the Khmers had to leave the compound. Legal arguments about territorial inviolability of diplomatic premises meant nothing to them. (These were the socialists who had smashed open the door of the Soviet Embassy with a bazooka shell.) If Dyrac didn't deliver the Cambodians, Nhem and his men would come and get them by force. If a Khmer woman was legally married to a foreigner, she could stay. If a Khmer man had married a foreigner, he should give himself up. Desperate to save the foreigners, Dyrac delivered the Cambodians to their fate. Exactly why Vann Ang had never bothered to get a French passport, Makara could not say. She had assumed it was some obscure matter of national pride taking precedence over expediency. Tepp's father left the embassy grounds, a smile clamped on his face, pacing slowly in a grim line of very frightened people. Odette, who knew that she would almost certainly never see her husband again, collapsed. Makara, herself Cambodian, was also forced to quit the safety of the embassy.

The question of Tepp's passport was still more complicated. Tepp actually possessed a French passport. All the children did. Marcel Vann-Delveaux was the name printed on it. But somehow Tepp had lost his passport. He said he had never had it at the embassy. Maybe. He may have actually had it at the embassy and conveniently mislaid it behind a bush. Whatever the truth was, Makara knew that the 18 year-old wanted only to follow his father. Come what may. Was it loyalty to him? A teenager's protective instincts for the father he loved? Something else — making him abandon his sisters when he could have stayed with them? She could not say.

The first thing that happened was that the women were separated from the men. Makara was herded on her way, the start of a punishing trek towards the rice fields of Kampong Cham. The boy stayed with his father. They were taken a short distance by truck to a shunting yard behind the railway station. At the station they were interrogated by two officials wearing black uniforms and *krama* scarves. Ang told his captors that he was an engineer and ready to serve the new regime. His young assistant was also ready to do what he could for his country. He was, of course, desperate to conceal the fact that Tepp was his son. The KR official told Ang that he had been identified by several people as a Lon Nol military officer. Why else would he hide in the embassy? The young assistant would be shown what happened to liars in the new Democratic Kampuchea. Ang was led outside into the bright sun and made to lie face-down on the railway track, his arms and legs spread in a cross so the hands and feet rested on the metal rails.

Ten minutes later, Tepp staggered away, his soul in pieces.

On 4 May 1975 Odette and her two daughters joined a truck convoy from the French Embassy which reached the Thai border the next day. From the border, they were taken to Bangkok, and from there they were airlifted to France.

15 September

Dinner tonight in an old place that I used to come to often with Sovany. I have flopped down in a chair right under the ceiling fan, pen in hand. This is a nice place run by a big family. Their restaurant has two shrines, one parked on the floor, with red lighting and a holy effigy which has been offered two glasses of cold tea, a Marlboro Lite and four pomelo grapefruit, and another mounted on the wall with smoking incense sticks. The young mother is doing English homework with her boy. He is accomplished. "Do you want to eat my sandwich for breakfast?" he asks. She giggles "No, I no." The chief waitress in a scarlet waistcoat sidles up to greet me, where you wife? I tell her that Sovany and I are no longer together. Sovany is with her mama in Prey Veng. Oh so sorry Sir. She then tells me she is sick with worry about her sister, who is going to hospital for to make cut. A swipe of the fingertips from sternum to groin shows me where the cut is to be made. The sister is due for a Caesarean. With careful miming I explain that the incision will be much smaller than she thinks, horizontal and not vertical. "Cut is bad" is all she says, and it's hard to contradict her. Then she quickly switches tempo and does a lewd movement with a green banana for the benefit of a male waiter. The sob story is reserved for the foreigner with the dollars in his pocket. I go for the *lok-lak*, and first a cucumber salad with hard-boiled egg. Fiendishly good mayonnaise.

Perhaps it wasn't a good idea to come here. I miss the old days. I miss Sovany in places like this. All the fun we had. I remember that fateful night of the napkin rings. The straw that broke the camel's back. That sudden moment of despair — was it really an illumination, or just a moment of stupidity?

This morning I went to talk to the people at the guesthouse reception. Where did they get the pretty bowl on my table? They didn't. Somebody came by and said it was a gift for me. And the funny thing inside? Also part of gift Sir. A gift? From who? Not the Criminal Law Round Table, it was too late in the day for that. It is not uncommon if you are attending a conference to have little trinkets deposited in your room, a token of appreciation from the organisers. But this was not like the usual gifts, which always had someone's logo on it and were obviously institutional. This was just a bowl with a funny disc in it. Who delivered it? Oh Cambodia man Sir he come on *moto*. Maw-toh.

The explanation will be forthcoming in due course, I suppose.

Yesterday I hired a RAV4 and drove 30 k to the temples at Oudong. I was not dying to see these temples, which I have visited before, but I did want to give Makara a 24-hour break from my presence and this was as good a thing to do as any. It can't be easy for her being forced to take her mind back to all that turmoil. Anyway it was fun chatting with the people selling fish and crabs in the woods at the bottom of the hill. A little boy gave me an unsolicited guided tour as we climbed the steps to the summit of the hill, he talking non-stop all the way (excellent pidgin English), me needing to pause for breath. Towards the top somebody took a picture of the two of us just as I was giving him a dollar for his pains. Then quickly disappeared. Who was this? Could be just some NGO twat who wants a photo for Facebook to vaunt his anti-trafficking/paedophilia exploits. Could be something more sinister. It left me feeling uneasy. Am I being watched?

This morning I went to see Makara again and asked her about what happened to Vann during the Democratic Kampuchea period. She said she did not know exactly where he went or when. Perhaps she had known once, but she had forgotten. He had been assigned to a village somewhere in Kampong Cham, and like all the "new people", which was the name they gave to the city-dwellers, he had been half starved while working to plant and harvest rice. Pol Pot wanted an output of three tons per hectare, which was unheard-of in Cambodia. Much of the rice they grew was trucked off to China in exchange for weapons and supplies. At one stage Tepp was randomly arrested and sent to a security centre (ie death camp) where he had been shackled by the ankles night and day, but later he was released to go and join the slave labour gangs building the airfield at Kampong Chhnang under the direction of air force commander Sou Met. It was a new airfield construction project where Chinese engineers did the plans and Khmer prisoners, many of them former soldiers, were sent to cut rocks and lay cement. The term they used was to "temper" people, which was supposed to mean bringing them to terms with Khmer Rouge ideology, and in practice meant instilling blind terror. Perhaps Tepp survived it all because he knew that nothing worse could ever happen to him than what he had been made to endure at the railway station. I could only imagine it must have hardened him and completely switched off a portion of his mind. By 1977 and 78 some strange things were happening among the ranks of the Khmer Rouge. The top brass were obsessed with defections, and the movement began to eat itself from within, executing a number of its own chiefs in energetic purges. The Vietnamese were also making tentative incursions, getting ready for the day in 1979 when they would invade Democratic Kampuchea and topple the regime. So great was the threat from the east that soldiers were needed in large numbers to fight the Vietnamese on the border, and Tepp was one of the ones who benefited from a generalised "pardon", ceasing his work at the airfield and heading off to the battlefront with a rifle in his hands.

"He went to kill Vietnamese. I don't know how many he killed in those battles. Maybe none at all. Everything was upside down in those days. Nobody knew who owed allegiance to whom. And when the war ended and the regime fell to pieces, it was the Vietnamese who took him. They took him to Saigon and put him in a university, of all things. They taught him everything: politics, philosophy, history, mathematics, everything. They were extremely patient and extremely thorough. They taught him to speak Vietnamese as well. Did you know he spoke Vietnamese?"

"I didn't."

"They wanted to train a new set of people to help tighten their grip on the whole of Indochina. They had beaten the Americans and nothing was going to stop them. Vann spent three years in Saigon. Living in a dormitory at the University. There were many like him. When he came out he was sent to Phnom Penh to be an army instructor. He was a completely new person."

"But he was surely the same man inside. What about getting back to the rest of the family? Letting them know he was still alive?"

Tepp had become part of a new Vietnamese-trained cadre that had been groomed to manage a starving, war-torn Cambodia as if it were an extension of Vietnam. The people who run Cambodia today, including the Prime Minister, all went through the same mill. Clearly, by Makara's account, Tepp had been tempted to assume a new persona, to encase the past in a dark cupboard somewhere in the recess of his mind, to step out and face the new world afresh. Perhaps it would have been intolerable for him to carry on as before; perhaps he simply could not contemplate facing his mother and sisters after what had happened on that first day of the occupation of Phnom Penh. Whatever the truth was, he stayed in Cambodia for a full five years before making the dreaded trip to France.

In 1987 he eventually went. He had no trouble finding their address — the Vietnamese kept good records. They were living in the southern edge of Paris in a place called Issy-les-Moulineaux. Vann (I don't want to call him Tepp) turned up unannounced. It seems that Makara was still in Cambodia at this time. She knew only the bare bones of the Paris story. When Vann turned up at the apartment in Issy, nobody recognised him. He was profoundly changed. So too was his family. Once they had realised who he was, the sight of him filled them with happiness and terror. If Vann was there, Ang was not. The hopes they had clung on to for so many years, that just possibly both father and son had survived, were finally dashed. Vann told them that their father was dead but he did not say any more than that. He was, moreover, talking to two people only. Vuthy was gone.

With every fresh detail she had heard about the Cambodian hecatomb, the weaker Vuthy had become. She had, it seemed, sought a kind of obliteration in physical love, and when sex failed to anaesthetise her fears, and when word had got around among the men that though she was pretty as hell she was also stark raving mad, and no-one dared go near her, she ended her short life under a metro train at the Solférino stop. That left Odette and Elise, the former in a deep depression, the latter pushing on with the business of surviving: an economics degree at Nanterre, a man called Victor who loved and respected her, and a vast amount of her energy devoted to keeping her mother on an even keel. Elise was exhausted, but Elise never lost her courage.

18 September

In the bookshop with two cups of coffee and a Danish pastry that has ginger and mango in it. On the nearby sofa, bloated Cambodian children are whining to their wealthy mothers for more ice cream. The two mothers, who want to examine each other's Louis Vuitton bags, are offloading the decision on the nanny. The nanny, a skinny village woman with a dark face, is unsure what to do next. She cannot make this financial decision on her employers' behalf. So the mums say yes, anything for a bit of peace. The children argue with each other about what colours and flavours they want. Already they are well on the way to obesity. The nanny is patient and smiling. She gets buffeted and bashed by the heavy children, picks up their discarded tissues, wipes food from their faces. You can see she is not just being dutiful. She actually loves them.

Time to check the emails. Becky wants to know when I will be back in the UK. October is looking as if it could be quite busy. Where *do* I want to be, I wonder. Good question. Part of me wants to be in London, slowly digesting this tragic Cambodian story, watching the autumn breeze blow the petals off my climbing roses, ovening a pre-basted fowl from Sainsbury's with Ro admiring her belly and Duncan uncorking a robust Nuit Saint Georges. With a really good Netflix to take us through to the evening, when we will put on woollen scarves and stroll down to the Whistler's Arms for a slow, garrulous pint. But that will all be there when I get back. The other part of me of me wants to be here in warm, affectionate Phnom Penh, in the restaurant in Street 118, with Sovany on the other side of the table laughing at my latest silly joke. But that is a vain hope. What's done is done, as they say.

There is a picture from Ro, taking an eternity to download on whatsapp, showing the beginnings of a bump. Ro in seventh heaven, and mum and dad apparently over the moon as well. Great. When will I be back in the UK? Next. Joao from the Portuguese Embassy is thinking of organising a barbecue on the weekend of the 20th. When will I be back in London?

Headed off from the bookshop and walked into Pasteur to get a Vietnamese *phô* for lunch. With a beer, which becomes two beers. It's hot and sleepy. I have an idea of what I will do tomorrow. I want to get more of a feel of this young Vann, this Marcel, this Tepp, this 18 year-old forced to do the ultimate abominable thing to the father he loved so much. I want to go somewhere where he was. I want to see things he saw. I want to track this man down, come closer to him somehow. He would have been about 20 or 21 when he was labouring on the Kampong Chhnang airfield. A completely changed person, a zombie of sorts. Working, eating, sleeping. Thinking nothing.

I don't think I'll drive there myself. I'll get a car with a driver as well. Come to think of it, I'll get Rithisak.

19 September

At Kampong Chhnang we had to get the locals to give us directions to the disused airfield.

The weather was hot and heavy; the countryside flooded. The tyres going flap-flap-flap along the concrete segments of the airport road. Beside the road, dark faces peering from inside cotton *kramas*. The children were fishing for bullfrogs in the emerald marshes. After a sharp right turn we pulled up at a wired gate. Soldier. Beret, AK automatic, flip-flops. The public are not allowed entry, we were told. We must turn around and leave. A dollar exchanged hands and the gate swung open.

So here it was. The airstrip. The runway was made of more concrete segments. From the end of the strip, the yellow central marker disappeared into a sweltering mirage. The clouds across the horizon seemed to have been exhaled by the earth. Over the years, between the runway segments, the bitumen had melted and scabbed, with the result that worms had been able to emerge to make journeys across the strip, only to be scorched and dehydrated on the concrete.

"So many worms dead." murmured Rithisak. "No birds sing."

It was an eerie place, no doubt about that. Here, in the beating sun, stone was carried down from the nearby hills, the terrain was levelled out, and the concrete was laid. The rations provided to the workers, rice floating in water, were wholly inadequate, and thousands died from exhaustion. Their deaths were of no concern to the DK leaders. Rather, they proved what they suspected, that these weak people were of little value to their revolution. As the evacuees from the cities were told in a chilling aphorism, broadcast over the radio: "To lose you is no loss. To keep you is no gain." To the left of the airstrip, a whitewashed control tower, now the domain of a rabble of peasant children. A herd of goats traversed the runway. To the right, a scruffy patch of palm jungle.

"Many dead people buried in jungle?" asked Rithisak. "Many, many" I assured him. He giggled nervously. "Now we go."

"In a minute Rithy. I just need a little more time."

Time for what? Time to absorb. Time to hear the silence that comes when words get tired. Time to admit defeat before this terrifying absence of meaning, to reflect on the utter fatuousness of human cruelty.

This airfield has never been used to this day. It was all a complete waste of time. One more killing field.

Time to look for Vann in the ruts between the segments.

As we climbed back into our car, a black Toyota Landcruiser V8 drove across the runway, about sixty metres from where we were parked. Then it turned to approach us, coming to a halt some ten metres away. The windows were tinted and nobody was visible inside. Nobody got out. The black V8 is the vehicle of choice for those who belong to the country's governing elite. It is a voluminous, tubby car, with huge tyres and no elegance in the design. It is like a battle tank. You feel that nothing will stand in its way. Once, driving to work on route 4, I saw a V8 drive straight over a cheap motor scooter that was obstructing it. The owner of the scooter was powerless as he watched his machine being crushed. It's like that in Cambodia. You are either rich, or you are poor. Untouchable, or defenceless. This is all by way of saying that Rithisak and I felt pretty uneasy when this car stopped in front of us.

"Ok Rithy, it's time to go now."

We drove across the concrete to the big wire gate. The Landcruiser tailed us. The soldier opened the gate as we approached. In the mirror I saw him saluting the black car when it purred through behind. We watched it following us along the approach road, past the children fishing in the marshes.

"Why is he following?"

"Keep driving Rithy. Easy. Don't speed up."

By this time, the Landcruiser was almost on our bumpers. Again, I told Rithisak not to speed up. Play it cool as if nothing was wrong. Eventually the wooded lane reached the main road. As we pulled into the next gap in the traffic, I heard a two dry taps and a whoosh. We drove ten metres before the car started to bump and Rithisak declared we had a flat tyre. Rear left. We pulled into the verge. I looked backwards in vain: the battle tank had already reversed back into the foliage.

We changed the tyre and drove south. There was about an hour of silence. During this time my legs were locked into this kind of uncontrollable trembling. I wanted to be sick. Then this:

"Mister Luc."

"Yes."

"Mister Luc..."

More silence.

"Those men shot my car."

"I know Rithy. I told you I will pay you for the tyre."

"No Mister Luc I'm not talking money. No. Why do they shoot? You must do a very bad thing to make them want to shoot the car."

"I haven't done anything bad. Don't worry Rithy."

"You don't understand these people Mr Luc. You don't understand Cambodia."

"Maybe."

"Not maybe! You don't understand! These people are very dangerous. Very, very dangerous. You make them angry, you pay the price. Next time they shoot not my car they shoot you."

Another long silence. By this time we were entering the outskirts of the city, gunning our way through a dusty Muslim district. Mosques. Pedestrians in veils. I just wanted to be home in the hotel.

"Mister Luc. I am very sorry. I have wife and children. Please never call me again. I am so sorry."

"It's ok. I understand Rithy."

20 September

Not much doing today. Taking it easy. I am trying to will myself up to go for a swim at the Cambodiana. I like that place. I know the hotel is a bit down at heel, but still. The things those walls must have heard... And the pool has an excellent view of the Mekong. Miles and miles of water.

I will see a couple of old buddies for dinner. Jean-Luc and Carlos, ex-French and Chilean police forces respectively. And if I know those two, we will end up in some karaoke dive afterwards.

21 September

I was planning to see Makara for one last time this morning. But I couldn't. Horrible hangover. A real A1 humdinger deluxe. Last night we ended up in Nero's. Aptly named palace of sin. Beer, far too much after the *magret de canard* at the bistro, the duck already extremely well lubricated with Côtes du Rhone. The Nero's girls kept putting ice in our beer, but that didn't stop us drinking about eight bottles each. Interspersed with vodka shots. Jean-Luc knew a lot of the soapy Khmer ballads and the girl who had attached herself to him had a great voice for the female parts. Carlos gave us an atrocious rendering of some Julio Iglesias love songs. I stuck to boring old John Lennon. My partner gave it her all:

"Imagine all-y peee pú...livvy ninny jhar mony! Ooh Ooh!" with ferocious giggles and stroking my leg as if she was dusting her mother's dresser.

Ok, so I will see Makara tomorrow. Good night Cambodia. And good luck.

22 September

Breakfast of chicken soup with banana flowers. I can't eat enough of this. I thought about the conversation I had with J-L and Carlos. In the bistro, while we were still sober. Told them about the tyre-shooting incident. They told me to watch out. I asked why

— I had done nothing to upset anybody. I explained the background: I had been visiting an old lady to hear about the early life of a Cambodian I knew in London who had died rather suddenly. I had thought I would go and have a look at the airfield he helped build.

J-L: Lucas you combed through Khmer Rouge records for three years. You're talking as if you had just found them in Wikipedia.

Carlos: Watch your arse Lucas. You don't know what you are dealing with. Or who. You know they don't like people digging around. Why do you think we carry weapons when we go to talk to these people?

J-L: Don't play games Lucas. You can't win. Visiting an old lady? Who is she? What do you know about her? The early life of a Cambodian? Oh yeah? Who? And now you say he has just dropped dead in London?

Me: He died in Myanmar. He had this sudden attack of convulsions. Collapsed on the pavement.

J-L: Jesus Christ Lucas! Open your eyes man! When are you leaving Cambodia?

Me: I have a flight on the 26th. I have stuff to get back to in London.

Carlos: That's four more days. Don't miss your flight whatever you do. Promise me you will be on that flight.

After breakfast, I went to pay Makara a final visit. I found her enfolded in her poverty, sitting dreamily on her old armchair, eyes glazing over, and I thought that the two ex-cops were being a tad over-dramatic. What danger could this dormouse possibly represent? People say things to make themselves feel more important than they are.

I did not go to extract more information out of the old lady. I had squeezed the lemon dry enough as it was. I wanted to leave on a note of respect and gratitude. I had prepared a gift for her: a nice lacquer box that I had bought in the Russian Market, and in it I put an envelope containing a good few dollar banknotes. That was my contribution, so to speak, to her getting some new curtains, though I knew she would use it for a multitude of other things.

"You are very kind" she said politely. *Il ne fallait pas.*

"It's a small token" I replied. "I can't thank you enough for sharing the family story with me."

"Well you know, it's only one story in thousands. You will know this already if you worked at the tribunal here. Thousands of families destroyed. Hundreds of thousands. These stories go on for ever. They never stop."

"You will understand why I am particularly interested in this one. I knew Vann."

"Tepp. Yes. I do understand that. But don't forget this was a cataclysm which swallowed up millions of people. Millions."

"It occurs to me that you never told me your story Makara."

At that point she laughed. A little tinkling laugh that showed the lipstick stuck to her teeth.

"My story? Ha ha! It's long and complicated. We Khmers are complicated people Mr Bellwether. My story will be for another time. If you happen to see Elise tell her to write to me. I have not heard from her for ages."

"I shall. Goodbye, Makara."

It occurred to me, as I gripped the bannister on those steep tiled steps, that I had never told her that my name was Bellwether. Somebody else must have.

23 September

Not much today. Swimming pool. Had lunch on a street kerb with Chanty. Bookshop Chanty.

Slight breeze blowing towards the end of the day. It had rained, and the trees were green and fresh, the fronds of the palms dripping at the tips. Along the river bank, the usual crowds. The standard, slightly tacky Riverside scene. In the bars, overweight expatriates were hunkering down, puffy hands clutching their jug of Angkor Draft and their Cambodian teenager, watching the replay of Huddersfield beating Wolves. The Mekong was fat and pink — it seemed to me that the river had never been so full. Beyond the big bridge the sky was threatening more rain. I walked across Hun Sen Park, down the street where the braziers were being stoked for the evening's grill. A few yards along the pavement, the sugar-cane woman was covering her cane crusher for the night and packing up her stand. We exchanged greetings. It is nearly five years since she first served me a cup of her juice. The swiftlets were dive-bombing each other one last time before going to bed in their spittle nests on Street 21. The city seemed to exhale. The Gendarmerie Royale guards in front of the Prime Minister's residence relaxed, lit cigarettes, flirted with each other's friends. I stopped at the grill for a drink. The beer girls hovered, plonking unwanted ice in my litre of Kingdom, curious about the single *barang* and where he come from, what he do, where he go.

In fact — rather than sit and mope about the loss of his wife — the barang went to see a movie.

At the Chaktomuk Theatre it was the last night of the film festival. The night when all the VIPs turned up. The atmosphere at the theatre was really buzzing. Children, hair combed and pinned, were romping around the staircases in their Sunday best. The audience was almost entirely Cambodian. We were all summoned to rise as Princess Buppha Dhevi entered, the once pretty dancer now a tiny dark figure encircled by bowing diplomats. Rithy Pan, the celebrated film director, gave an opening speech to introduce the evening's choice, *Apsara*, a film made by Prince Norodom Sihanouk in the 1960s and starring a cast of royal family members, the only non-royal in the cast being the sulphurous Sak Sisbong. Sihanouk loved making films, by the way.

It went like this. Rattana (Sak Sisbong) is the unfulfilled widow, and Rithi, her lover, is a five-star general. Rattana wants a marriage proposal, and she is stepping up the pressure. But the general is a busy man. That evening he is guest of honour at an *apsara* dance show at the very same Chaktomuk Theatre, where he is mesmerized by a teenage performer (played by the very same Buppha Dhevi). This teenage dancer, Kantha, whose heart is pledged to a glamorous fighter pilot, is embarrassed by the older man's attentions. But the general is smitten, and drives off to see the girl's mother to ask for her daughter's hand in marriage. The mother, who knows a socially advantageous match when she sees one, gives the girl away without even consulting her. A lavish wedding follows. Rattana sizzles; in her anger she brings a young man home with her, but he disappoints. Meanwhile, the newly-wed dancer negotiates a 24-hour moratorium on the physical consummation of the marriage. Tragedy then looms when her brave lieutenant boyfriend takes a hit in his Dassault Mystère while defending Cambodia's skies against an unknown aggressor. Kantha rushes to his hospital bedside. Miraculously, he will survive; neither his nor the plane's vital parts have been hit. The young lovers embrace with passionate abandon. General Rithi knows when he is beaten and jumps into bed with Rattana after releasing the ballerina from the marriage. This time Rattana makes sure she gets her marriage proposal before surrendering to Rithi.

The whole drama was really an excuse for the Prince to paint a portrait of his beloved Cambodia, a place of stately cities with grandiose avenues uncluttered by traffic, patriotic pilots in their Mirage jets, lots of Mercedes and Jaguar saloons, and sumptuously costumed ballet pieces dating back to the Khmer golden age. It was also a tribute to 1960s Phnom Penh architecture, all angle and shadow, juxtaposed with the racy geometry of open-roofed sedans.

I was really struck by how much the audience in the Chaktomuk was thirsting for illusion. All disbelief was quickly suspended. They applauded the 1960s corps de ballet as if they were there in flesh and blood (as the lead ballerina was, somewhat less fleshly).

At the general's wedding party, Son Sisamouth and Ros Sereys-othea, the great singing duet of the era, were warmly applauded as they appeared on the screen. The singers with the "golden voices" came magically alive instead of being skeletons in a Khmer Rouge pit. These film-watching Cambodian families were out for a good time. They chatted and commented. When their mobile phones rang, they answered them. Snacks were being munched. Each time Sak Sisbong oozed on to the screen, bouffant sixties hair-do and boob-spilling dress, she got a hearty clap. Just when the post-marital bedroom scene began, a baby tore the air with a cry so primal that I wondered if it had just been born in the cinema. Probably had.

Apsara is an urban story, showing the metropolis in an idealized light. There were temples and fountains and avenues and gardens, and no smelly peasants, villages or huts. Rice-growing featured nowhere. The protagonists dressed with chic, were evidently possessed of large amounts of money, and sipped coffee from tiny golden cups. This was the film, they say, which persuaded the peasantry of Cambodia that the entire urban class was corrupt, dissipated and worthless. The Prince didn't know that he was sharpening the spur for revolution. The people knew in their hearts that the city elite were rotten; now they saw it on the screen. What further proof was needed?

Leaving the theatre, I was struck by the contrast between the city facing me and the one Sihanouk wanted to show in *Apsara*. As I stepped on to the pot-holed pavement, the heat whacked me like a body-blow. Heading up the road, I observed the Mekong at night, mesmerized by its slow movement as it carried all those billions of gallons of Himalayan water. Two street children came towards me, scampering and giggling, switching to a beggar's whine when they saw me, clutching their tummies in anguish. I told them to piss off, and one of them did just that, urinating in a proud arc into the water.

This was a film about the before. The pre-Democratic Kampuchea era, those sun-drenched days of Vann's childhood, grilling sea bass on the beach with his sisters, sand between their toes. Vuthy daydreaming. Makara in her 60's cat-eye sunglasses, cadging a light off Ang, his broad back sheltering them from the breeze as the cigarette repeatedly fails to light and she leans closer into his chest. She would have been a stunning beauty. Who would her admirers have been? She must have had a few. I gave up smoking several years ago, but just the thought of Makara on the Kep beach makes me want to light up.

Oh Makara. Enough riverside meditation: I was hungry for fuck's sake. The time had come for some dinner. I settled into a vigorous stride through the night, curving round the Sorya Mall and north up street 19. I called Carlos to ask him what he was up to and we decided to meet for a meal in the Korean place. Carlos asked me if I had been staying out of trouble. I said so far yes. Afterwards he growled off on his 650 cc. I wanted to walk home. By now it was about 11.30 — not so desperately late. That was when I was attacked by the two bugs.

It was by the national museum. There is an open field where they cremated Sihanouk when he died in 2013. Now it's just a mess of unused land. Along the wall of the museum it's quite dark, but it's hardly a shady backstreet. You get a couple of drunks hanging around, a few people snoring in hammocks, maybe a scabby ladyboy in a greasy wig that hasn't been washed for six months. But even so, don't get me wrong, it's bang in the centre of town. Anyway up comes this motorcycle, a small one, not a monster like Carlos' thing, with two smallish guys on the back in full-face helmets with tinted visors down. They were insect-like, short torsos and the absurd bulging heads, and they would have been comical in any other situation. They pulled up at the pavement, one of them hopped off the back and head-butted me in the kidneys with his helmet and while I fell down fighting for breath the other gave me two nasty hoofs in the belly as if he were scoring for Huddersfield from the mid-field. Then the first had a bamboo stick and was beating me hard on the right arm. Then they got on their ridiculous motorbike and drove away. None of the street denizens came to help. I just lay there for a bit. I only discovered I was in pain when I tried to get up about ten minutes later. I remember thinking in the tuk-tuk how glad I was my balls were intact.

25 September

I checked out of the guesthouse and checked into the Sofitel. I want to spend my last 24 hours here in comfort and this is the fancy hotel in town. Ok, yes, I'm getting scared. My chin has a rough graze from where I hit the pavement, but that is all you can see when I am wearing clothes. So when I checked in, the receptionist asked me if I had had an accident with a *moto* and I said yes without having to lie. She told me where the nurse had her sick bay if I wanted to get it looked at. I might just do that. I realise that my beating-up could have been a lot worse. It hurt like fuck at the time but in retrospect I can see they could have done a lot more damage. It was token, kind of. As if to say, we'll let you off lightly this time, but no guarantees about future beatings-up.

26 September

Packing finished. Body in slightly better shape today. The nurse clearly didn't believe me when I said I had fallen of a bike but she asked no questions and used some balms which did a lot of good on my arms and hips. Then some hefty painkillers. God I'm blue. Blue and grey. Look at me. Some people pay tattoo artists to do this to them. Well guys, all I can say is you get it for free in any dark alley in Phnom Penh.

Of course, the decorative bowl is there on the coffee table. Well done boys, good job. Five discs this time. I packed one disc in my suitcase, and trashed the rest. Then I smashed the pottery thing to fragments on the bathroom floor.

Just time for a nocturnal swim before the midnight flight. It was a dreamy swim, and after about three lengths I caught sight of Sovany sitting at the far end with her legs dangling in the water. I dived deep under and came up in front of her. She was very like her, but of course it wasn't Sovany. She looked at me with curiosity but no fear; I apologised before letting myself sink back beneath the water. I went down to the bottom, holding the breath in my lungs, and I knew at that moment that — whatever I may have thought in the past — I would return one day to look for the real Sovany.

II

Sambath sprawled across a deck lounger made of tropical hardwood. He stroked his hand along its lissom surface. Many of hours of sanding had gone into smoothing those legs, into sculpting the raw timber into the precise forms he wanted. The showroom was looking good. There were different sections, each upholstered as mock-up decors: master bedrooms, seigniorial dining rooms, living rooms with immense couches accessorised with tumbles of silken cushions. Above, there were large framed photographs of tattooed villagers that he had picked up in Myanmar. Srey Bopha, who managed his store, sat opposite him, trying to look relaxed, her responses attuned to every move of his head. This was the master, and the master had to find that all was satisfactory. A blemish here, an ill-matching picture there, and heads would roll.

A foreign couple entered the showroom. Australians, he assumed. They were large-boned people, raised — thought Sambath — on cow milk and pig meat. People who were big in every way, who actually fitted the oversized furniture as if it were made for them. Beside them, Srey Bopha was a dark midget. The manager performed her set-piece, showed them around, invited them to try the furniture, smiled her sweet Khmer smile, and nodded to an underling to produce two fresh lemon juices with ice. It was a blistering hot evening in Phnom Penh.

The couple went their way after placing an order for a teak dining set. He could see the delight on Srey Bopha's face. Silly girl. As if this was where he made his timber profits. As if these beds and dressers and wine-racks were anything more than a veneer of respectability. Idiot.

"You managed them well Srey Bopha. I like the way you got them to take eight chairs instead of six. Who invites only four friends? Ha ha. Who has only four friends? Very good."

"Thank you Bong Sambath." Rapture. She would take her clothes off now if he told her to. But no need. He did not undress

Khmer women. He was much more partial to paler meat. Light-weight pale meat, of course, not the elephantine kind that had just bought his dining room set. There was one exception to this principle, and one only. Later he would go and find her at the Blue Mekong Club, but first he had to talk to one of his suppliers.

A Cambodian man, casually dressed, passed through the sliding glass frontage. He held a small cardboard box. Sambath ushered him to the back office and told Srey Bopha that she had earned herself an early evening. He sat down at the table in the small office: a ceiling fan revolving slowly, shelves with ledgers, a magnetic board with unpaid invoices. No window.

"Show me."

The man pulled out a cutter blade and sliced open the box.

"You will see. Perfect air freshener system. I think you will like this."

From the box he produced a white plastic cube. Into the rear of the cube he fitted two double-A batteries and, inside a groove above the battery chamber, a transparent capsule containing a pink liquid.

"Cherry blossom in the springtime."

The man ran his fingers down the two black strips. "Auto-adhesive. Just peel off the film."

"Will it hold on raw plaster?"

"Raw plaster, tiling, wood, paintwork. Believe me, it sticks."

"Activation?"

"Activation precisely as you ordered, my friend, simple as pie. Remote."

The man stood the white box against the wall at the far end of the small room. From inside the packaging he extracted a slim remote control unit. "On. Off. Aim. Press."

The box emitted a discreet puff of air freshener.

"Range? Show me the same thing again. This time, right over there. By that coffee-table."

*

Romduol, usually called Romy, was named after the Cambodian national flower that is fragrant only at night. She was preparing herself for the late shift at the club. First, however, she had to attend to her mother. She mounted the flight of worn teak stairs and crept along a neon-lit corridor, inhaling the smells of breath and urine and old fruit that lurked behind the curtains. Before she got to her own compartment she already knew that her mama was sleeping from the rumbling noise she was making. She pulled aside the curtain. Dear mama, poor sick mama. Look at you. Like a great big fish in a tank, waiting to be eaten for lunch. She pouted her cheeks at the woman, imitating her snoring fish-mouth, then let the pout metamorphose into a kiss.

Romy sat down beside the sleeping woman. Her mother gave a deep grunt and shifted her body. A man sleeping in a cubicle further down the corridor replied in his sleep, muttering something she did not understand. A third person, disturbed by the noises, rose to urinate in a metal pot, the piss drumming against the sides. Other people stirred, whispered, snored their way back to sleep. There were six families living in rented compartments on this floor, all breathing the same old air in promiscuous closeness. Romy found it reassuring to be so near other people. Nothing bad could happen with so many good people surrounding you. She took the washrag and dabbed her mother's temples. Her mother opened one eye, whispered "Go carefully, my little baby" and slept again. Snore snore. Rattle rattle. Old fish, I love you.

Romduol had left school at twelve to help her parents in the rice fields. That did not mean she was not educated, however, because she was cleverly tuned to what people said and she knew how to piece together the important facts that governed people's lives. Health, for example. Obviously her mother was ill. This was caused by the cells in her body. Every human body was made up of cells. Most of them were in the blood, but a few were in the other parts like the legs or the liver. In the blood there were two

[99]

kinds of cells: red blood cells and black blood cells. The red were good and healthy; the black were the kind that pulled you down towards the earth and made you melancholy. The red lifted you up towards the sky. For people to be balanced and stay upright in the fields, you needed some of both cells, but trouble started when you had too many of one or the other, especially the black. Once the black got a hold, they increased and multiplied. That was what had happened to her mother when her auntie had died. Her auntie was in the earth and she was pulling Romy's mama towards the earth as well when mama was meant to be alive.

The reason for being alive was to do good. That was what we were on the earth for. If the great Lord Buddha had wanted her, Romy, to be in the sky, he would have given her the wings and tail of a swan. But he had not. He had given her gravity, just enough in each of her black cells to stay down upon the earth and do what kindnesses she could to people who were not happy. Most of these unhappy people were men. Men were predisposed to having too many black cells, in her experience.

One of the girls had told her that the Japanese understood her mother's illness and they had invented a kind of device which shot invisible bullets at people's blood and killed the black cells. Romy had been delighted to learn this. She also found out there was a device in the Khmer Soviet Friendship Hospital where people could go and be shot. She telephoned a nurse there and was told that every time you went for the shooting treatment it cost three hundred dollars. And you had to be treated many times, not just once. That was too much. She could never afford all that. Nevertheless, she was going to take her mama next Thursday morning for an appointment in the blood device department and she was going to ask them how to get a cheaper deal.

Romy snuggled beside her warm mother. It was like being a child again. Don't swallow me you great big whale! Let's hide under this fin. She was deeply happy. Surrounded by living, red-blooded people, carried away to a planet of love. The air was so sticky you could almost touch it, but soon the rain would come again and make them cooler. Life was perfect. Maybe it had its faults and its troubles, but she knew that all these people, concentrated together like a heap of warm mangoes, were so full of goodness, so ripe with truth and honesty, that no harm could ever come to any of them.

She had to keep an eye on her mother. Who else was there? Papa had died when his tuk-tuk had been pulverised between two large trucks on the big highway in Chom Chau. Neither driver even knew there was a man being mangled between their vehicles. Mama had had two sisters, but they were both gone in the dark times, killed by exhaustion when the salt had eaten into their legs at the Ambal salt farms. When Aunt Im stumbled from the weight of the salt sacks, the Khmer Rouge guards had slung her in a suspended bamboo cage as an example to the others. Without food or drink. She died soon after. Uncle Heng had had his brains smashed out on some worksite. She did not know where, and she did not care to find out. Then there were all those cousins who starved in Takeo. So who did that leave? Nobody. It left Romy. And Romy was damned if she wasn't going to take care of her mother.

She got up from the bedside. Time to choose a work outfit.

*

A Fidel Castro lookalike parks himself at the Blue Mekong bar. He has the costume and trimmings — the beard, the military cap, the field-green tunic. He is tall and manly. A Khmer girl with dyed straw-blonde hair approaches and climbs on to his lap. She is lanky and elegant, with rude good looks, and her movements are overplayed. She giggles wildly at a joke she has not understood, stretches her skinny arms upwards and slings them dramatically around the man's neck. He clasps her waist; she nestles her head on his shoulder and shudders. Sambath cannot resist giving her the conspiratorial eye and she returns a flashy wink. Was that a methamphetamine tablet she knocked back with the glass of water? Yama, *thnam kamlang*, the power drug that keeps you going during the long working hours and anaesthetises your mind during the sex. A tremor crosses her face: she is confident, yet ready to cry. She grinds her buttocks against the groin of her customer and closes her eyes.

A lumpish girl appears from nowhere and places a cold hand on Sambath's thigh. No, dear. Please. Do go away. Standards are really falling in the Blue Mekong. Who is that ridiculous movie extra over there anyway? This is meant to be a proper, exclusive place with a hefty subscription charge and a thug at the door, not one of those buttock-squeezing places on Street 103. It's time to discover a more exclusive venue. And where is Romy anyway?

Romy, it turns out, is behind the bar. She is having a chat with the bar woman about how to get a bit more coke and a bit less vodka into the drinks. She is dressed as if she is ready for a game of tennis, except that her clothes are not cut in white cotton but in black velveteen. The top has a zip that is undone down to her navel, and below there is a tiny skirt. She holds her legs in a way that does not betray whether the outfit includes underwear.

Romy is very beautiful. Most of the girls who work here are run-of-the-mill pretty. It's a basic on the CV. But Romy is beautiful. Sambath examines her as he orders a cocktail. Real rum, if you please darling.

A classic beauty. A face which, with little interpretation, would be ready for a museum of Asian art. Her eyes are large and dark, but not vulgarly so, slanted but not excessively, her nose long and slim while retaining its sensuousness, and her lips rounded without being thick. Her skin has not been subjected to any fashionable whitening treatment. Her complexion is burnt gold. Instead of hair she has jet-black silk. She sits down next to Sambath, relaxed and leggy.

"Romy."

"Oh. Jo Clayton. How are you tonight?" She knows it is not his real name.

"What's new, my night blossom?"

"Nothing. Mother still sick."

"You certainly know how to win a man's heart.'

"She is sick. If she sick, she sick."

On a couch on the far side of the room, Sambath has recognised a deputy director from the ministry of agriculture and fisheries. A decent family man, into whose hungry face a plump under-age girl is pushing her young breasts. Useful. Always useful, this sort of stuff. Sambath has a memory like a trap. Once in, never out. Maybe no need for a change of geography after all. You don't want to miss out on any of the news.

After sitting around for an hour at the bar, chatting with Romy about nothing at all, they take a spiral staircase leading to a small private room upstairs. For this privilege, he has to pay a "fine" for temporarily removing Romy from the bar downstairs. Once in the room she removes the top of her velveteen sports outfit to show him her perfectly formed upper body. He lights a cigarette. She then slips off the mini-skirt, and it becomes clear that there is nothing else to remove. Except the shoes. Lacquered red sandals with four inch heels. She stretches on the couch and lifts a leg on to the upper rim of the sofa.

Sambath only wants to look. Nothing else. Romy's body is without a doubt a vision of paradise, but it is the vision, only the vision, that he wants. That exciting kind of sex, where you cut your way into a person then discard her like dirty packaging, he reserves for the English girl.

III

It was called the Oncology Department. It was the head count that reassured Romy the most. So many people, everywhere. They were seated on rows of wooden benches and they waited and chatted and laughed. There were large fans to keep everybody cool, like aircraft propellers in a movie, mounted on the floor, aimed at the lines of people, blowing winds of health at them. In all the corridors there were people, waiting for a shooting or resting afterwards, and Romy found this atmosphere to be very convivial. It was easy to start up a conversation there. Everybody wanted to talk about their cells. There was a whole community of people who did nothing else all day. So many of them had mothers or fathers or sisters or brothers who had the wrong balance of body cells that Romy felt herself surrounded by sympathy in the Khmer Soviet Hospital, as if all the good she had done to others in her life was now being rewarded by a gush of benign providence.

The doctors were very kind and very patient. The one who looked after the old fish was called Doctor Sathea and she wore a special badge and a white coat with buttons and had a caring face which was not surprising considering that her name meant compassionate. Romy was not allowed to go inside the room when they wheeled the old fish in on her trolley because they said there were lonely cells flying around the machines which could come and stick on you, so the families had to be outside. When her mama came out she was not very happy and she would often vomit in the tuk-tuk on the way home, but Sathea had said not to worry it always happened and actually the old fish was doing well and soon they hoped she would be out of the worst danger. You must understand, little sister, Sathea told her. The road is long and she must walk slowly.

Romy was happy to think that she would be married soon. She had only met her future husband a couple of times at the village parties, but he seemed like a good man and he had a well-built wooden house with three rooms near the marshes. He had a small holding for rice but he had also bought a flock of ducks and was making quite a living from the duck eggs. He seemed to be a man with prospects. It would be so good to go back north to the village, and take her mama with her out of the city, and stop her job of having to please people.

But that was for later. The important thing, right now, was to get just a bit more money to help pay for the hospital. Because she was already bathing in good karma, Romy was barely surprised when the next stroke of fortune came her way in the shape of a call from Clayton. He sometimes called her in the evenings. Clayton! What a name, as if he were from Texas or Europe. He was just a Khmer man, not a *barang*, but she knew he was wealthy and he tipped her well. He said that in all the statues in all the temples in Cambodia there was not a body as beautiful as hers. She thought that was a pretty stupid thing to say. What would the statues think? She went to burn incense at the shrine when Clayton said things like that. She could tell he was rich by the generous cut of his shirt and the smell of his perfumes, but men were sometimes very stupid. You shouldn't upset anybody in the temples. Not the monks, not the ancestors, not the spirits in the carvings and statues. Anybody knew that. She was just a farm girl, but she knew that.

"Romy?"

"Yes?"

"Clayton speaking. Look Romy, I am going on a trip. I am going away for a few days to a place called Yangon. Do you know where it is?"

"Indonesia."

"Wrong."

"Frankfurt?"

"It's about two hours away by plane."

"I can't imagine that."

"You won't need to imagine it."

"What do you mean?"

"Romy, I want you to come with me. It's an important meeting I have to attend with some people who I must have some discussions with. In two weeks. Some financial discussions. Just the usual business things. When I go to these meetings in foreign countries it is not good to be alone. It is good to go with a woman. That is what they expect. They think there is something wrong with you if you go by yourself. So they find a woman for you and that makes all sorts of trouble. I want to go with someone I choose and I can't think of anybody I wish to go with apart from you. You will just be with me and be beautiful. I will take care of you."

"Why don't you go with somebody else? I cannot do this. It is too high for me. I am not a high person. Sorry Clayton."

"I will pay you well. And we will buy some nice outfits for you. You will choose what you want in the Aeon Mall."

"Hotel with bath or shower?"

"Hotel with bath *and* shower. And a room so big it takes a whole minute to walk across it and a bed so wide you can sleep like an angel when you are tired of me."

"Still I cannot, Clayton."

"Sleep on it. I will call you in the morning."

"Ok bye."

That evening, Romy spent a tedious two hours in the private room being fingered by a retired dentist from Dusseldorf. Later, she went home to lie beside the old fish, who was still wearing her new wig, so the daughter eased it off and when she did she saw her perspiring scalp streaked with strands of hair like an old man. Poor old fish. It has been hard for you my darling mama. The girl drifted in and out of a troubled sleep. In the morning Clayton called her again and asked if she had made up her mind. She said yes she had and she would come to that city with him.

PART IV

Hampshire and London

I

Iт was a hushed landing, almost supercilious in its ease. Five hundred tons of Airbus swaying into the descent, just topping the perimeter fence, a tilt of the nose, a wheeze of thrust reverser.

In the event, she re-routed from Zurich because Wystan wanted her to come to Little Jarrow. It wasn't excessively difficult from Gatwick. Up to Clapham Junction, down to Farnborough. A taxi would cope with the rest. It would give her time to acclimatize to England, to put the loose details of her thoughts into perfect order. And grant her a huge moral advantage in the amount of fatigue she could plead when the M-in-L got overbearing, as inevitably she would. As it turned out, she didn't need to find a cab when she got to Farnborough. Wystan had come to meet her in the Volvo.

"Darling! There you are at last. It seems like such ages."

"Wystan! Goodness, are you driving already? Are you sure you should be?"

"I'm right as rain darling. Never felt better. Look at me. A new man."

"Hampshire must have done you good."

He pulled away from the station car park. Outside the window was England, a place of soft, waterlogged colours, kindergarten road-signs and decent people allowing you the space to merge into the central lane. There were pretty brick cottages, the wood-work picked out in white gloss, and corner stores called Frobisher's and Kwik-Buy where things were for sale at nine pounds ninety-nine. The light was bland and undemanding and the air smelt of autumn and car exhaust.

"I thought we might pick up a bite of lunch in the Poacher's

Plunder in Hollington. It's where they do that pheasant pie you once liked. I'm assuming you are hungry, though maybe it isn't lunch time for you at all. Maybe you are in the middle of the night."

"Maybe. I have no idea what time it is for me Wystan, dear. But lunch would be nice."

Olivia's game plan had been quite simple. As she had strapped her exhausted body into her Qatar Airways seat at Mingaladon airport, she believed there was one option and one option only. Tell all.

She had been far from home and she had made the most appalling error of judgement. For which she was deeply sorry. She had had a fling with a local man which was completely and totally over. She must have underestimated the strain she had been under. The winter had been long and full of worry. Her husband had been diagnosed with cancer. Then she had been sent to investigate a sudden death. It had all been extremely taxing for her and she had blundered into making the most dreadful mistake. She understood if he was angry with her and even if he needed some time on his own, but he must know it was a foolish but meaningless interlude and she would never make the same mistake again. Her place was by his side and that was where she would remain. Buttressed in her decision, she had pivoted her seat two inches backwards and fallen asleep.

She woke about four hours later. The route map said they were over Pakistan. She stretched, went to the toilet, looked herself in the eyes, gave herself a clownish grin, emerged and turned to the refreshments bay to ask for an apple juice. Refreshed, she picked her way back up the aisle, until she was forced to halt by an oncoming drinks trolley. Momentarily squeezed in a vacant seat, she stared down at a middle-aged white man sleeping by the window. The man's lips were puffy and the dribble had crystallized on the corner of his mouth. The airline blanket had slid from his body to expose an unbuttoned shirt, a round belly and a fly zip that was half undone. His body hair was like tumbleweed, scrappy and wispy. This, she thought, *this* is what we are asked to love. She went back to her seat. The plane flew over Afghanistan, then a segment of Iran. By the time it got to the Caspian Sea, something had become clear to Olivia.

You are nursing a sick man, said the voice in her head. Getting better, I grant you. But I'm not sure this is the kind of thing he needs to hear right now. Cancer isn't just about drugs, it's also about morale. Now that your Wystan is back on an even keel, it's your job to keep him there. You have been under terrific strain and it did cloud your judgement and you went for the full whammy, no doubt about that. Dear me yes. Like rabbits in springtime. But it was a passing fancy that is already finished. You have your needs Miss Trelawney. We all do.

I know, headmistress.

We are all animals at heart Olivia. We may talk of our higher nature, but we growl like any other beast. The fittest survive, the rest are forgotten. These bodies of ours, they govern our every move. From the moment you wake and stagger to the bathroom to the moment you slide back into a coma. They determine our moods, prompt our reactions, dictate our decisions, and decree our fate. We hunt like cheetahs and when we see some dumb warthog we murder it. We sink our fangs into its throat and we suffocate it.

I've not been to the Serengeti, headmistress.

That's enough of your lip, girl. Now button it. You know I'm right. When have I not been right?

Wystan and Olivia stopped at the gastro-pub and ordered the pheasant pie. They drank sparkling water. Defying the wisdom of the publican, they ate outside near an old copper beech. There was some sunshine playing hide-and-seek behind the cloud cover, and the temperature was clement. Olivia could see it was raining over the hills to the south, but Hollington was out of the squall. Wystan set his jaw to the breeze, his square face and hooked nose and unruly grey hair facing the wind like a mariner from a storybook. But Wystan was no seaman. Those ashen locks had been earned in libraries, and there was nothing seaman-like about his favourite shapeless tweed jacket. Wystan was a man of the indoors, a man of museums and galleries who liked nothing better than to be hunched over a nineteenth-century charcoal sketch with a magnifying glass in his hand, glasses tipped upwards on his broad forehead. There were tiny scarlet capillaries on the sides of his nose.

"Dear..." he began.

"How's the pheasant?" she asked.

"Just right. Piping hot. Dear... I wanted to say, before we got any further to home, that, well, I think you knew that mother invited my old friend Antonia round for dinner, that night, and it seems silly to hide this, we sort of re-established things a bit, took a couple of walks together, you know, she had been feeling a bit excluded, and we ended up going to see that rather romantic Thomas Hardy film down at the City Flicks in Great Jarrow."

"Go on."

"Well, things got a bit cosier that I might have wanted, she rather took advantage of me. Only in the cinema, I mean. I think mother is complicit with her in some way. Anyway, I wanted you to hear this from me dear because if we see Tony and she is endlessly flashing her eyes in my direction, well that is all that happened and I'm very sorry. I didn't want you to think we dived into the nearest hostelry for a romp in the hay, because we didn't."

"Okay. Well thanks for telling me Wystan. I need a bit of time to take this in."

"Nothing to take in dearest buccaneer. I just don't want you think there is something bigger than there is..."

The pheasant pie had cooled and the branches of the beech tree were beginning to sway. The damper air was approaching. On the farther end of the garden another couple, also seated across a timber picnic table, were buttoning their wind-cheaters. They were cyclists with little green shoes: outdoor ballet pumps. They ate with their helmets on.

"Let's go inside."

Indoors, they found a horseshoe window seat and placed themselves with their backs to the rain-pocked panes. Wystan asked, with that ever-so-slightly smug smile of his, if he was forgiven.

"Don't rush me Wystan. I'm tired. I need a little time. Let's not talk about it anymore."

Seated in silence beside her husband, Olivia sifted through her emotions. There was anger, anger with Wystan for surrendering so easily to the situation, anger with that repulsive pouting Antonia who had known her husband longer than she had, anger with the conniving mother-in-law who had nothing better to do with her time than invite her son's old girlfriends to dinner in her absence. Shame that she had been caught off her guard; that the tables had been reversed so unexpectedly. But her indignation was not dressed in solitary and unalloyed grandeur. Alongside it, there was something else, something less painful and more private, the inner vibration of one who has a secret and feels richly vindicated in not divulging it. She knew now that Sambath was hers, and hers alone, and he would be kept protected in a very secret place and not, my God not, exposed to the embarrassments of confessions over pub lunches with cyclists sitting at the next table. Sambath was a finer thing than that. She knew immediately that there would be no reckoning, no consensual allowing of bygones to be bygones. She would forgive Wystan his squeeze with that woman, their grope in the Jarrow cinema with Bathsheba Everdene all across the screen. Yuck. Of course she would, she was sailing so high in the moral ascendant. But she would not in a million years reciprocate; not in a million years disclose anything about Sambath. Not one word. She was sure of that now. Wystan did not deserve it. Sambath would be kept in the tabernacle of her heart. Sambath was her official secret.

They ordered coffee. Then they made their way to the car under the pub owner's umbrella, and drove home to Little Jarrow in silence. The gentle sweep of the wipers lured Olivia to sleep. When she woke Mrs Green was opening the door for her. Mrs Green was having a good day, because she called Olivia her poor dear child, and said how tired she must be, and told her to sit in the best armchair with a nice amontillado, and not to move one little finger. And dinner, when it came, was very tasty, a lemon sole with lovely young potatoes, and she had put Olivia in the cowslip-yellow room which was the one with the big bed and the gorgeous soft mattress, and by the time Wystan clambered into the other side in his Peter Jones pyjamas she had fallen asleep to the thought that maybe they really did love her after all. She slept like a goddess, and when she was woken by the sun peeping through the curtains, she experienced that strange and rare sensation of utter happiness which comes before one is sufficiently awake to ask oneself what the cause is. She turned to lie on her back, stretched her legs long and straight, then relaxed, her hands clasped behind her head and her knees apart. Her first semi-conscious thought was that there were no cowslips in South Asia. Why should that matter? Where the bee sucks, there suck I.

II

Lucas wrote to Elise very soon after he was back in London, but she did not reply for a good while, and by the time she did he was in Spain, in Santander, where he was moderating an EU panel discussion on refugee rights. The Spanish event was rewarding, and outside the diplomatic gathering he enjoyed brisk evening walks along the front, watching the rough tides in the bay. One morning, somebody introduced him to the English report-writers who were doing the write-ups for the meetings, and one of them was the woman called Olivia Trelawney who had written the professional linguists' report about Vann. Neither had the time for a long exchange, but he was able to explain how he figured in the story. She told him she was staying for a while with her husband in Hampshire and she would love to talk it all through with him if ever there was a chance. Lucas agreed they should definitely meet up in London.

Meanwhile, in her letter, Elise suggested lunch near the British Museum, where she and a friend would be visiting an exhibition. The friend would not be able to stay for the lunch. There was nowhere to get real Cambodian food in London but there was a reasonably satisfactory Vietnamese place in Drummond Street. She hoped he was available on the date proposed.

Lucas was available. It would mean losing the two free days he had planned to spend exploring the area around Santander, but so be it. There was a commanding tone to Elise's invitation that he found intimidating. He also suspected that if he said no to her once, he might not get another chance. That too was why he arrived fifteen minutes early at the Vietnamese restaurant.

Elise swept in, greeting the waiter as a person she knew. She was dressed more gaily than at the memorial. Hardly surprising. She had a pale blue dress and a light-hearted necklace — a jumble of beads and glass fragments. Over it there was a pale linen jacket. This time she wore her hair in a simple neat bun, with a parting in the centre of her forehead. For the family member who was closest to her French mother, today she paradoxically looked the most Cambodian. Well, it wasn't really a paradox, thought Lucas, but she did look more Asian than Vann did.

"Hello Mr Bellwether."

"Hello! Do call me Lucas. So tell me how was the exhibition?"

"Oh. That. I enjoyed it actually. It was a little display of heads, sandstone heads, from the Empire era. I mean the Angkorian period, all that. To be honest the French have more of these things than you do here in Great Britain, but what you *have* got are very nice."

"I see. Great."

"There was a lovely torso of Lakshmi in the Baphuon style. Exquisite grey sandstone. You almost wanted to stroke her belly." She laughed drily.

"Heavens. I ought to go and see."

"You should."

The waiter appeared, wielded menus. Elise thanked him in Khmer and asked what was good today. He pointed to various items on the white card then left them to choose.

"Yes, you guessed right. He's from Cambodia. I got him the job actually. He's always happy to tell me what's freshest. Would you be alright with the *bún chá* to start with, it's very light, and then maybe the *cha ca Hanoi*, it has a lot of fresh dill, they marinade the fish in turmeric. Maybe a mango salad to go with it. What do you think? We will need something with pork, too."

"Whatever you say."

"You need to get the right balance with Vietnamese dishes, I find."

What was Elise's game? From Angkorean sculptures to *bún chá*, she wanted it to be clear who was in charge. It didn't take years in adversarial courtroom hearings to see that she was unsettled. She saw him as an opponent; she was laying down a barrage of fire. He would need to be patient.

"Talking of France, would you say, all in all, that you prefer this country to France. Or vice-versa, perhaps?"

"Well. That's a good question."

The waiter served an assortment of slippery white vermicelli, tufty herbs, sausage cakes and bowls of complicated sauce.

"I confess to enjoying England. It's gentler. People are often less demanding. For me France was always a place of suffering. It was a terrible time we had there in Issy. By which I don't mean it was the fault of the French. I remain tremendously grateful to the French. They got us out."

"Yes. They took care of their own."

"They took care of their own. But they took care of a lot of others too, you know. Many of the foreigners owe them their lives."

"And how was it to live in a suburb of Paris after being in the centre of Phnom Penh?"

"You should dip that meat in here. Try and wrap it in the vermicelli. I know it's not easy."

"Here we go. Mmm. It's really delicious."

"Well as I say they don't really do Khmer food in London. You can find any amount of Thai, of course. And any type of Thai too, from Mongolia to Colombo, if you see what I mean. Most of it is to be avoided. But luckily we have a few good Vietnamese places."

"That's a very pretty necklace."

"Oh. Thank you. It cost next to nothing."

They continued in silence, picking at the bits and pieces with their chopsticks. A fresh course arrived. Lucas knew that Elise was stringing him along. She did not trust him. He gave her a sudden smile, looking her in the eyes, and she smiled back, at first naturally before her face quickly hardened. He wanted to look at her more. She had a brittle grace that was impossible to ignore. The brittleness belonged to the mistrust. He needed to find a way to earn her consideration, to rise in her esteem. Any trick would do.

"Do you have any idea what this is?"

He took from his pocket the last brown disc that he had saved from the hotel and placed it carefully on the white table cloth.

"*Should* I have any idea?"

"Not at all. Just curiosity. It's from Cambodia."

"May I?" She took it in her hand, tapped its hard shell, then held it to her nose. "Well. What's the answer?"

"If I knew that I wouldn't have asked you. Elise."

Her head bucked nervously at the mention of her name.

"I know what I would do" she declared.

"What would you do?"

"I would put it in water."

"In water...?"

"See if it grows, Mr...er...Lucas. You never know. See if it grows."

She returned the disc to the table cloth. Their plates were empty.

"There are lots of plants and herbs in that part of the world that we don't know about here. And if you like, just to prove it, I suggest we try a Minh Mang liqueur. It has all sorts of roots and herbs and it's very strong. If you are an Asiaphile, I'm sure it will appeal to you."

"Why not? Sure."

Elise ordered two glasses of the liqueur from her Cambodian waiter, who bowed and smiled. The glasses came, filled with a thick, dark liquid. On the nose it was sour and muddy.

They briefly raised their glasses and sipped in silence. God! What is this potion? Lucas turned his face to conceal his distaste, taking in a poster of Halong Bay hanging on the wall. Clunky sailboats and rocks poking out of green water. On the farther wall there was a large lacquer painting showing women in slim dresses plucking chickens and winnowing corn while Ho

Chi Minh's militiamen stood guard. The leaves of the bamboo trees were painted in gold and the mountains in the backdrop were a deep crimson. It was a beautiful painting. Customers at the next table were being served some sort of fish hot-pot. Elise was frowning at her fingers, her mouth betraying the occasional twitch. The silence was difficult, but this time he was not going to be the one who broke it. If it meant saying goodbye and going home none the wiser, then so be it. In the courtroom, there is no better way of getting a witness to talk than simply saying nothing. Just waiting. Creating an expectation.

"It's very hard, Mr. Lucas" she eventually said "It's very hard to go back in time as you are asking me to do. At some stage all that grief and pain has to be laid to rest."

"I don't mean to trouble you by..."

"Makara wrote to me. She said that you really cared about Tepp. I don't resent you as much as you think. Makara finds it easier to talk than I do. About certain things, at least."

"She..."

Elise raised a hand, held it suspended.

"When we arrived in Issy-les-Moulineaux, we had a lot to organise. We had to invent a new life. Vuthy and I busied ourselves and put an awful lot of effort into keeping mother occupied. Setting up a home, choosing curtains, painting the walls, finding the best supermarket, how to get food from home, all the usual émigré things. They, I mean the government, helped us find the apartment. They gave us a grant of six month's rent, to be repaid over ten years at no interest. It was a ground floor apartment, looking on to a small courtyard, and at first that was no worry, but when the autumn came there was very little light. We missed the beautiful strong light of Cambodia. Mother was our great worry. Eternally. We had to keep her occupied all the time, tire her out. She may have been back in France, but she didn't get much support from her family. They had never really forgiven her for running off with a Cambodian man in the first place. And don't forget when we arrived, nobody believed us Franco-Khmer fugitives when we said what the Khmer Rouge were actually doing, what they were capable of. François Ponchaud published that book, the..."

"*L'année zero.* The Year Zero."

"The Year Zero. That was when people started to take us seriously. But even then intellectual heavyweights like Noam Chomsky accused Ponchaud of talking reactionary rubbish. People who dreamed of revolutions thought the Khmer Rouge were just fine and we were mere apologists for the old bourgeois ways. The wicked USA was dropping napalm on Vietnamese villages, and a lot of people thought that Democratic Kampuchea was a brave new world. You know what the French are like, wrapping themselves in their own fairy stories. Only bit by bit did people begin to understand that the Khmer Rouge were covering the entire country with mass graves. At the beginning we too clung to the hope that the revolutionary government wasn't so bad either, and that father and Tepp would be toiling in a cooperative somewhere and maybe having a rough time but still alive. Still alive. Then bit by bit the real news filtered through, even though no journalists were allowed in, apart from one or two from Yugoslavia and Romania and places like that. The news filtered out in dribs and drabs. Cambodians were dying. Dying in huge numbers, all over the country, while the elite were treating themselves to banquets. Pol Pot wanted a new Khmer Empire, and he was prepared to pay a big price to get it, and the people became his tools. Slaves. They ceased to matter. They were completely expendable. People starved, watched their children die, got arrested if they were sick, had their heads smashed to pulp by idiot peasants with sticks. Put an impressionable man in uniform and he will do anything you like. Anywhere. I don't just mean in Cambodia. But in Cambodia it was worse. They had to make fertilizer — everything had to be done to get the rice production to thirteenth century Angkorian levels; I imagine Jayavarman VII disposed of human lives just as freely — and making fertilizer in Democratic Kampuchea meant mixing rice husks and human excrement, and then blending this mash with the chopped remains of human bodies. Mothers had to make fertilizer out of their own daughters Mr Lucas. I don't know if you realise."

"I worked in the tribunal."

"Of course you did. I forgot. But as we learnt these things, mostly through the few refugees who came through the Thai border, we still clung on to hope. Hope dashed with a good measure of despair, because my father was on the wrong side, don't forget, he had fought in the war against these people, he looked every part the bourgeois army officer they hated so much. Mother crying, night after night, night after night, refusing to take her anti-depressants because she said that if Ang and Tepp were alive there was nothing to be sad about. All she wanted was them to be alive. When death comes so close you stop caring about the state in which your husband, your brother, your child is delivered back to you. All you ask for is life, maimed broken life, anything will do, a few parts missing, amputated, anything, just as long as that person returns to you alive. And for three years we went on hoping, day after day, then all of a sudden, the whole thing was over. The Vietnamese had invaded and all those half-witted sadists who had been running the country scuttled off into the jungle and their Democratic Kampuchea regime collapsed like a pack of cards and the country was opened up again. But instead of it being easier, those times were even harder for us, they turned out to be the worst times of all because there was still no news and we thought that if there was no news when news was allowed, they were well and truly dead. They were lying in the bottom of a stinking death-pit in the ruins of some extermination centre. That was when little Vuthy started to go downhill. She had been a brave girl up till then but after '79 she started to stop believing. Vuthy suddenly went wild. She screwed all the boys on campus at Paris III. Every one. They asked nothing better, she was pretty as hell. She came home and cried all night when she wasn't drunk out of her mind. She began to go insane, slowly at first, just saying things out of turn and illogically, and the boys got a bit wary and one by one they left her. She had weird outbursts and broke into their rooms while they were studying and ripped off her clothes. More than once she was raped. Then she threw herself under the metro and that was that. Mother stopped talking altogether. I was reduced to spoon-feeding her. She wouldn't take food from anybody else. She wanted rice, she said, only rice. She wanted to feel what it had been like for the others back in Cambodia. I ground vitamins into that rice Mr Lucas because I knew that if she stopped eating... well. You can imagine."

"I don't know how you did it."

"And then, and then, the day arrived when Tepp came home. I can't describe that to you. It was very strange. We did not know him, I mean, we did not recognise him, he had changed so much in the way he was, and looked and talked. He had suffered awful things. At first he said he didn't know where father was and I knew he was lying and I pushed and pushed him to tell and he would say nothing. He refused to say what had happened to papa. I became deeply vexed and frustrated by the way he was guarding this secret for himself, and one night we had a terrible fight and I hit him with a tool, a spanner or something, and he was bleeding and he gave up. He promised to tell me once mother was asleep. He did tell me. He told me very brutally too and I remember his words to this day.

She paused. "I remember to this day. They handed him a revolver. He had to prove himself."

"Do you want to say what he said? You don't have to, Elise."

"I fired the revolver into his skull and it was as if someone had hit it with an axe."

Lucas took a further sip on the liqueur.

"*Someone? Someone* was *you*, I said. Someone was you. Someone was you! *Merde!* When I knew that Tepp had killed our father, I was speechless. It was too much. My mind was completely confused. There was, it is true, immense relief at knowing he was dead and that the waiting was over at last. But I was deeply, deeply angry with Tepp. Utterly humiliated. We had been waiting since 1975, and papa had been killed within an hour of when we last saw him! Though I understood now why he had kept us waiting for those long years. His secret was too terrible to tell. It was untellable. Now he had come, and I had forced him tell it, and it had made everything much worse. We became estranged. Luckily I was studying at Nanterre and I had Victor there, he was a professor there, he supported me, because otherwise I would have had nobody."

Elise ordered herself another glass of the muddy liqueur. They were alone. The other customers had left. The words continued to flow.

"Tepp stayed with mother and I moved in with Victor at Nanterre. Tepp wrote to me. Once, twice, three times a week. The letters were always the same. A bit of news of mother. Tepp managed better in getting her to eat. Today she had some vegetable. Yesterday a little piece of minced steak. Stuff like that. But each bit of health report on *maman* always ended with a plea about him. He wanted my forgiveness. He wanted me to understand. He explained time and again that he had been forced to kill our father, that he had had absolutely no choice at all. I had to forgive him. He said he was not a killer. I told him I could not. I refused. He had murdered our father. All the time, for months and months, he wrote to me. *Maman a mangé du chou-fleur.* Yesterday I got her to choke down some grilled chicken. She had some boiled fruit on Thursday with a sprinkling of sugar. Tepp looked after himself and mother by doing translations. He got involved with the refugee groups and he became one of their main translators, which just about paid for the rent and the grilled chicken. More letters. *Maman a mangé un morceau de tarte aux poires! La première fois! Elise tu dois me pardonner.* Over and over again. Feed mother, beg forgiveness. It was Victor who swayed me in the end. He said I was becoming cruel and hard. He could barely recognise me, he said. The greatest of human attainments, he claimed, was to be able to forgive. Victor kept pushing me like that and gradually he turned the tide of my anger. Eventually I agreed to meet Tepp in a café at Solférino. I deliberately chose that place; that was where Vuthy killed herself, and he knew that was why I had chosen it but we said nothing. It was called the *Brasserie Solférino.* We ordered coffee. Then I just let him know he had my forgiveness and he clasped my hands and wept like a baby. Like a baby he wept, his head all drenched. Then I stopped him. I explained to him my forgiveness was not unconditional. He asked me what I meant, the tears running down his face like rivers. I told him that two of our family had died. Democratic Kampuchea was not getting off so lightly. I told him that he had two lives to avenge. And when I said avenge, I meant avenge. I was prepared to trade two lives for one, but if he wanted the blame to be transferred to the man who *forced him to kill papa*, then I demanded a killing. I wanted that man's head on a plate. On a silver plate."

"How did he react?"

"He was horrified."

Outside the restaurant, the sun was shining on the bricked buildings and leaves were beginning to gather along the kerb. Elise said she would take a taxi; Lucas decided he would pop in to the British Museum and get an eyeful of the sculptures. He took a deep breath. He had to give it a try.

"I'm terribly grateful" he declared. "I understand it was very hard for you to go over that ground. I was wondering if you would accept to come to my place down in Fulham next Saturday evening. Nothing special, just a couple of friends coming for a light supper. I don't know if you could ever face any cooking by a British man."

"Oh. Heavens. I don't know either." The breeze disturbed the hair at her forehead, blew a lock backwards then returned it to its place. Her long fingers went to her necklace. She gave him her first genuine smile of the day.

"It's a nice idea. I'd love to come. Where did you say you lived?"

III

When the day came for the party, Lucas had to force himself to get into the right convivial mood. His mind was not in the mood for dinner conversation, still less for producing a meal for six with all the trimmings. He almost wanted to feed them all glutinous sticky rice with dried gar fish flakes, one of the more malodorous of Asia's breakfast condiments. This was not because he had any particular wish to upset his dinner guests; he just needed to keep his mind on Cambodia. There wasn't room for idle socialising. In the event, he did not feed his guests anything dried or fermented, but he did pass the job of designing the meal to someone else.

He had invited Izzy, an old friend from past Fulham days, to go in the morning to an art exhibition. Naturally enough, the subject of that evening's dinner came around, and she asked him who else was coming. Apart from you? A mixed bunch, Lucas had explained. A man in his early fifties going by the somewhat effete name of Wystan who was a habitué of art dealerships in Geneva. Probably rather a pedant. Equally probably, used to refined eating and very able to tell the difference between a good meal and a mediocre one. Okay, said Izzy. Next? Next was the art dealer's wife, younger than him, English, quite well travelled, rather mousy and serious. Next? Next comes our Blessed Duncan, awaiting canonization, betrothed before God to the equally saintly Ro, who can be trusted to eat just about anything. Duncan, that is. Rowena is in her eighth month and too tired to come. That's hardly a way to talk about a brother, huffed Izzy. It's because he's my brother and I love him so dearly that I can talk of him like this. I see. Then there is you, Izzy, a medal-wearing veteran of the Cordon Bleu course in Bloomsbury Square and also not likely to accept poor food gladly. And I suspect there's you as well, she said, which makes five. Who is missing? Oh, yes, said Lucas sounding unconvincingly distracted, there is also a friend called Elise. She teaches Khmer literature at the university here. Sounds absolutely terrifying, said Izzy. Yes she is, said Lucas. That's why I could use some help.

They were at the gallery in Dulwich. The Jonkind oils were oddly exhilarating: beach scenes with boiling skies that would have seemed laboured under a less expert hand. Outside, real life was in watercolour, the soft English sunshine painting long rectangles across the lawns. Izzy questioned him about himself. Did he miss the courtroom side of international law? Yes, he said, he did miss pleading in court. Did he miss Cambodia for that matter? Yes, he missed Cambodia too. What about the girl he married and then — er — stopped seeing? To be honest, he missed her most of all, though it had been quite the wrong decision to get married. He could see that quite clearly. He had underestimated the extent to which in Asia you marry the entire family. You marry the entire family in this country too, she retorted. No you don't. Not to the same degree anyway. You can have some sort of independence.

Izzy was dressed in a coat of dark grey wool with fur trimmings, cut in a military style as if it had belonged to a junior hussar. The centrepiece of her strong face was the Roman nose, set off by a pair of apple-rosy cheeks. When she listened to Lucas she tilted her head slightly to one side and a non-committal smile played about her lips. She punched him playfully on the upper arm.

"You need to think twice before making such big decisions, you silly boy."

"Sometimes I think it could all be repaired. We would reconcile. We would live a quiet life together here in England."

"You don't sound too convinced."

As for the menu, Izzy did eventually create it, while having the tact to respect the idea behind some of Lucas's suggestions. They went shopping, then home to prepare the food. The cooking was strenuous but fun. Well aware that Lucas had taken advantage of her, Izzy stood by with a drink while she issued instructions, confining herself to dipping a spoon in the mousse, immersing a finger in the soup, inspecting his nutmeg, and, as a concession, peeling the pears.

"I met her because I knew her brother." Now Izzy was asking

about Elise. "Her brother was this professional interpreter I used to hang out with at international conferences."

Why didn't you invite him then?

Because he's dead. Probably murdered.

What!

It's true. That's also why I'm a little wary of the sister.

Christ, Lucas. The people you hang out with...

By the time the guests began to arrive, the rain was spattering, the wind was up, autumn was unashamedly outside and warmth and welcome and alcohol were on offer within.

Saturday 8.30 pm: Wystan is going great guns with Elise. Wystan sits at the end of the long table, powerful classical features that have been sustained with rather too much melted gruyere, a flirtatious hook to his eyebrow and unruly greying curls, the effect being that of a Roman emperor considering whether to delegate the task of massacring yet another tribe in The North to one of his generals or handle the matter himself. He is full of consideration, of *fascination*, for Elise, so much so that they have slipped into French without even noticing it. Elise is pale tonight. She is in a black sleeveless dress and pearl earrings. Her arms are like sticks next to Wystanus Maximus. The clever sod happens to know a lot about Asian art. Right now they are both chuckling about André Malraux, who once stole a slab of bas-relief from Angkor and got arrested for his pains.

Olivia, the wife of the art man who wrote the linguist's report, is toying with her mushroom soup. She seems to be asking Duncan a lot about Brazil. She is very much in favour of eco-tourism and wants to know if he organises bird-watching safaris out there. He doesn't. But if she has any suggestions, it sounds like a tremendous idea. Smiling and nodding, acquiescing, just being terribly nice. Just being Duncan. And this Olivia woman, look closer, she has something about her, a kind of glow of inner jubilation. Is she hiding something? Izzy is hopping nimbly between two conversations, one with Duncan and Olivia and one with Lucas.

With D she is claiming a *droit d'ancienneté* over Olivia by asking after poor darling Rowena and D is having to break off his talks about toucans and parakeets (which he is genuinely enjoying) to make suitable noises about Ro. You know. She's at that stage where there's no position that's really comfortable for her, and so on. Big baby, I fear, and Izzy counters by saying it's not going to be a midget with a Dad like that, is it? Great laughter. Quick burst of congratulations from Olivia, echoed by Wystan and wholly ignored by Elise, then Olivia literally forces the conversation back to bird-watching in Brazil and Izzy whispers to Lucas that it's time to check the meat.

Back in the main room, Izzy takes advantage of the oohs and aahs about the incoming beef wellington to engage Duncan once again on his life as an expectant father. Lucas carves the beef. He registers that Olivia is now out on a limb, so he asks her if she has any interesting work coming up in the near future. She says it's the usual stuff, mostly in Geneva, with the exception of one nice thing that has come her way from AWF.

"AWF. Asia Woodland Foundation, *if my facts are correct, er-hum.* That's in Bangkok isn't it?"

"*If my facts are correct, er-hum,* it's not to be confused with LAWF, the Latin American office" added Duncan. It was a family joke; the brothers were imitating their father.

"Yes it is." answered Olivia. "Long way away, I agree."

"So where will the meeting be held? At the Bangkok headquarters?"

"No. In Yangon."

"Ah. I see. Myanmar again."

"Someone talking shop down the other end of the table?" barks Wystan. "I think we should propose a vote of appreciation to the chef tonight!"

They all clink their glasses. Elise is still on the white — her first glass.

"It's Izzy you should be thanking" he says, but his voice is conveniently drowned in the growls of approval. Wystan, who has emptied his plate very happily, along with more glasses of the Burgundy than his doctor would have recommended, then takes the floor in the role of the entertaining art connoisseur.

"Now if I'm not mistaken that looks very like a Wilhelm Kleen" he announces, pointing in the direction of the side table by the TV where there is a clear glass of water containing a circular brown disc. "Come on Lucas, admit it. It's an early Kleen."

"Clean?" asks Lucas. Wystan's pseudo-erudition is lost on the gathering. Taking his cue from the general perplexity he has sown, Wystan explains that k-l-double-e-n Kleen does "things in stuff". "A cockroach spray can in a bowl of custard fetched a considerable sum at Sotheby's only last month. A length of copper wire in a carafe of face-cream; a dipstick in a puddle of wax. Things in stuff."

"Or in this case, a simple plastic disc in a glass of Evian."

"Oh come on" laughs Izzy "You're having us on! Pull the other one you old rogue!"

"A gullible man walks up a garden path" offers Elise, somewhat enigmatically.

It is a strange gathering. In some ways very successful, considering what a heterogeneous crowd they all are. They all seem to be getting on. Everybody loves Wystan's art charade, and Lucas joins in the laughter. The only person who does not is Olivia. She, he notices, has abruptly crawled into herself, as a snail does when you touch its antenna. Shoulders hunched, she is watching the disc in the glass of water. Transfixed. Lucas focusses on her. The sight of the glass and its contents has stirred some fell premonition deep within her. The bloom of happiness has vanished. She is stricken with gravity. As her fear communicates itself to the other guests, a silence falls on the room and nobody can think of anything to say. Then, as if the one person who is from a distant land can elucidate something they do not understand, they all turn towards Elise. Elise says nothing, though she does acknowledge their attention with a lingering smile of satisfaction.

The dinner proceeds, and slowly the good cheer returns, if rather more muted. Eventually there are one or two questions thrown Elise's way about whether she is Asian or French or what, and she manages to tell everybody she is half Cambodian without letting anybody breach her inner secrecy. Wystan, scrambling to repair the awkwardness, asks Lucas some heavy-handed questions about trials of war criminals. Olivia remains plunged in thought. Izzy toys with her i-phone before leaning over to Lucas and telling him she has to rush but really doesn't want to break up the party. Her departure sparks a wider movement. Olivia announces that she has to get Wystan home as it is well past his convalescent bed-time. They will get a cab, no hassle, they are staying with his aunt in South Ken. Duncan declares that Ro should be left alone not a minute longer. Within minutes they are all gone, all except Elise. It is only 10.30. Lucas is doubly vexed, both because the festivities broke up so early, and if he cares to admit it he is unsettled to learn that Olivia is going to Yangon.

A voice beside him. "Do you have a cigarette?"

"I don't smoke anymore."

"Nor do I. Do you have a cigarette?"

"I'm sure I can find some."

Rifling through a drawer he discovers an old packet of Winston. Together they step through the sliding door that leads on to the balcony. The wind is bracing. The common is alive, raindrops swarming around the auras of orange light from the streetlamps, the grass quickened with leaves tumbling from the plane trees and scudding into the darkness. He widens his jacket to shelter the flame as they light up.

"What's annoying you?"

"They all packed off so early. It was as if the artsy joke about the seed in the glass spooked them all out. Wilhelm Kleen, indeed. I only put the damn thing in a glass because you suggested it."

Silence follows. In due course they drown the cigarettes in a waterlogged ashtray. Inside, the chaos of the meal spreads before their eyes. A table cloth marked with magenta splashes, soiled cutlery, wine-pigmented bowls, half-empty claret glasses, dead bottles. Over on the far wall, a spotlight lamp illuminates a turquoise canvas, and on the oak coffee table in front of the sofa (which matches the painting) sits a bronze Buddha head which he once picked up in the market at Tuol Toum Poung. The Buddha is looking effeminate and contented. Alongside the bronze is a richly illustrated book on Khmer sculpture which Wystan had fingered avidly two hours earlier.

"Don't worry Lucas." Elise is eyeing an unopened bottle of Armagnac. "I can talk for a while, if you care to listen."

IV

"I must have driven Victor mad."

He had made a token attempt at tidying the mess. She was seated on the blue sofa. Both held cigarettes. They had dropped the niceties about smoking outside. Beside the Buddha, the Armagnac bottle was half empty. Elise wanted to talk.

"That's quite sacrilegious you know. Having the bottle right by the head."

The rain hit the windows in sudden angry spits, and each time the wind shook the pane mountings. Bad weather outside, and comfort in the apartment. Elise showed no signs of wanting to leave. Her white arm clasped a turquoise cushion, the liqueur nestling in the other hand.

"Poor man. Poor Victor. It was he who got the job in London, not me. I just followed."

She paused.

"They asked him to be a head of studies on a course about matrimonial patterns in Asian societies. I thought it was very silly, the way they dissected our societies from outside, but I wasn't going to say no, was I? Mother had her illness by then and she was being nursed as a residential patient at the centre in Villejuif. She used to ring me every day asking why I had gone to live in such a godforsaken place as England. I was asking myself the same question. I had no links with this island whatsoever. But England did its work on me. You know, Lucas? London had a softer edge to it than Paris. Don't look so surprised. The pressures to conform are much stronger in France. France is a nation of uniforms, conventions, rules. That's why it's so totally stuck in the past. Anyway. I came to London a deeply troubled person on the verge of a breakdown. Five years later, I was starting to mend. Not really mend, I don't mean that, but starting to accept. Starting to think that I would try and live, instead of just waiting to die. It was a process, as you are supposed to say nowadays, a process of healing. Victim number one of the process was Victor. Way back in Nanterre he had stepped in as the rescuer, as men often do, and by the end he ran away, beaten and bruised. Defeated. Some pretty girl in the oriental languages department scooped him up and gave him the mothering he wanted. I didn't mind. I had really put him through the grinder. God, poor Victor. By the end we couldn't talk, we could barely eat together. We couldn't do anything. Go for a walk. Fuck. Anything."

Two stiff glasses of Armagnac. That's all it takes. She's a different person.

"Yes. I got my job after that. Pulled a string or two. Mugged up my Khmer epic stories, the Reamker and assorted writings, and gave my own modest classes at SOAS. No security of tenure, never was, but perfectly decent money for all that. Still is. I had a life. I had an apartment. I was quite alone. No more Vuthy. Mother passed away. Victor screwing an Indonesian girl. Tepp on the other side of the world."

"Tepp?" Too eager, thought Lucas. Too eager. Go gently.

"Tepp. Bloody Tepp."

She leaned her body towards the packet of Winston. This woman was familiar with the delusional choreography of the smoker. Pull the cig from the packet, tap it on the side, fling the packet away with exaggerated indifference, balance the cig on the lip, light up suddenly, chomp the mouth around the first lungful, move hand plus cig quickly to the back of head when the nicotine kicks in, reach for the booze. The bottle and the cigs were old friends for this woman. No new acquaintances here.

Tepp.

"Was he back in Cambodia?"

"Of course not. Why should he go to Cambodia?"

"I don't know."

Now the smoke was doing a reverse Niagara Falls, out of the mouth and straight up the nose. Held in the lungs, then a sudden coughing exhalation. Clouds of the stuff. Oh God, Elise.

Don't conk out before we get to Tepp.

"Tepp" he said, firmly, as if to suggest there was nothing else on the agenda. It seemed to work.

"I told Tepp I required revenge. I told you that. So Tepp turns to me and he goes (why the sudden British vernacular?) and he goes... Just pour me another glass Lucas."

He filled their glasses. Elise downed hers in one go.

"I feel awfully lonely at times Lucas. I know I'm not showing you my best side but you are an honourable Englishman and you will surely forgive me. If you don't mind, I'm going to take a little nap on your sofa. Not for long. Just need to catch up on a bit of lost sleep. Do I have your permission?"

"Of course you do."

She kicked off her shoes and straightened herself across the sofa. Lucas went to the bedroom cupboard to find a blanket. He laid the blanket across her, tucking in the corners, assuming she was already out for the count.

"Lucas?"

"Yes?"

"Would you mind if we... if we ...? It's cold outside. I...."

"Stay warm Elise". He kissed her gently on the cheek. "Sleep tight."

Lucas went to bed.

In the morning, he rose and arranged the breakfast. Intent on pre-empting any embarrassing apologies from her, he claimed he had drunk far too much wine and spirits and could hardly remember a thing from last night. He just hoped she had managed to have a reasonably comfortable night on the couch. Any decent person would have given his bed and slept on the couch himself. For this he was duly sorry. The storm had been quite appalling; there was even something about it on the news this morning (untrue, unless he meant the typhoon in Luzon). Thank God she had made the wise decision and stayed put. Now breakfast, there was bread and toast and jam and stuff and coffee. Of course there's Earl Grey as well, don't hesitate. Fruit? How about a fried egg? Not very Asian, admittedly. I love the soup with banana flowers they do in Phnom Penh.

"So do I." She began to weep, then restrained herself. "My country Lucas. My country."

"Don't cry Elise. Have some coffee."

She sipped the coffee and suddenly launched into her narrative as there had been no intermission.

"I asked him if he knew who it was and he said of course. How could he not know? Everybody knows to this day who the people are. Who did what and when. Who did what to whom. There is no anonymity. Tepp knew exactly who the man behind papa's murder was and where he was living. And he knew who his family was. You are not a person in Cambodia without being a part of a tribe. You are never just an individual. You belong. Tepp had researched the whole crowd from inside his government job in Phnom Penh. They had done well. Practically anybody who held any command responsibility in the Khmer Rouge was either killed in the purges or came out on top. Dead, or in a position of power. His man was not in Phnom Penh, but two of his siblings were, one in the Foreign Office and one in the Interior Ministry. High up. Very high up. Another cousin was a judge. Tepp's man was in Long Beach. In California. Did you know that the greatest concentration of Cambodians outside Cambodia is in Long Beach, California?"

"I did actually."

"Tepp went to America. He waited for a while in New York, staying with a friend he had known from the Vietnam days. Then he flew to Los Angeles. I don't know the full details, Lucas, and I never asked him. But he marked his man. He stayed somewhere in a place called Torrance. His target was a family man, three children, with some kind of anonymous import-export business connected with automobiles and another to do with furniture warehouses. Quite predictable actually. His wife was a Khmer woman from another important family. Nothing very unusual for that type of overseas Cambodian. Sitting pretty, blending in with the local culture just enough to make a lot of money. He also had a stake in a company making pornographic videos and helped to supply young Khmer girls. Nieces, cousins."

"Sounds like quite a savoury character."

"You know, Lucas, I used to think as you do. More recently I have understood that he was just one more facet of Democratic Kampuchea. One more face among so many. Like those smiling, sneering faces sculpted all over the Baphuon monument in Angkor. Faces that have lost their humanity. He was just one more of the seeds carried on its winds which had happened to take root in America. You can't keep that amount of carnage, that intensity of hell, bottled up in one country. However hard you try, it breaks loose, it flows like lava from village to village, crosses entire continents. This man was merely exporting and reproducing the Khmer Rouge assumptions that had been drummed into his head by others. Complete and total brutalization. I say this with hindsight of course. At the time I just wanted Tepp to kill him."

She pauses.

"Anyway Tepp decided what he would do. And did it. His wife found the corpse with the head missing. Mannlicher Schönauer."

"What?"

"It's such an odd name. It always lodged in my memory."

"Jesus Elise! That's an old Austrian hunting rifle!"

"He blew his head off at close range. I admit that when I heard that, it made me very happy."

"Christ! Tepp must have stood out like a sore thumb, carrying a thing like that."

"*Mais non. Que penses-tu?* He was too clever for that. Tepp was back in Queens the same day and on a flight from JFK to London by the time night had fallen." She could not repress a smile.

There was a lot of admiration for that big brother. For that episode, anyway.

Elise tucked into her breakfast with surprising relish. Oxford thick-cut marmalade on Sainsbury's wholemeal was entirely up her street, she declared. And what a beautifully lit place this apartment was when you saw it in the morning. Those plane trees across the road had taken quite a buffeting from the storm. How sad it seemed when so many of the leaves disappeared overnight. She had never quite been able to reconcile herself to the onset of winter, though autumn was so beautiful, so glowing. You had to completely rethink your emotions when you lived with seasons, she had realised. It made you understand things about the European poets that you could never grasp just by sitting in the Foreign Languages Institute in Phnom Penh. Nice place and all that, Vann Molyvann at his best, but how were you supposed to understand Mallarmé if you hadn't experienced the seasons?

"Or Keats, for that matter" added Lucas. This witness has a definite tendency to go wandering off at a tangent. "But did Tepp stay in the UK after that?"

Tepp had stayed. Coming and going, but eventually gaining permanent residency status on the basis of an asylum application. The Home Office was happy to poach a few Cambodian refugees off the French and the Americans. Elise was convinced he was safest in the UK. He could go to ground. He wanted to live with her in London, but she refused to allow that. She looked around on the south coast and chose Worthing, a sleepy town full of retirees where nothing ever happened. They found a quiet place for him, a flat above a corner store. The locals took him for a Vietnamese — that was what they assumed most Asians must be, if they weren't Philippine nurses. The TV had broadcast reports on the Vietnamese Boat People, and their plight had entered the public consciousness, while nobody really understood anything at all about the Khmer Rouge. The Khmer Rouge was all too bizarre, too intricate. At the height of the Cold War chicanery, Margaret Thatcher even gave an interview in which she said they were quite reasonable people. Can you believe that? Vann played on the confusion, happy to be the local Saigon Viet if that's what floated their boat (pardon the pun). Nobody minded him among the old pensioners of Worthing. He was obviously an unobtrusive chap, not out to make trouble. So he carried on doing translations by mail for the refugee groups in France, and he worked hard on his English and gradually he got into the interpreting trade through the informal route. Translating agencies in London and so on. This was quite a few years later mind you. He had to keep his head below the radar for a long time.

"Ok, so — to summarise — he brutally eliminates his enemy, flies back to the UK, settles in by the seaside, sows a bit of innocent confusion about who he is, where he comes from, keeps his head down, earns a modest living translating here and there, upscales later on to conference interpreting, and lives happily ever after on fried eggs and wholemeal biscuits above a corner store in Worthing."

"In a nutshell, yes."

"Well it's all moderately believable, Elise, except for one bit."

"Yes?"

"The family. The target. These people who you have been so careful not to name. The man had children. Those children grew up into adults. Someone murdered their father."

Elise placed a paper napkin across her lips and held it there. Her hand relaxed, then reached for the cigarettes on top of the fridge. She winced as the fresh smoke stung her eyes. Lucas found an old saucer for the ash.

"There were two daughters and one son. One of the daughters returned to Cambodia. She works in the entourage of the Prime Minister's wife. Part of her staff. She arranges things for her. The other stayed in the USA and married a Cambodian man there and has a couple of children, but I don't know much more than that. Her husband has a car import-export business. As for the son, he went to live in Cambodia but he moves around. A well-connected Khmer entrepreneur in Cambodia. A man of style you could say. He is reputed to be very wealthy. His speciality is furniture made from rare varieties of tropical wood. Rosewood, that kind of thing. He has forest lands in Mondolkiri where he grows the wood and cuts the trees."

"Hmm. He sounds like a Westminster choirboy."

Elise stubs the cigarette. "I really ought to go Lucas. I have abused your hospitality far too much already."

"Stay for lunch."

"I can't. It's sweet of you. I have a whole slew of dissertation papers to read. I'm behind already."

"Before you go. I need a name. What's his name, Elise? Our tropical forester? Try and help me."

She made her way to the door, fussed with her coat, said goodbye, turned on her heels.

"Sambath. I think that's what he is called."

She refused to let him accompany her downstairs. He watched her from the balcony, striding across the common with her long arms, a gangly Khmer effigy carved from tree branches. He picked up last night's ashtray from the wrought-iron picnic table and tipped the waterlogged contents down a gutter. The big plane leaves that had alighted on his balcony were brittle and curled. He would have to clear them before they started to rot and block the drains. Rosewood, eh? How disingenuous was Elise being? Rosewood was a very highly prized commodity. It was also a closely protected one and fell under all sorts of international treaty bans. The Chinese were prepared to pay huge sums for it. You didn't fell tropical timber with impunity, not even in Mondulkiri, Mr Sambath. Unless someone was protecting you, of course.

The phone rang. Olivia Trelawney.

PART V

Yangon, Myanmar

I

THE HOTEL WAS MARBLED, SHINY and forbidding, but it had a place called The Stagecoach, a kind of mock-up English bar, which was not so bad. Nothing to compare with the Old Saltmarsh back home, perish the thought, but for Yangon it was quite welcoming in its way. The club chairs were upholstered in plastic red leather with shiny tacks, the bar had a kind of regency portico to it, and the pool table was elegant, not made for dwarves. Ceiling fans revolved above like chopper blades in a Vietnam film. Inevitably, there were framed photos of child monks and smiling waifs, faces splurged with sandalwood paste, but they were quite pleasant pictures when all was said and done, not too kitsch. You couldn't devote a whole life to hating sentimental pictures of the poor. Go with it, Olivia, navigate the flow. Don't fight everything.

Sambath had said he would meet her in Thailand. In Bangkok. Excellent. First, the rough, and then the smooth. Get the conference done, then head south to Bangkok, where an exciting weekend awaited. That would probably be the last time she saw him — there was no point in prolonging all this. That much was obvious to any fool, but one last meeting would do no harm. One last night in the arms of her Asian lover. It almost hurt to think of the pleasure. She stretched her legs. Who would have believed all this three months ago? Nobody. Least of all her. Her, Olivia, having an affair? But common sense should prevail. And must. After one final night she would bid goodbye to the whole affair, announce to Sambath that it was over, and settle back into proper matrimonial life with Wystan.

Wystan, whose attitude to life seemed to be far from proper these days, if that dinner party with Lucas Bellwether was anything to go by. He had really kept everybody entertained that night. In the cab to Aunt Dorothy's she had held her peace, leaving him to cogitate his own wine-fuelled performance, until the ride eventually concluded in Eldon Road with a tentative enquiry about whether she was angry with him. No love. Not angry. Just preoccupied by stuff. A penny for your thoughts he had pleaded, and she had replied that her concerns were not up for auction. Well that was a bit bitchy, wasn't it? Yes, it was, he hadn't done much wrong except drink too much, but she needed to put a block of secrecy on the whole business of that so-called artistic object on Bellwether's side table. The artistic object was one she had seen before, and it had had the power momentarily to freeze her. Moh-Moh had shown her something exactly the same in Café 99. Yes, exactly the same object, and she had identified it, not through any expertise of her own, but by reading a note written by the policeman the girl said was her boyfriend. Constable Michael Maung. This was not an artistic object at all, I'm sorry Wystan, it was a humble seed sitting in a glass of water, failing to sprout.

The bar waiter approached, forcing Olivia to cut her recollections short. She became briefly flustered. She had not devoted one second to the bar menu, so she fell back on her old favourites, one mojito and one club sandwich. Certainly madam. May I repeat your order? One mojito. One club sandwich. Yes.

The evening bar crowd were starting to congregate. The music was pushed louder and the lighting grew softer. People were barking above the noise to make their jokes heard, and others responded on cue with noisy male baying. It was a mixed Burmese and expatriate throng, almost all young. Some of the Burmese were in traditional dress. Most wore Western suits. Some of the westerners had Asian women with them. She had observed these mixed couples on her earlier trip to Asia. International businessmen, generally a little bulked out from too many overnight flights and expensive dinners, eyes shadowy and complexions a tad too pale, would sit opposite exquisite diminutive Asian women, bright-eyed beauties who looked delighted with their catch. It was the fairy story of the successful foreigner meeting the local maiden. These women set a standard in feline attractiveness that she could never dream of approaching. They were

[144]

utterly captivating to look at, though the loveliness seemed too perfect to last. Did the relationships endure? Would they survive repatriation to the London drizzle and pilgrimages to Boots for Night Nurse, Paracetamol and Sudafed? The girls looked fragile; spring bloomers who would have already wilted by mid-June. She took satisfaction in the thought that she and Sambath were an exception to this pattern, or rather a reversal of it. She the fair-skinned outsider, he the dark-eyed endogenous basilisk. And with all these perfect little pimpernels to choose from, he had cast his eyes wider and selected her, an English peony. It would be a pity to say goodbye to all this, really, just when she was getting started, but common sense had to prevail.

A seed failing to sprout. Yes, she had seen the same seed before. Moh-Moh had one wrapped in tissue paper. Her boyfriend had given it to her. It came from the fruit of the *Strychnos Cardomemsis*. Moh-Moh was only a messenger. Moh-Moh had been sweet and simple, definitely not heading for a Nobel prize in anything particular, and Olivia had taken a liking to her. The text that Michael Maung had given her to read referred to the very high toxicity of the seed when refined to crystal form. When Olivia had learnt she had been hired for a meeting in Yangon she had written to the email address Moh-Moh had given her. Police constable Maung had agreed to see her in Yangon. His message also said:

Strychnos Cardomemsis *seed is employed to give warning in old times of Khmer empire. The highest man in the pagoda use this style. He send seed. If man or lady get seed they know straight away is a disaster for them. Disaster mean always dead. Style used by Khmer Issarak rebels against French peoples or against traitors who must die in the pit. Later this style is finish. Khmer Reds don't use this style. They kill with no warning. They prefer.*

Very decent club sandwich. She was hungrier than she thought.

High priests of the Khmer empire used an object to announce to offending individuals that their punishment by death was imminent. Olivia had found the historical anecdote entertaining. It increased her fondness for Moh-Moh and her man that they should find it necessary to tell her this. It was certainly nice of the priests to give their victims a sporting chance to run away. Or — who knows — perhaps the offender just froze on the spot. And it was a clever touch to convey the message in the form of a toxic plant seed. The melted cheese in her club sandwich wove a yellow thread between her hand and the bread. No doubt if one were to study other high-achieving, despotic civilisations, the Mayas and Aztecs and so on, one might encounter similar uses of seeds as tokens of meaning to a non-literate slave population.

Of course the point at which this became more than mere academic distraction was when she saw that Lucas Bellwether was the owner of one of Maung's seeds. The morning after the dinner party she called him and told him the whole story as recounted by the Yangon constable. Lucas was amazed. He told her that when he had been in Cambodia, he had found these things in his room wherever he stayed. It was her turn to be shocked.

"Do you think somebody is trying to tell you something?"

"Well, why? Or how? To me this warning language is meaningless. I'm not a sixteenth century Khmer who has offended a high priest. For God's sake. It's like something out of Hergé. Ancient curses shall strike those who invade the inner sanctum... It's baloney."

"Tell me I have nothing to worry about. Don't forget I'm booked for a tropical timber meeting down there."

"You're going to Myanmar. Not Cambodia."

"Yes. Where Vann died."

"I know that. But, I mean... what possible worry could there be? It makes no sense at all."

"Then I will put it out of my mind."

"Olivia?"

"Yes."

"I — er — I've been thinking. Thinking of going to Asia myself. I have one or two things to do in Cambodia, and now you have told me this, it seems as if we might have a few strings to tie up in Burma too. Myanmar rather. It might be good to actually sit down for a chat with our Constable Maung. I'm just thinking aloud here. I could hop across quite easily from Cambodia. No intention of getting in the way at your forestry thing, but we could touch base, if you felt like it."

"It's expensive to go all that way."

"True. But I know the cheapest routes. Cattle class. Don't forget my wife lives in Cambodia."

"I didn't know you had a wife, Lucas. But that's none of my business. If you want my opinion, I would be delighted to see you if you could make it to Yangon. It might even be quite reassuring, frankly. But I will be leaving for Thailand as soon as it's over. I have people to see in Bangkok.'"

"Ok. Let me work on it. Let's keep in touch."

The club sandwich devoured, Olivia toyed with the idea of another mojito and then decided against. She signed the chit and took the lift to her room on the fourth floor. From the window she surveyed the busy streets. Nine at night and everybody still out. She drew the curtain and went to the bathroom where she studied her face before starting to undress. In front of the mirror was a curving half-moon slab of grey marble. This was not a cheap hotel. The soaps, conditioners, shampoos and fragrances were nesting in a small towel within a hand-crafted basket. In the centre of the half moon was a big embossed crystal jar with something pink inside. She lifted the lid. The lid was heavy enough; the whole jar must weigh a ton, she thought. As I suspected. Bath salts. Pink bath salts for her ladyship. She undressed and stepped into the shower, washed, dried her hair in three minutes, counted the freckles on each breast, no change in the previous 14/11 score, put on her cotton nightdress, enveloped herself in the rich duvet, extinguished the lights, sat up, removed the nightshirt, cuddled the duvet and went to sleep.

In the morning Olivia donned a brown two-piece suit. Serviceable, nothing fancy. H&M. But enough linen in the mix to give the right tropical note. She breakfasted in the room. From the window the landscape looked as fecund as it had by night. The Foundation was starting its business at nine. She arrived at the second floor basement half an hour early, gauged the geography, the typical hotel committee room, each place ready with national name plates and flags like a royal banquet, the mineral water bottles, flowers, document piles, pencils, notepads, headsets; the technicians tapping microphones and saying *one two one two* to other technicians sitting in the interpreting booths. Thick-pile Chinese carpeting. It was a landscape that was familiar to her. Positioned to one side, at the Chairman's end of the room, was the table where she would work along with another précis writer, an American woman called Vinny Rosales, who had been sent up from Bangkok.

Vinny came in, plump, smiling. They report-writers shook hands, exchanged notes about the various languages they worked from, and took their places at the table.

The delegates began to appear. Men with swagger and heft and expensive suits. Indonesia first. That would be the minister, to judge by the names on the list. Cambodia came in next: she was a lavishly dressed, intimidatingly permed, diamond-clad woman. Lower rankers fretted around the heavyweights, answering phones for them, sitting them down, pouring their water. Philippines. Another minister. Hand-shaking with the Cambodians. Eruptions of exaggerated laughter; clasping, hugging. The whap-whap noise of fat people patting each other on the back. She saw some of the pimpernels from the bar last night, fussing around the men, smiling anxiously. Thailand now. Large numbers of Thais, it seemed. One of them in a dark green military uniform with stacked shelves of medal ribbons. A flunkey carrying his cap. More laughter; the opening of arms in sudden recognition. These were men and women who understood each other, who were bound by a sense of purpose deeper than the bland prerogatives of a multilateral forestry meeting. You could smell the power of these people. A trio of the Cambodians turned to welcome one of their delegation, who, Armani-suited and suave, had just walked in, tailed by a very attractive female assistant.

A clawing at her throat. Olivia wanted to vomit. No! Not possible! She blurted out to Vinny that she had to dash to her room. She had left some notes behind.

"Sure, I'll hold the fort down here. Hey, you doing okay girl?"

Olivia scuttled out of the meeting, hugging the wall, head down. When she got inside her room she sat on the bed and breathed as deeply and slowly as she could. What on earth was going on? Was she seeing things? Sambath? Here?

Calm down Olivia.

Calm down your fucking self! Sambath is here! And he's got a woman with him! She wept tears of frustration. Her neat plan was hopelessly upset by this totally unscheduled apparition. Her lover! With a Khmer doll sitting next to him.

And have they fixed the where and when? quoted a familiar voice in her head.

And shall Trelawny die? she responded mechanically.

There's twenty thousand Cornishmen will know the reason why. Brazen it out girl! Take it in your stride! And for heaven's sake get out of that silly H&M trouser suit. And get a move on. You don't imagine that ditzy Rosales woman is going to write the report for you, I hope.

Olivia rose, removed the trouser suit and put on a cream dress in Egyptian cotton with raw silk collars, cuffs and belt. The dress showed off her figure to perfection. She painted her lips a chalky pink to match the trimmings and anointed her collarbones with Versace. That's a bit more like it. Eyelashes next. A decent pair of heels. When she returned to the conference room, Olivia walked slowly, gracefully, glancing neither to left or right. All those Cornishmen watching her every step — she could hardly let them down, could she? She took her place beside Vinny who stared at her with eyes stretched wide and jawbone dangling.

"Everything okay here? Other outfit was just too tight on the boobs. You know what I mean…that kind of day." Vinny nodded, speechless.

The part up to the first coffee break at 11.15 was mostly taken up with courtesies, introductions and formalities. Under the leadership of a Danish forestry expert, the AWF team laid out the objectives of the meeting, which was to hear species-by-species status reports, both endangered and non-endangered. After that, the other government observers introduced themselves. Three tidy women from Beijing in heavily accented English. One man from Moscow (yes, who spoke Russian). A Sikh civil servant in a blue turban. Then the non-government attendees: two different conservation groups and one Bangladeshi man representing the Asian Trade Union Federation of Forestry Workers. This was material for the annexes; very little of the introductory details would need to go in the report, so the two précis-writers enjoyed an easy warm-up. Save your guns for the national statements, they told each other, which will be read without feeling by people who didn't draft them. That was always the tough bit. When all the preliminaries were done and the Burmese chairman announced a coffee break, Olivia fixed her gaze on Sambath. She watched as he rose, said something to the girl beside him, and marched towards her table. Oh my God, he's coming. She steadied her hand, tilted her head to one side.

"Sambath. What an extraordinary surprise."

"What a surprise for me, you mean" he answered. Gently, perhaps a little too suavely. "The nicest surprise I could ever have hoped for. So this is the work that you do?"

"For my sins, yes."

"Sins?"

"Oh, it's just an expression." She managed a fetching giggle.

"Olivia they are waiting for me outside. I can't talk now. As I say this is a wonderful surprise. What are you doing tonight? Please tell me you are free."

"I might be. What about you and your girlfriend?"

The man frowned and tut-tutted. His hair was oiled back; he gave off an aura of sandalwood scent.

"Please. Assistant. Not girlfriend. Fully professional." He glanced down at the documents spread across her table. "You don't think I can manage all this paperwork on my own do you? Now listen. There is a very good restaurant I know three streets from here." He smiled his slow, knowing smile. "So tonight let's go there. They say the food's not too bad." He wrote the address on one of her documents.

"I see. Very well then. I'll see you there."

"Seven thirty? Don't be late, English angel." He gave a little flutter with his hand as he departed.

For the rest of the day, Olivia was floating on air. Her mood improved dramatically and she devoted her lunch break entirely to Vinny, who described how she had had a run of bad luck with several husbands dying on her. Touch wood, the new Swedish accountant in the AWF was going to be a survivor. Life was like that. You had to take your chances. Touch wood, honey. Touch teak. Touch jelutong. Touch kapur. Or touch something really nice. Touch rosewood. Vinny emitted a giggle and Olivia decided she approved of this woman. Like her, she was a fighter.

II

Sambath had a lot on his mind. Fortunately for him, there was enough time to weigh up the different questions that were troubling him. The speeches were continuing in steady succession and he had no wish to listen to any of them, so he was free to think. *Dalbergia Cochinchinensis.* Cambodia Rosewood. Siamese Rosewood. Vietnamese Rosewood. Endangered species, listed in CITES Annex II. Convention on International Trade of Endangered Species. Endangered. Illegal.

Negotiation of untroubled passage, for a start. The sheer logistics of moving truckloads of rare timber out of northern Cambodia and into Thailand. How to deposit the timber in Thailand for the time it took to age it before moving it across to Myanmar. How to negotiate the border crossings in Shan State so as to get the trucks into China where the merchants would fight tooth and nail to buy his Dalbergia. He had the system in place. It was up and running. The trouble was that it needed constant maintenance. He needed a whole host of people on his side. Some wanted monetary compensation, some wanted a percentage of the wood, some (the Chinese) wanted nothing except the knowledge that he owed them a very hefty favour in return. Meanwhile, the human rights and the conservation groups were becoming more and more vocal. Killing Chut Wutty in the Cardamom Mountains had only helped in the short term. The citizens' patrols would soon be back again, confiscating sawing equipment and making bonfires of the illegally cut wood. The whole logging thing had got caught up in the climate change agenda. Climate. Nobody talked about anything else these days. Journalists went out into the woods to film the felling. You had to make sure that these people got properly intimidated, with the right leeway of deniability for you. It was all possible, quite practicable when you got into the way of it, but it took a lot of work. What rank were those three Chinese women over there, for example? He didn't know any of them. He would have to corner them in the coffee-break, try to get a feel of how much influence they carried in Beijing, find out which of them knew the border routines into Yunan, see who they knew, gauge how they operated. That could be classified as a cross-cutting issue, as the AWF diplomats liked to call them. He smiled at his own wit. General, on-going administrative headaches were now called cross-cutting issues. Brilliant. Seated beside him, radiantly beautiful and monumentally bored, Romy smiled back.

Headache number two was sitting writing notes on the other side of the room. Writing like a demon. Look at her. That English woman. What on earth was she doing here? In a forestry meeting, of all things? Tonight. Tonight we will lay all this to rest. A quiet table and a lot of wine and pick her brains very aggressively. Yes, admitted; she was okay. Well-dressed too. Sambath conceded to himself that he was turned on by Olivia. She was so wonderfully white. The whole body, when you got her clothes off, was so pure. He knew. He had inspected it with care on their first night of sex after the meeting at the pool. She had been so reserved over dinner that he had never imagined that she would agree to a drink afterwards in his room. And yet within six minutes of his closing the door, she was naked on the floor. That body. It was screaming out to be defiled. She excited him in the same way as northern European tourists had before. Pale flesh and fawn freckles. The dull brown skins on offer locally simply bore no comparison. Romy, for example. He just couldn't do it with her. Couldn't raise the interest. One more Khmer whore, even if she was a very pretty one. But Olivia was a different story, though first and foremost her presence here called for urgent damage control and that was what he was going to apply tonight.

Issue number three was the actual instruments of general (cross-cutting) damage control. For Olivia it might be limited to a bottle or two of expensive wine. We will see. There were enforcement instruments of another kind too. Mannlicher Schönauer made a very nice SPP 9 mm handgun. They were quite rare nowadays. He had bought one several years ago in Sihanoukville as a personal tribute to the hunting gun he had inherited, a kind of memento in miniature of the rifle used to murder his dear father. But guns were for boys and Sambath had done enough with guns for one lifetime. He had subtler things in his arsenal.

Far subtler things. Things that people connected not with assassination but with neutralising toilet odours. Yes, that's right. Initially he had wrestled with the concept. Impact-activated systems never really worked that well. There was one type in use that was activated by the air movement when the door opened. He found that functioned better. Then there were systems activated by the light impulses when someone opened the door, but what if they had left the card key in the slot when they went out and the bathroom light stayed on? Unreliable. Slowly he had realised that the best system was much the simplest. People activated the air conditioning with a remote control, so why not the wall-mounted freshener unit? Simply trigger a signal manually. It made so much more sense. His ideal would be to have the remote signal built into his i-phone, but he (or Apple) hadn't got there yet. For the moment it required an independent device. The unit was very slick and small and it fitted nicely into his chest pocket. There was also a timer — anything from thirty seconds to two minutes. The capsules of crystalline alkaloid suspension clipped snugly into the back of the plastic dispenser unit, which you could hold easily in one hand. And the auto-adhesive fixation band that meant that you could put it where you wanted, when you wanted. It really was a brilliant piece of work, not of his own manufacture but certainly of his own design. He imagined his father's grunts of approval. Clever boy, Sambath. Clever lad. Takes after his dad. Heh heh.

Romy smiled back.

*

He wore a pink shirt, the same one as he had been wearing when he first met her. He had pale linen trousers. He wanted to look pastel and caring, avoiding the intimidating "national delegation" look. She was in a dark dress with a spiky collar and no sleeves, as if she sensed his liking for her long white arms. She seemed to have put something oily in her short hair which made it stand up a bit, reminding him (agreeably) of a Ukrainian dancer he knew from the Blue Mekong. The Indochine Fusion Lounge provided a passable menu, a bit of a mish-mash between Burmese, Thai and Indonesian, with an option of steak and fries.

It also provided very discreet velvety booths where you could eat undisturbed. He told her he was going to make his life easy and go for a fine rare Angus steak, plain and simple, and she told him that was a brilliant idea and she just might do exactly the same. This played nicely into his hands, because wine with Asian food was always complicated, while a self-respecting Lafite with an Angus steak was the most natural thing in the world. Over the first bottle he discovered that she was doing her report-writing job for the first time in Asia and she was actually terribly excited to be breaking into a new market. She garbled something about three official languages which he didn't attempt to understand. As for her previous trip, no the first time she hadn't exactly been doing that sort of report but a kind of professional thing for her colleagues. He told her that he owned a number of exclusive furniture outlets in the region, which she knew already from their last encounter, and that he sometimes travelled with Cambodian delegations as an advisor on anything to do with timber, which she did not know. A man of the world is my Sambath, she had replied.

The wine was flowing fast. The claret glasses were very large and he made sure hers remained full. She seemed to be successfully letting the tensions of the day drain away. At one moment she asked him about his assistant, saying (by this time her voice was slurring very slightly) that she hoped she was nothing more than an assistant. He said she was the wife of one of the big timber merchants in the north and she sometimes came to help him with conferences. At this point she appeared relieved. He poured her wine again and she gazed at the gorgeous rush of crimson sailing around the vast perimeter of the glass and she leaned towards him and Sambath, she asked, can I trust you? Can I confide in you? He took her hand and whispered of course my darling Olivia. That was when she started talking about things that made him irritated at first and, as she continued, violently angry. White-nerve angry.

There was a whole thing about some seeds, she explained, which actually she had had explained to her in Yangon by this rather silly girl, but on behalf of the police, so maybe not so silly, strychnine seeds which grew only in Cambodia, and her friend, or rather colleague, had been bedevilled by these seeds, he was the friend of Dermott Vann, an interpreter, and then Vann had died, obviously not of eating the seeds or anything as crazy as that, but the fact remained that he had died, of, of eating something and Lucas was trying to track down the killer and it helped to know a bit about the Khmer Rouge because he thought it was linked up and he, fortunately for him, or maybe not so fortunately, come to think of it, actually knew quite a lot about the Khmer Rouge because he had worked in the reconciliation commission out there, and although she couldn't put her finger on it, she felt she was in some kind of danger. Or maybe he was. Or maybe they both were. To be honest, Lucas was a bit of a nutcase. And if her Sambath was the sweet man she thought he was, he would tell her she was talking complete nonsense.

Sambath could feel a nerve on the left side of his face quivering insistently. It was a symptom of burning anger that he got when he felt cornered. Once it had occurred with his dentist in Phnom Penh while he was locked in the chair, and the man had rushed to find a mirror to show him the nerve, perfectly mapped by a white line running behind his eye, over the cheekbone and down to the jaw.

"Are you okay Sambath?"

"Of course my dear. If I were a ruder man I would say you were talking complete nonsense." He gave a dry laugh, attempting to relax the sudden cramping he felt. "But I will simply say you are being rather, er... European."

"What do you mean?" She ran her index finger across his palm. "I didn't mean to upset you my sweet. I was just being stupid. Forget it. Forget it this moment."

"Asia? What is Asia? Oh, Asia is so exotic you know. If you cut your way through the jungles, you will find fabulous Khmer ruins. Peasants in gorgeous woven silks toiling away in the paddy fields beneath mossy carvings of ancient Buddhas. Monks in saffron robes spreading peace and karma. But Asians have another side, as we all know. They are deeply peaceful until the day they want to cut your throat. Or massacre each other, as they did in Vietnam or Cambodia or Indonesia or wherever. No foreign powers need meddle with them, oh no, they just kill each other for fun. And in the dark alleys of Cambodia's cities, they are still killing each other, these people, my people, because that's what yellow people do, don't they? They smoke opium and drink rice wine and poison each other for fun."

"Oh Sambath I'm awfully sorry. I really shouldn't have mentioned it. Just put it out of your mind. I'm just a silly tourist."

He gave a laugh, more genuine this time. "I am being silly as well. How about we forget all this talk of Agatha Christie and poisoning. Let's look at the dessert menu." He took her hand gently. "It's okay Olivia. Really. No offence taken."

"I'm frankly not sure I could manage a desert. Shall we just, er, head home?"

He had shown he had a vulnerable side and now she wanted him more than ever. There was only one way to heal a wounded man.

"Okay. Let's just… head home!"

He shouldered his grip (somehow he had paid, though she saw no transaction) and they walked out into the baking night. In the reception area of their hotel, somebody recognised him and hailed him towards their group. Let's not make it too obvious, he whispered furtively, I'll see you in your room in ten minutes. He went to join the group. She took the elevator. When he knocked on the door twenty minutes later, she had already changed. Underwear and black stockings below, and only a white towel on the upper half. He took her straight in his arms and kissed her.

"Do you always carry your condoms in such a big bag?" she whispered, licking the hairs on his navel.

"Depends how excited I'm feeling" he answered, then excused himself and went to the bathroom. The bedside phone rang. Bloody phone. Olivia ignored it.

They made love, starting on the bed, quickly continuing on the floor, her arms pinned down so firmly by his that it made her armpits burn. She lay there for a long while afterwards, breathing heavily and watching the side of his face which had that strange pale streak. Afterwards, when the carpet was starting to scratch her shoulders, she got up and walked to the bathroom to wash. She closed the door. He rose to his feet and grabbed his jacket from the chair. After a while she came out of the bathroom wearing nothing, sat on the bed and beckoned him to her.

"Stay Sambath. I don't want to be alone."

"Relax Olivia. You need some sleep. This is only the first night. We have time."

"What were we drinking tonight? This wine is having a funny effect on me."

"Wine does that my love. Makes you sleepy."

"Dizzy. Oooh. Hold me. I'm unstable. Migraine. Lights flashing. Sambath!"

"Lie down. Here. Take this blindfold to block out the light. That's better, isn't it? Soothing. Take a good nap. Call me if you need me."

"I'm feeling terrible."

As he inched out of the door, Sambath turned his glance back to the room, in time to see Olivia, blindfolded, give a sudden backward jerk of her torso so her entire body from pubis to jawbone was curved outwards like an Italian marble sculpture. He walked down the corridor without bothering to fully close the door; he took the lift two floors higher. It was such a beautifully exciting way of killing. Perfected, in all its beauty, by him. His libido was charged by the sight of the woman dying, and, indifferent to the fact that he had made love ten minutes earlier, he wanted more, much more. These chances were so rare. Romy was watching a popular soap on TV when he came in. He pulled her roughly from the bed, grabbed the cord of his gown, dragged her towards the bathroom, put one arm around her stomach, lifted her body from behind, balanced one little brown foot on the toilet cistern and left the other leg dangling while he tied her wrists to the metal shower frame above his head.

"Clayton you go mad!"

He penetrated her from behind, and when he had finished, leaving her sore and wet, with grey suds drooling down her leg, he couldn't be bothered to untie her. That would teach her to put on airs. A whore was a whore. He went to sleep, leaving her sobbing, still suspended by the wrists in the shower.

III

Passing the Dragon Guesthouse on his way home, Constable Michael Maung saw a foreigner standing by the check-in desk. He recognised him immediately as the English witness who had come in to the station for questioning the morning after the poisoning case. So. Great Britain was here again. The Great British man was in a very cheap hotel, while Mrs Trelawney of England, who had emailed him recently, was in a very expensive one. Michael could smell the danger that was lurking round the corner. They should not be back here in Myanmar, those two people, quite so soon. It was tempting fate too far. He had no clue of the motivation or reasoning behind the killing of the Khmer man that those two were associated with, but he had a powerful grasp of the method that had been used. And, being the thorough man that he was, once he had researched the subject of Cambodian strychnine poisoning, he went on to research the antidotes. This was to prove a frustrating exercise. His hopes had risen when he had found articles in The Lancet stating that opium was the best antidote to strychnine, and then waned again when he understood the article dated back to the nineteenth century and was entirely superseded. What a pity. There was certainly no shortage of opium in Myanmar. Nicotine was also once meant to be a cure, but you could hardly tell somebody in the throes of asphyxiation to smoke twenty Rubys. The modern day antidotes were written up in medical terms that he found difficult understand. It seemed you needed hefty amounts of barbiturates if you were to relax the patient's muscles enough for him, or her, to survive.

Watching Lucas from the shadows, Michael saw him leave the guesthouse and march off with a map in his hand. And, policeman that he was, Michael followed him.

*

The guesthouse single had rattan furniture. To Lucas it had seemed tidy and functional. There was a shared bathroom down a recently mopped corridor. The area was devoid of attractions or charm and he was not convinced that his decision to come here had been a wise one. He missed the softer touch of Cambodia. Something had prompted him to fly to Myanmar. Olivia Trelawney was clearly reserving her weekend in Bangkok for her private needs, and she did not seem to have plans for being anywhere else. Yes, it was Olivia who had prompted him. She had said his presence would be reassuring. He was here to reassure. He resolved to make an ally out of Olivia. Safety in numbers. They would sit down together in the bar of her hotel and make a joint plan. They would decide whether to go any further with the pursuit. Or let the whole story die a gentle death, and go home. He knew enough about Vann's death to understand that he did not wish to know more. Did that make sense? Not really. These Asians were right to resent all the international people who came to solve their problems. It was time to return to his flat and batten down for the approaching London winter. Enough was enough. Lazing around in charming Phnom Penh was one thing. Sitting here on planet Mars was another.

He took a cold shower. The fuse inside the electrical water heater had blown. The shower room was musty, with sand encrusted on the window panes. Behind the sand, the sun was weakening. He returned to his room, stretched out on the bed with a towel around his waist, and fell asleep. When he woke it was dark. His watch said twenty past eight. He dressed, went to the reception and asked for directions to the Myanmar Park Grand. The route (he intended to walk) took him round the Kandawgyi Lake. In fact, if he chose to circumnavigate it by the top road, it would take him past the very place where Vann had died.

He walked fast at first, but quickly he became too hot and he slowed his pace. The lake road was longer than he remembered. The traffic moved fast, taxi drivers darting from lane to lane. Pedestrians ventured across the road at their peril. Only the dogs seemed unperturbed. There were other people on the pavement, teachers in long green skirts, monks, loitering couples. A thin girl with ginger hair gave him a smile and a suggestive tilt of the head as he passed by. When he got to the place where he had last seen his friend, he was momentarily filled with grief. This soon gave way to a new longing to know more about him. No, he realised, the pursuit was not over yet. On he walked.

There were phalanxes of black diplomatic cars aligned in the parking area of the sprawling luxury hotel. Perspiring and tired, Lucas stepped into the cold marble lobby. People were milling around dressed in the smart-casual attire required for conference evening events. On the far side of the hall there was a mock English tavern called The Stagecoach. At the concierge's desk he asked to be put through to Mrs Green's room. The concierge, who was dressed in white silk knickerbockers and had a pointed spike in his hat, flicked at the keyboard on his computer. He wrote a number on a slip of paper which he handed to Lucas.

"This is the room number sir. Just add a nine and you will get through. There is an internal phone right there."

Lucas called. There was no answer. Wearily, he turned his steps towards the pub. Their arrangements had been casual. He had assumed he would find her in the hotel. He had no Myanmar sim card and did not know if she had a local number. But she ought to be back from dinner soon. The bar was rowdy. He took a place at the end of the polished wooden counter and ordered a beer. He felt badly under-dressed in this place.

"Carlsberg, Budweiser, Heineken Sir?"

"Myanmar beer."

"Very good Sir."

He picked at a bowl of peanuts and wondered what to do next. Drink the beer first. Check the newspaper. The Myanmar Times. Pictures of tennis players having tantrums. He wanted a cigarette but decided he would find some later, in a less pricy outlet. He yawned, paid eight dollars for his half-finished beer, and left the din of the bar behind him. Half an hour had passed. Let's have another try with the hotel phone.

Someone picked up the receiver. He heard breathing.

"Olivia. It's Lucas."

"Lucas. Come here. Come here. Quick."

Was that Olivia's voice? Was it a joke? Was she in the middle of a spasm of dengue haemorrhagic fever? A spasm of...? Oh holy fuck Olivia! Gripped by sudden urgency, he ran to the lift, pushed the fourth floor button, saw that it needed a room card to unblock the commands. Shit! As he stood there, an elderly Asian man hobbled in, accompanied by a well-permed woman. He had seen this woman's face before somewhere. Perhaps in a Cambodian newspaper. The man's quivering fingers fiddled hopelessly with the card and the lift button. Lucas leaned over, excused himself in Khmer, took the card from the man's hand and pressed the fourth floor before asking them which level they wanted. Too befuddled to work out why this shabby-looking foreigner was speaking to him in his own tongue, the man merely nodded his head. The lift was slow, stopping at the third floor, opening for nobody, before finally reaching the fourth. Lucas strode out, ran down the carpeted passageway, turned on his heels, ran in the opposite direction. He spotted 422 and knocked. Then saw that the door was ajar.

"Lucas!"

"Olivia... what the..."

Olivia lay on the bed, her head dropping over the side of the mattress. She was clasping a pillow to her body, attempting to conceal her nudity. Saliva drooled from her mouth, one long string reaching down to the floor. She was breathing in short grunts. Her face was grey and perspiring. Lucas stared at her, paralysed by the spectacle, then took a deep breath, lifted her back on to the bed, propped her head on a pillow and pulled a sheet over her. He reached for the phone.

"Reception how may I help you."

"I need a doctor in room 422. It's an emergency!"

"We have no resident doctor Sir. Please wait while I try to find somebody. What is the nature of the emergency?"

"Poisoning!"

"Food poisoning there is not much we can do Sir. Patient should be doing better by the morning."

"Real poisoning you arsehole! Now get a doctor!"

"Let me see what I can do Sir."

He cracked the phone receiver down. Went to the bathroom to douse a towel in cold water. Cleaned her face and told her everything would be alright.

"Lucas... It won't be alright."

"Yes it will."

"Lucas I told him about everything. He did this to me."

"Who did?"

"Ss..."

Before she could say the name, Olivia gave a growl, spat foaming saliva on to the sheet and started kicking her legs energetically. She turned on to her stomach and pushed her head backwards, the growl rising to a bellow. Then she gestured towards a tote bag on the floor. Lucas called reception again and told them to hurry. They replied that it was complicated finding doctors who were free at night time. They were doing their best. Olivia's next spasm was almost identical to the back-arching movement that had been imprinted on his mind ever since Vann's death. Did she want something in the bag? He turned it upside down and out tumbled toiletries, a paperback, a souvenir back-scratcher in polished wood, paper handkerchiefs.

"Sambath? Are you saying he is here? Sambath? Answer me Olivia!"

Olivia was unable to speak. Her breath was coming in very rapid bursts. Crazed with anger and frustration, Lucas left the room, ran down the staircase to reception, and yelled at the reception people that someone was dying in 422. A tall Burmese man appeared from nowhere.

"Is it Mrs Trelawney? Is it asphyxia?"

"Yes! And yes! Who the hell are you?"

"Leave this to me."

The man took the phone from the receptionist, and spoke fast and insistently. He hung up.

"They need six minutes to get here. I told them it's strychnine. If they are very fast we may save her. Michael Maung. Yangon police."

Exhausted and confused, Lucas mumbled his own name.

"Let's go to her. There is very little we can do. Go very gently. Any stimulation will give further spasms. Very, very painful."

"You go. I have someone else to see."

Lucas turned away from the desk, then suddenly swivelled back to face a horrified junior trainee. "What room is Sambath?" and without daring to ask him why he needed to know, she tapped her computer and said "Mr Sambath in room 635." Lucas rushed back to the stairwell and legged it up three floors, paused for breath, and walked the other three. At the top he took a deep breath, too exhausted to run any further. Once he was standing outside 635, he breathed once, twice, pressed his elbows to his side and launched his stocky shoulders against the door. The cheap latch gave way immediately. He stepped into the room to see a man sitting up in bed.

"Who on earth might you be?"

"Sambath! You poisoned her!"

Sambath seemed unperturbed. "Ah. So you would be the Englishman I heard about. You haven't wasted your time."

Lucas heard a voice and turned to face the open door of the bathroom. A woman was hanging from the shower door.

"Jesus Christ! What is this?"

Sambath, in t-shirt and boxer shorts, opened the drawer of his bedside table. He extracted a large hand gun.

"You stupid little English fuckwit. Flying around the world to save people from themselves. Helping nations out of darkness. Pardon, reconciliation, justice, and how proud of it you all are. How very pleased you all are. We told you to go home and you decided to stay. Ok stay if you want. Stay you fucker. I'll teach you to stay, you truth and reconciliation arsehole."

He shoved a magazine clip into the handle. There was white smear pulsating down the left side of his face. Lucas retreated backwards, entered the bathroom, shutting the door behind him. He untied the wrists of the suspended woman. For a reason he did not try to understand she immediately began to run the bath. At that moment Sambath smashed the door with a kick from his heel. With a hand as steady as ice he levelled the barrel of the gun at Lucas' head. Lucas stepped slowly backwards. His heel hit the shower basin and he toppled, coming down in a limp heap. Soap, pipes and showerhead clattered down on top of him. Sambath laughed and raised his gun. Lucas caught the girl's eye. He grabbed the shower head and she hit the lever control, projecting a spray of hot water in Sambath's face. He was momentarily distracted, stepped back, and that was when Romy, still behind him, lifted the crystal glass jar of bath salts and swung it hard against his head. Sambath groaned, curved in a deep bow, and she drew back the jar and beat it hard into his skull a second time. Blood sprang from his ear, contrasting sharply with the white nerve line. He bowed deeper, only half conscious. Then Romy grasped the back of his head and plunged it under the bath water. She held it there. Sambath's body folded on the bathroom floor.

IV

Township Commander Captain Win Maw Oo was having a good evening. Good would be an understatement. It was better than good. He felt like an old-fashioned alchemist, a *zawgyi*, who from the base metal of his life had successfully completed all the stages in the manufacturing of his own immortality. It was, to be frank, a golden evening, marred only by one dark cloud.

Time to pour a Wincarnis.

It had all begun two weeks ago when he had received a call from his friends in Special Branch. There had been a serious incident involving foreigners, right in the midst of a diplomatic conference. How could he be of service? He could be of service, said the caller, by overseeing a major damage mitigation exercise. He had proven his skills in working with foreigners, the British in particular, and the Interior Ministry wanted to see him in the top job, the job of making sure that nothing got out of Yangon about the fiasco.

Sensing that his great aim might be finally within his reach, Captain Win Maw Oo replied that he would be glad to oblige.

There was a lot of talking by phone with Special Branch. A British woman was in a coma. He was to liaise with the Consulate. She must be extracted from the country as soon as she recovered. No need to talk to the Ambassador, others would take care of all that. Another Englishman was involved, the Bellwether he had come across before. Yes, precisely, the same specimen. Get him out as well. Permanently out. We do not wish to see him again. There was a Cambodian delegate enjoying special privileges and immunities. Male. Seriously injured. The Cambodians were making arrangements to remove him, and the Captain was to liaise closely with them. There was also a Cambodian escort woman. Expel immediately. Liaise, negotiate, conclude. His duty was to avoid all actions that would raise the notoriety of this event, and to persuade others to take the same approach. A report was expected in five days' time. A room had been reserved for him at the Myanmar Park Grand, and another for his sergeant. No uniforms, please, *pasoe* and formal shirt only. And, finally, pass on their commendation to the constable who alerted the emergency services.

He continued with his report. He had covered four of the witnesses so far. Dr C An Punlok, government advisor, delegation of Cambodia. Ms Honey Su Aye Min, trainee receptionist at the Myanmar Park Grand Hotel. Mr Desmond Win-Win Hathaway, pro-consul in Naypyidaw attached to HM Consulate in Yangon. Ms Victoria "Vinny" Rosales, international report-writer. Now the doctor.

Dr Tun Tun O, Registrar, Dept of Toxicology, Victoria Hospital declared that he had been summoned by the policeman in question to treat a case of strychnine poisoning. Speed was essential and he had been driven to the hotel by ambulance. On arrival he immediately administered an extremely strong barbiturate sedative to the patient and emptied her stomach, not realising at that stage that she had not ingested the poison orally. Artificial respiration techniques were also applied. The woman had "a very strong constitution" he stated. He also performed emergency first aid on Mr Sambath prior to dispatching him by ambulance. Mr Sambath had suffered a cheekbone fracture and damage to the cranium.

Now the woman. The whore.

Ms Ong Romduol said that she had revised her opinion of Mr Clayton (the name she used for her Cambodian companion) when he had treated her with great physical cruelty for the purposes of his private gratification. She claims to have reacted instinctively to protect Mr Bellwether when Mr Sambath levelled his handgun at him. She knew that he had a weapon in the bedside commode because she had inspected the drawers in his absence. She was not unduly alarmed to discover the gun because she said it was common in her country for men like that to carry handguns. She clarified that she had run the bath water in a reflexive fashion because she had felt soiled and wanted a bath. She had held the man's head under water only to neutralise him. She opined that men could be relied on to do enough killing on their own and she did not intend to add to the tally. She let it be understood that financial inducements could enable her to divulge further information, at which point the sergeant issued her with a sharp warning. She became emotional and stated that she was only trying to help her mother. After she had recovered her equanimity, this officer informed Ms Romduol that the Myanmar Prosecutor's office intended to bring charges against her for the wilful intoxication of Mrs Trelawney. She would be liable for a sentence at Insein Prison in Yangon; a minimum of eight years' duration. At this point the woman wept bitterly and denied any involvement in the attempted murder. She could not, however, prove that she was telling the truth. She would also be charged with causing major bodily harm to Mr. Sambath. At this point she collapsed on the floor. The sergeant revived her and took her into a separate room where, after some persuasion, she agreed to sign a document attesting to her guilt in the attempted murder of Mrs Trelawney. It was an act of jealousy, she admitted, perpetrated when she had become aware of Mr Sambath's growing attraction to the English woman. Her emotions had taken control of her rational faculties. On receipt of the signed confession it was agreed that the charges would not be pressed if the woman returned to her native Cambodia and remained in her village and never attempted to return to Myanmar.

That just about covered her. Now for the English witness.

Mr Lucas Bellwether has been known to this officer since he interviewed him in the case of the death of a staff member of the Euro-Asian narcotics convention in Yangon earlier this year. At the time, Mr Bellwether had left a favourable impression. He was concerned to see justice done in the case of his deceased colleague. At no point did he intimate that he might be naïve enough to take justice into his own clumsy hands. Yet this appears to be what he has done. Mr Bellwether recounted at some length his encounters with certain individuals in Phnom Penh (Cambodia) who had led him to believe that the death of his friend and colleague had been the outcome of a historical vendetta. In other words, that Cambodian reckonings were being settled on the soil of Myanmar — an unwelcome eventuality if it were to prove true. It appears — if any credit is to be given to this very colourful account, which may or may not be a fabrication — that Mr Bellwether identified an individual belonging to the Cambodian vendetta network in the very person of Mr Son Sambath, and trailed him to the Myanmar

Park Grand Hotel which he was attending as a logging consultant at-
tached to the delegation of Cambodia. Mr Bellwether claims that Mr
Sambath discovered from Mrs Trelawney, in a manner that remains
to be elucidated, that he was imminently to be unmasked, and in a fit
of fury he found a way to poison her. In that room he found not only
Sambath but the woman by the name of "Romy" who was working as
an escort girl and was suspended by a dressing gown cord from the
frame of the shower and in considerable pain. Mr Sambath attacked
him in the shower with a hand pistol. Before he could discharge his
weapon, however, Romy struck Mr Sambath laterally in the cranium
with a glassware vanity vessel, causing him to collapse. By that stage
Mr Bellwether was in a high state of agitation and had to be forcefully
restrained by the hotel security agent who was present on the scene,
and then sedated by the doctor.

*

Scene: A quiet corner in the Stagecoach Bar. Midday.

Desmond Win Win Hathaway: The spouse of the patient has been informed about the items.

Captain Win Maw Oo: I am glad of that. I am very sorry it should come to this. You informed him of the bodily evidence as well as the items?

Desmond Win Win Hathaway: Through the normal channels, yes. Captain, I believe I am talking to somebody who understands our British preoccupations. The need for extreme discretion.

Captain Win Maw Oo: Thank you. I have always felt a certain fondness for Great Britain. Its myriad ways.

Desmond Win Win Hathaway: These myriad ways include an extremely aggressive Fourth Estate.

Captain Win Maw Oo: Just update me so I am clear.

Desmond Win Win Hathaway: Mr Wystan Green has been told that along with other personal effects, items discovered in his wife's bedroom included a wooden beating stick, a book of sadomasochistic literature, and a blindfold. Mr Green has also been informed of the nature of the bodily samples taken from his wife.

He has been told she had bruising on her body. Captain, Mr Green has put in a strong plea, which is endorsed by my superiors, that there be no criminal prosecution in this case. Mr Green is deeply distressed and naturally wishes to avoid these events becoming public knowledge. We are requesting that the matter be treated as a case of acute food poisoning. I need to know if I have your understanding.

*

Let us pour a second Wincarnis. Why not? No, my dear spouse, you would not wish me to be drinking a second glassful like this, but you must accept that exceptional events call for exceptional behaviour.

Everything had gone very well. Bellwether was out. Gone. He had accepted to sign a paper pledging to not apply for a visa to visit Myanmar for five years. When the Captain has seen him off at the airport, he had been surprisingly courteous, extending his hand and expressing deep apologies for all of the trouble he had caused. There was not a lot of bad in that Bellwether fellow but he was certainly barking up entirely the wrong tree. He needed to put his mind elsewhere. Or, as Moh-Moh would say, he needed to adjust his settings. The escort woman was also out, and he had submitted her signed confession to the proper judicial authorities and served her the extradition order. They had shipped her back to her native village in Cambodia and told her to stay there on pain of something very nasty. The Sambath individual was being treated in Bumrungrad Hospital in Bangkok for cranial fracture. The Captain's parleys with the British pro-consul had meant that the British Embassy would not be raising a riot. Rather the contrary. They were not even aware that someone had been charged for attempted murder as the Cambodians had requested. A master-coup. Apart from that, inducements and threats of the usual kind had been distributed among the hotel reception staff who may have witnessed the agitation on the night in question. Good old Sergeant Myint Tin Tin knew his way around that particular zone. They would not talk. Trainee receptionist Honey Su Aye Min was granted a 3% salary rise.

There was only the one remaining stain on his skyline, but that could be dealt with. He would find a way.

And then back home to little Moh-Moh, who made a great fuss of her big, brave papa once they were safe together in the little house in Thayawaddy Lane. She was wearing *thanaka* paste on her face and a green outfit in the traditional cut. What a dear she is.

Then, exactly one week later, as he was relaxing in his rattan armchair, the phone call came. Congratulations on a job well done, said the man from Special Branch. The Minister had been impressed. Had even asked for the Captain's name. Had told them to make sure the police Captain was properly rewarded.

"Obviously it was not single handed. I had my Sergeant to help me."

"No false modesty, Deputy Township Commander. We are very grateful. Exceedingly grateful. Shall we start by dropping the word Deputy from the title?"

He gestured excitedly at Moh-Moh to lower her music. This was too good to be true. But there was more.

"What about the family, Township Commander? How is your daughter doing after your tragic bereavement, what was it, three years ago?"

Township Commander!

"Well, Sir, she's holding up well. Not so young as she was then of course. Ready for University now I fear. Have to think of somewhere safe to send her now."

"Any plans?"

"Well, of course in an ideal world, it would be Singapore, for Business Management, but that's only a dream financial-wise. Or closer to home in Yangon, of course."

"Why don't you send us a budget for Singapore, Captain? Fees. Living expenses. Scan her secondary school diplomas for us while you are at it. Copy of her passport. One or two academic recommendations. Make us a little file. I am sure we can arrange something."

Captain Win Maw Oo had to work hard to quell the tremor in his voice.

"I... I don't know how to thank you."

"Don't worry. It's not the first time we have extended a helping hand. Richly deserved in your case, I would say. Just send us that file."

Win Maw Oo's face moved to the darker corner of the room, away from the fretted windows, to where his wife's shrine was. The colour photograph already a little bleached by the sunlight that stole over the wall in the morning, the brass statue of the great Lord Buddha above, with its red flashing halo-lights and the left hand raised, the glasses of water and tea, and (yes, she had been a smoker) the packet of Red Ruby Filter: all were dissolved in an aqueous blur.

"If only you had lived to see this day my darling. If only you had lived to see this day."

By the time Moh-Moh came over, his shoulders were shaking and he was sobbing his grief into his handkerchief. His daughter took him in her arms, patted his back, sat him down, poured another drink.

"What is it, father? What *ever* is the matter?"

"Moh-Moh. You are going to study in Singapore."

V

They did not chase him away. He went of his own accord.

Maung's people had been Christians ever since the Portuguese had arrived in Bangladesh, or whatever it was that Bangladesh had been called in those distant days. His father had come down the coast to Rakhine State when he was still a child because there were opportunities there for Grandfather Maung, grandfather Daes as he was called then, to teach classical languages in the Catholic schools there. Even nowadays, Michael Maung's father still liked to say that he hailed from the archdiocese of Chittagong. He was a man fuelled by the nostalgia for the land of one's birth that is often the greater for not having experienced much of it. Chittagong was not too far away of course, a boat ride up from Sittwe, and every two or three years Michael's parents would take a private ferry to visit the people in the old country. On their return they would complain that it was not such a good place after all, going downhill really, but soon they would forget the harder realities of their trip and return to their longings for Chittagong, for being respected people with an education in a place that recognised them for the fine family they were.

Michael, for his part, was not a devout Roman Catholic, but he did enjoy the idea of a creator who had made the world with a loving and tender hand. His studies of the wonders of botany had confirmed his faith in that divinity rather than undermining it. Immaculate pregnancies and virgin deliveries were less to his taste, however. This upset his mother who said you couldn't pick and choose with the tenets of a religion. It was a matter of finding enough faith and then you could believe in these other things as well. You can't know everything, Michael, she would say. Some things are a Mystery, with a capital M. He knew there was a capital M by the tiny frisson that would shake her when she spoke of the Virgin Birth.

When Michael sat with Hoo Tin Maw in the police station and tried to explain what it meant to be a Roman Catholic converted four centuries ago by Portuguese priests, whose lineage was

Bengali and who hailed from Bangladesh but whose family was now Rakhine and spoke Rakhine and lived in Sittwe, the capital of Rakhine State, his fellow constable got so completely lost that it was almost comical. We are all Burmese, moaned Hoo Tin Maw, and if you want proof of that then...

"Then...?"

Hoo Tin Maw stretched out his arms in feigned exasperation. "Then just look at how we all wear *longyis* and we all smoke Ruby Red."

Michael agreed, for the sake of discussion, that they were all Burmese. The newly promoted Township Commander was Burmese too, for that matter. The Captain had accepted Michael's congratulations without referring to his own role in the drama, and they had gathered round in the station over a few beers to celebrate his promotion. It had been a tough week, the Captain said, and, now on his second bottle of Myanmar Pale, not a beverage he normally drank, he had allowed himself to hint at some of the challenges he had had to grapple with on his mission. He described Honey Su the trainee receptionist and her look of terror when the Sergeant had approached her — her face had just blanched — to tell her the good news of her salary rise. And when she had finally latched on that it was good news and not bad she had clasped the Sergeant by the arm because that was all she could reach, she being so small and he being so huge! Everybody had a good laugh over that, and the little celebration in the police station had gone so well that the Captain had gone on to confide that none of the Burmese people present on the scene had been found responsible for the murder, not one of them, it was all to do with a different country. He was not entitled to divulge which country it was. A woman in fact, a woman of low reputation and loose morals who had committed the crime that he had been brought in to investigate. He and the sergeant.

That was the moment in the merry chit-chat when Constable Maung offered his grain of salt, saying that if it was a nearby country this murderess was from, she had to be from Bangladesh, or failing that India, or if not India then China, or perhaps

Thailand, or even Laos or Cambodia. Could the Captain give them a clue?

The Captain had replied very gruffly that if the constable wanted to teach geography there were jobs going in the local schools. He was not in the business of giving clues, he was paid to investigate them and the Sergeant laughed, guffawed in fact, before stating that escort girls came from many places but Khmer tarts only came from one. And the whole group of them burst into laughter at that.

In the following days the thought that there had been a Khmer prostitute murderess on the rampage in Yangon began to do its work on Maung's endlessly curious imagination. And for this particular Rakhine man with his Catholic upbringing there was a tradition that said that the prostitute was often victimised. Not a tradition so much as a parable. The prophet Jesus of Nazareth was always looking for ways to reverse things, to stand them on their heads, to make the unimportant important and vice-versa. And in order to explain that humble people mattered a lot more than you might think, he told a story that was not about a lottery ticket seller or a toddy palm climber or a tooth-puller or a trash-picker or a foreigner's Lexus driver, although it could have been about any of these, but about a hooker. An ordinary bargirl such as you might meet in any of the alcohol shacks in Sittwe port. And the story was that this bargirl was about to be bludgeoned by the men of the town and then who should come round the corner but Jesus of Nazareth and he said kill her if you want but just as long as you have never shafted a bargirl yourself. And they bowed their heads in shame and went away. He was quite outspoken and blunt this Jesus when he needed to be. It said much about Michael Maung's romantic nature that he imagined that he was out to help this Cambodian woman because he was inspired by the story in the New Testament. More prosaically, Michael was a man who smelt a rat when there was a rat to be smelt, and the Township Commander's version of events was too easy to be true.

His method, simple but tried and tested, was to rifle through the boss's desk drawers. There it was. It was a Wednesday afternoon, as hot as any Wednesday afternoon had ever been, and he was full of valour and daring on that day because the results of his application would be posted on the internet by the end of the week. The Captain was having a cup of tea down the road and the Sergeant was snoring in his office. The report was there, in a foolscap envelope, a brown one so damp it was almost furry to the touch, and he eased it out and began to read about the evidence that had been gathered. When he found the part about the Khmer woman, his concentration doubled. This woman had agreed to sign a document attesting to her guilt in the attempted killing of Mrs Trelawney. The report said it had been an act of jealousy. But before agreeing to sign the document the woman had passed out on the floor and she had had to be revived by the sergeant who had taken her into a separate room and used methods of persuasion on her. After that she had signed. Maung skimmed through the other paragraphs which gave a description of the carnage in the hotel. It was idiotic of him to read the document there and then instead of rushing it straight to the photocopying machine, because he had been standing there in the captain's office for less than five minutes when the Captain himself marched in. Constable Michael Maung was caught in *flagrante delictu.*

"Would you mind explaining to me what you think you are doing there, Constable?"

"You framed the Cambodian woman."

"I did what?"

"You framed her. She didn't do it."

Captain Win Maw Oo looked the constable hard in the eyes.

"I don't know what you are talking about."

"Yes you do. You framed the Cambodian escort girl."

"Now look here, young man..." The captain approached the policeman, began to roll up his right sleeve, thought better of himself, exhaled.

"Sit down." The constable did as he was told.

Now, thought the Captain. At last.

"There is an awful lot that you do not know about life, young Constable Maung, and it seems this is not the right place for you to learn it. We have made an effort, the sergeant and I, to knock some sense into that dumb Rakhine head of yours, but now you have gone too far. There is no longer any place for you at this police station. There is no longer any place for you in the police forces of Myanmar. I am dismissing you for multiple misdemeanours in the performance of your duty and for sticking your nose into things that do not concern you. Gross insubordination. What you have done today is an offence for which you could be made to serve a lengthy custodial sentence. Charges can be brought."

"I did not mean to cause such offence, Sir" said the policeman, suddenly contrite. Then something bolder. "I merely seek the truth. You did frame her didn't you?" Only now did he put the papers down on the desk.

"What I did, Constable, was obey orders. I did what I was told. I know the concept is foreign to you, but it is what I have done all my life. Obey orders. The identity of the person who actually attempted murder in that hotel is not necessarily something I am paid to discover. I don't know if you appreciate my point. I doubt it. What is more, this Cambodian guttersnipe for whom your heart bleeds so nobly is now back in her country and alive and well. She has recently married. So dry your eyes you impressionable young man and get my point. You do not get to where I have got in the nation's police services by questioning orders."

"I do understand, Sir."

Captain Win Maw Oo's tone was glacial. He was brimming with anger but the secret with this Maung prick was never to lose your temper. Stay calm, and the stain would be wiped forever from the horizon.

"I am so glad that you do. In that case, Constable, I am prepared to reach an agreement with you."

"Yes Sir."

"Constable, you will resign forthwith from the police force. You will return to civilian life. You will remember nothing, I repeat nothing, about this case. Whatsoever. I am fully at liberty to press charges and have you locked up for ten years. Do you read me, Constable?"

"Yes, Sir."

"Sergeant!" yelled the Captain "Come and witness a statement by the constable!"

*

Aunty Lilly and Uncle Richard bring the girls along to see him off at the airport. Little Aye-Aye is excruciatingly sad to see him go but she is determined to be brave about it. Her sister has refused to come but Aye-Aye wants the full emotional onslaught of Michael's departure. Only when he heads for the escalator beneath the huge mural of the kings and queens at Kandawgyi Lake do the tears start to fall.

"Now are you sure you will have enough money?" asks Uncle Richard.

"Now don't be silly Dicky" retorts Auntie Lilly. "He has told you already that he will get a scholarship."

"Yes Uncle. A stipend, more like. But the College of Saint Barnabas is very generous. I will have a room of my own and they will give me breakfast and dinner. All I have to pay for is my sandwich at lunch."

"A room of his own" repeats Auntie Lilly, who has never really had a room of her own. She is wearing a fine outfit of Rakhine cotton to see Michael off, all dark blues and emerald green zigzags. At that moment a covey of Bangkok Airways flight attendants breaks away from the check-in counter. They pass the little group at the foot of the escalator. Four women, each of them sweeter than a cup of fruity *faluda*. Almost as sweet as his M...

"Now you take care" says his uncle, reading his thoughts. "Don't get into any mischief in Kuala Lumpur. It's a big place you know Michael."

"I won't Uncle."

"Study very hard" orders Auntie Lilly. "You will become Doctor Maung. How proud your father will be!"

"Anyway I won't be in KL. So no distractions. The Further Education Foundation of Saint Barnabas is outside the city, in Putrajaya. It will be botany in the morning, botany in the afternoon and botany at night."

"Don't forget to go to confession once a week" counsels Aunty Lilly.

Tall, dark and very handsome, Michael Maung reaches down and takes Aye-Aye in his arms, lifts her up and squeezes her tight against his chest. He whispers in her ear that she will have a story sent to her every week and between her sobs she asks for not all the stories to be about Jesus and some about the Kachin hornbill and his beautiful plumage and he says yes the hornbill too, there will be stories about the hornbill. After that he says he must be going and Auntie Lilly is crying too now, they hug each other, and he turns and stomps up the metal escalator. He stares hard at the romantic scenes on the mural, and when the escalator switches direction by 180 degrees and he can see them below him again, he gives a last wave before they are lost from sight.

In the hallway at the top of the escalator is the place with all the desks where you have to present your passport and have it stamped. Before that, he has one final encounter. She is waiting by the far wall.

"Moh-Moh. Darling..."

"My prince."

There are too many emotions inside him from all the farewells and he is not able to say what he wants to say to her. But Moh-Moh knows her man. She knows she is loved.

"Come soon, Michael."

"I will right now if you don't take your hand away."

"Ha ha. You be a good boy and don't even look at one single

Malaysian woman. Understand? Anyway they are very ugly."

"Understood."

"I have something for you my love. In this envelope. Take it. It's sixty-six Malaysian ringgits. Return train fare KL to Singapore. First of many."

"Moh-Moh..."

"I will be waiting for you."

PART VI

London, UK
Phnom Penh and Prey Veng, Cambodia

I

IT WAS HE WHO HAD SUGGESTED a walk in the park and Elise who had proposed One Tree Hill because it was not too far from where she lived in Lewisham. Before the call there had been a much longer one in which he had told her all about the Yangon debacle. They had agreed to meet up at the Honor Oak overground station and he had joked about wearing a red carnation. She saw him coming, old duffle coat and scarf, and they set off together uphill. There was no immediate need on her part to catch up on his news after the conversation of the previous day. They walked silently; she pensively, he pausing to kick stones or pick up branches before flinging them across the greenery. The grass was greasy and messy; neither alive as it was in summer nor frozen hard as it sometimes was at Christmas. Ahead of them loomed several brown trees. Her eyes took in the outline of the copse against the sharp colourless sky.

"There was a time when these drab colours depressed me" she said. "Not any more."

His eyes looked fatigued. He was in a professorial mood, it seemed. "At the top, there is a special oak tree. If you sit under it, you will be under the tree that replaced the tree that replaced the tree that Queen Elizabeth I sat under. She was on her way to Lewisham and she needed a rest."

"There is a large shopping centre there."

"And from the top" persevered Lucas "the —er — summit was used for a beacon in the Napoleonic Wars to signal the presence of enemy shipping."

She caught her breath. "I always thought it was silly, this British and French thing. I often wonder why you all despise the French so much. The French don't hate the British, you know.

They think you are good-natured and a bit eccentric, with a really disorganised political system and unspeakable food and all that, but they don't loathe you like you loathe them."

"Don't judge by the tabloids" he retorted.

Had she upset him?

They walked on; scarves, coats, no hats. The acorns crunched satisfyingly under their feet. A rook followed them, hopping in strides like a triple-jumper, picking up the pieces. They were going uphill and the effort made her un-pop her anorak. A dog, some woolly sort with bushy eyebrows, came to crouch alongside Lucas, its spine quivering and hunched. He bent down to it and yelled woof! straight in its face. The dog stared back, amazed, before expelling an umber turd. Elise was surprised, then burst into laughter.

"It really is time you learned to behave yourself Lucas!"

Her laughter remained floating in the air, perhaps no more than a mocking remonstration to his tomfoolery with someone's dog, yet carrying suggestions of much greater things, more terrible warnings, as if his misbehaviour in the park was a trite echo of the cataclysm that he was unleashing in Asia. Olivia. This rather serious young woman she had met only once at a dinner party. She had spent four days in a coma before she began to recover. The doctors said that she must have absorbed only a small dose, otherwise she would be lying stiff in a morgue. Elise knew that Lucas was turning it over and over in his mind. He would be thinking that if Sambath had tried to kill him, Lucas, it would fit into some sort of perverse logical path, but to try and wipe out innocent Olivia? That was too difficult for him to grasp. But murder never really made any sense. Don't look for the meaning Lucas, there isn't any. There never is.

"Let's sit on this bench."

"Lets."

Through the oak trees they could see London; the panoramic flatness of its suburbia and the bristle of towers around the Thames wharves. Something was breathing through the trees although there did not seem to be any wind. The city stretched away for miles and miles.

"The whole thing seems so incomprehensible."

"I know Lucas. But you chose to do this. Remember. Nobody said you had to. Now it has turned round and bitten you."

"I can't make any sense of it. That poor, poor Olivia. What on earth could she represent? As a threat I mean?"

"If Sambath attacked her he had a reason."

"What reason?"

"We don't know. We may never know."

"I can't believe she could have done anything to upset them. Try as I might it doesn't make sense."

"Well if you want some advice from somebody who knows what she's talking about, don't rush it. Don't push your mind into places it doesn't want to go. It will get there in the end. Give it time."

"Stop thinking?"

"Stop thinking. As I say Lucas, the mind will do its own work. Unaided."

"Thanks Elise. I value your advice."

Taking her by surprise, he placed her hand on hers. She made no attempt to remove it.

"The subconscious mind may need to be left well alone, but the other bit has been doing a major rethink."

She was pleased he was taking the conversation on to a more practical note. "Tell me more." She turned her palm upwards and clasped his hand fully. He looked with his tired eyes towards a distant glass tower shaped like a cucumber.

"Well, I mean meddling in other people's business in South East Asia, I think we can say I have learned my lesson. I've gone in with my eyes wide shut and worse than getting myself killed, I've caused the near death of an innocent and, from what I hear on the grapevine, a relapse into infirmity of the distraught husband. With a track record like that, you need to review your options a bit, I suspect. It may be time to do something constructive for a change."

"Agreed."

"So I have done some thinking. London. The job. Me. What am I doing; the whole boiling. I have realised it's time for a new start. No more international justice. Let's leave it to the NGOs and Facebook to save the world from its own darkness."

"Goodness. Major rethink. And…"

"Well, I have been thinking, I'm half Brazilian, I speak Portuguese like the best of them, and I thought that rather than London, somewhere on the edge of Europe would be better. I have always been the more unsettled brother and I've come to accept that, but I do need to put down some roots somewhere. So why not try my luck in Portugal? I've checked the real estate prices Elise, I could pay a mortgage on a nice place in Oporto with the income from renting the London flat. And just, I don't know, go into business. I'm looking at import-export, possibly fine alcohols, not just the Portuguese fortified wines but…"

"Do you mean Port wine?"

"Yes of course but also stuff from Brazil, a two-way traffic in and out of Europe, and I know my mother could give me a few introductions into beverages in Brazil. You could live pretty well, actually, out of harm's way."

"I see. Blue drinks. And tell me, when would this Portuguese job be swapped for the next one?"

"Not as soon as you think. I need to settle Elise. I've learned my lesson."

She withdrew her hand. "It sounds like it might be a good plan Lucas."

She turned to face him. No wonder he barked at dogs, this man.

He was all canine and alert himself, the south London breeze picking through his tawny locks, the thrill of his new life project making him smile his labrador smile, in with the new, out with the old. Nothing like a good purge. Huff huff huff. Then a quizzical, rather despondent frown replaced the smile. Of course. There is one little problem that remains to be resolved. Is he going to tell me? Or are we going to hope it will go away by itself?

"But?" she asked.

"But it has a loose end. There's a string that is still untied."

"Which is?" For God's sake. She wasn't going to say it for him.

"Oh Elise. Elise. You know anyway. Don't be disingenuous."

"When did you last see her Lucas?"

"I dunno. Almost a year ago. More, maybe."

"I think you can assume she is out of your hands by now."

Silence. Until he declared:

"According to Betjeman this is a better view than from Parliament Hill."

Somewhere above them a pair of squirrels was rattling around the branches, filling their acorn larders, or perhaps emptying them. Little bits of bark, disturbed by their scurrying claws, floated down across the sweeping vista of the metropolis. Small passenger planes circled the urban map like well-fed butterfish, dropping inch by inch on to City Airport. It was a wonderful thing to behold, London, on this clear, chilly day, London from outside, from the top of One Tree Hill, from beneath the oak where Queen Elizabeth I took some repose before heading on to the shops in Lewisham. Oh, these English. But Lucas had not finished.

'If there is one responsible act I can perform, if there is one last duty in which I must not be found wanting, it is to do something about Sovany. Elise, I wake up at night worrying about her. It was once or twice at first, now it's almost every night. I wake up thinking they are coming to get Sovany. They can't get me here but they most certainly can get at her in Cambodia. I think Sovany is in danger. If anything happened to her I couldn't live with myself."

"Do you care for her?"

"I owe it to her."

He was beginning to irritate her. She played the old non-sequitur trick.

"Well if Betjeman says so then we have to take him at his word."

"Do you know who Betjeman is?"

"The fact that I lecture on Cambodian poetry does not make me utterly ignorant of other countries' literatures."

His pelt was too thick for her darts. Boyish, enthusiastic. Huff huff huff.

"Here's the plan Elise. I go in. I go out."

"SWAT team" she replied.

He sighed. "I get a return ticket for five days in Cambodia. I go to Phnom Penh; check if she's there. If not I go on to her village in Prey Veng province, ask around, locate her. Tell her I'm here to take her away to a new life in Portugal. A small town, friendly, a bit like Phnom Penh. I will tell her she can have the child she wants. I will care for her. I will make sure she has a comfortable life. We will go to the civil registry and all that stuff. We will be happy."

"Oh Lucas, for pity's sake stop. What if she says no? Have you thought of that? What if she has somebody else? Another half bonkers foreigner. Why assume she has waited through thick and thin, unravelling the great tapestry while her suitors get drunk on palm wine?"

"Look Elise, if she's taken, I will bow out gracefully. If she's free, she will come."

"Then what about visas and all that? You can't just put a

Cambodian woman on a plane and expect them to let her in at the other end."

"I know. It will take a bit of arranging. Obviously I would miss the return leg of the flight. It would all take a little longer than five days. That's one of the reasons I like the idea of Portugal. Easier for a person with an un-white skin and no money to get into. Easier than the UK. Which I assume would be almost impossible."

"Indeed."

He turned to face her, gave her that silly happy grin.

"Elise would it be alright if I sent you the flight details when I get them? I would feel safer if somebody knew where I was. Would that be alright? As things stand right now it's literally five days on the ground and out again."

"Of course it's alright."

Lucas removed his phone from his pocket and chuckled unconvincingly. "Actually, er, I have got the flight already. I might just as well send it to you now."

She laughed, genuinely, spontaneously. "You silly idiot." Seconds later, there was a bleep on her phone. She read the mail. "Ninth to fourteenth. Via Ho Chi Minh."

"Yes. New Year with the parents. Two days at some death penalty congress in Manchester. Then I'm off."

"Oh, Lucas."

She took his hand again, shifted closer to him on the bench, then laid her head on his shoulder. They remained sitting there, just one more London couple taking a rest on their Sunday afternoon walk.

"One question Lucas. And I will only ask it once. Do you love her?"

"I will know when I see her."

What a fool this man was, she thought. Was it just being British that gave him this incorrigible sense of his own invincibility? A genetically inbred myopia? His people had barged into Asia so many times before, trumpeting their importance at every street corner, turning people's lives upside down, proclaiming their inherent superiority from every department store and public library. This man's disregard for personal danger, his hard-wired naiveté: was it not the same affliction that had driven Gordon and Clive and Kitchener and all the rest of their red-coated troopers? This lawyer who practised his arts in the court they had set up to try her country's psychopaths: from whom did he inherit his sense of entitlement? From his own history books? From the United Nations, perhaps? Did he not know that Cambodia didn't play by their rules? That Cambodia doesn't play by anybody's rules. Surely he had learned that. *At least that.* Hadn't the so-called international community chalked up its costliest failure ever in Cambodia? And did their evangelical zeal to heal sick countries, organising themselves on *missions* as they called them, apparently without embarrassment, not stem from precisely the same red-coated zeal, albeit enshrined in a newer and altogether more turgid scripture?

Elise took a deep breath, fatigued by her own private rhetoric. In truth, there were no morals. People slaughtered each other. They always had and always would. There was no ethos, no imperative, other than self-preservation. Join the survivors at any cost, and when you are safe behind their portcullis, never leave.

"Lucas?"

"Yes?"

"Just promise me you will be careful."

II

The temperature continues to rise as the year ends. The rice harvest is almost gathered. With the dry season at its height, weddings are being celebrated in the villages. People leave the dust and the bustle behind, going home for the festivities, bringing with them the hard-earned cash from the daily grind in the metropolis. Opposite the café where Lucas takes his breakfast, the allemanda thicket has gone into overdrive. Every morning the guard sweeps up more of the yolk-yellow petals with his coconut broom. Each day more flowers bloom, while others drop from the tree like ripe fruit. Lucas studies the guard as he works. Khmer sweeping is an art in itself. It has none of the shovelling of western broom-work. The soft palm fibres are caressed along the ground; a gentle calligraphy is executed with serifs and swirls that coax the detritus rather than command it. He remembers the cleaning lady in his office who would swirl her brush around the floor, merely displacing the dust. It was pretty to watch, almost totally ineffectual, and very Cambodian.

Sipping iced coffee, Lucas checks the newspaper. On the front cover is an article about a demonstration of garment workers who are demanding a better wage. Somewhere on the fringes of Phnom Penh. There is a photograph of a woman being pulled away by scruffy security men wearing motorcycle helmets. Their black visors are down. The woman is bleeding from the forehead and the stream of blood has divided up her face like a jigsaw puzzle. The backdrop to the photo is burning tyres and coils of razor wire. Lucas turns the page.

Here is an article about the on-going Khmer Rouge trials. My old employers, he thinks. Good morning to you. There is an older photograph here: the opening page of a prisoner file from the S-21 detention centre at Tuol Sleng. One prisoner among thousands. The page carries a few typed biographical details and a small photo. The photograph of this young woman is striking because the light and shade are overstated as a result of crude photocopying. The mould of the cranium beneath the teenage face is clearly evident in a bar of light above the eyes and in the black pits beneath the cheeks. The girl has just been delivered to the centre; all Tuol Sleng prisoners were photographed on arrival. She has weeks, perhaps months of torture to endure before she is finally killed, but in the photograph it is as if she is already dead, already the bleached skull that will be heaped with hundreds of others in the monument at Choung Ek. Her torturer, Duch, has not yet finished his breakfast with his wife and children, let alone had time to issue instructions about needles and fingernails. But the camera has already claimed her. It flashes her numbed expression and she becomes another statistic.

The war crimes tribunal has already sentenced Duch to life imprisonment. It has done the same to the two surviving Khmer Rouge overlords, Nuon Chea and Khieu Samphan. But the indictment is hundreds of pages long, and these latter two have only been tried on a limited number of the crimes they are accused of. So the hearings continue, and the two convicts sit in the courtroom, spectators to their own continuing damnation.

His mind harks back to the days when he would take the car out to the tribunal every morning. He can feel himself in the plastic upholstery on a fresh October day, slightly carsick from the stopping and starting. Rithy driving. The big road that goes out east. The baked earth and the red dust billowing up. The daily grind; the snail's pace. Chom Chau. All the usual gridlock, the Crocodile Cement flatbeds blocking the way in one direction, the Sihanoukville container trucks blocking the way in the other. A couple of hefty black Lexuses straddling the lane markers like bullfrogs, moving very slowly. That benign Cambodian chaos. The roadside market that spreads on to the main road and compresses two lanes into one, slowing the pace even more. The tuk-tuks and motor scooters puttering through the traffic, loaded up with merchandise, heading for the market at a steady 2 mph.

All of a sudden one of these scooters overturned in the middle of the road. A woman, perched on the back, went tipping into the middle of the road and her flat basket of fish went with her. So there she sat, looking more puzzled than hurt, as the live fish jumped and twitched and flopped on the tarmac. The other drivers did their best to avoid her. The fishes' sticky bodies were coated with grit but still they flipped and jumped. Then a cement truck squelched over one — even now he can still see the silvery fin ligaments lodged in the ruts of the big tyre. Another fish became pink slime when it was pulverised by a car. And then, in the way the mind makes these sudden connections, his thoughts had switched to the latter days of Khmer Rouge history, when Pol Pot murdered Son Sen and a dozen of his family with him, and had a truck drive over the body of each one.

He remembers Rithy laughing at the woman's misfortune.

"Fish."

"Yes. Fish."

"No sell dead."

No sell dead. The sky is a sharp blue this morning. The guard has finished sweeping the flowers and he goes inside the house to tidy his broom. Mocking his exit, a yellow flower flops to the pavement as he leaves. Growing along the same wall as the allemanda, there is another species of hedge-flower which has a pleasant perfume and a cosmetic pink colour. The flower has grown into a thicket around the sharp wire protecting the outer walls of the house, so the metal teeth are barely visible.

Lucas orders another iced coffee. Yes Sir. Wham, click, clonk. The woman at the Gaggia machine enquires: "When she will come back Sir?"

There are no secrets in this country.

Lucas pays his bill and leaves. He strolls down the street, declining offers of tuk-tuk rides with a broad smile and a shake of the head. He is not exactly sure of why he is in Phnom Penh. All that he knows is that he is happy to be here. The mid-morning sun warms his strong shoulders as he walks. His solid calves are exposed: he is wearing a cotton shirt, shorts and sandals. He could be one more white-skinned tourist off to book a flight to the ruins at Angkor or volunteer for two weeks in a bogus orphanage. But he is not. Lucas is tied to this country by bonds stronger than those of the tourist. He has spent many months probing its pain and helping to prosecute those who caused it so many years ago. He is not foolish enough to think that he has suffered alongside the people of Cambodia, because it takes more than a sharp brain and an international salary to do that. Any pain the country may have caused him is almost entirely to do with his wife and the failure of their union. Talking of which, is Sovany still his wife? Or does customary law now absolve him from such bonds? Does this country accept a non-existent relationship for what it is? Give the legal imprimatur to the fait accompli? For all he knows, she is married to somebody else by now. In which case good luck to you, my darling, and if I ever meet him I will tread on his head.

Strolling down Rue Pasteur, he remembers the dressing down he received at the hands of the Burmese police officer. *In this country at least, Mr. Bellwether, it would be considered that she had legitimate grievances.* He passes some of the numberless coffee bars and restaurants of Bong Keng Kang. Some new, some still going from before. This is expat territory, the zone where the development agencies have their offices, people live in serviced apartments, exercise in gyms, and put their toddlers in progressive play schools. He ducks his head into the Khmer Dream coffee bar and is greeted by a chorus of *hello Sir welcome!* This is the café where Sovany's cousin Thida works, but she is not there today. Maybe she has left. Maybe she has gone home.

Eventually he gets to the little side street at the bottom. The lane is calm and quiet, sheltered from the traffic on the other side. One of the houses here has been gutted. On the adjacent pavement, ragged women shovel cement. Probably building another boutique hotel. Lucas stops in front of the three-storey house with its fan palms and its toblerone-triangle air vents. He gravitates towards Makara unerringly, as if only she can give some shape to his ill-defined purpose. Makara has more to say to me and that is why I need to be here. It is for Makara that I have come, for her that I have rejected several offers of work and flown across the world in considerable discomfort. It is thanks to her that my spirit will find clarity. It is nothing to do with Sovany.

[196]

He climbs the stairs slowly, as if acting the part of an older man. There is in fact a real older man, hunched on the tiled landing, busy watering the largest of the fan palms. The man wields a green hose. His curved back is turned away from the visitor. As Lucas ascends the last flight of steps the man watches him from behind.

Makara is surprised to see him, but opens her door nonetheless. He takes a seat on the couch and she offers tea. Lucas notices that the curtains have not been renewed since his last visit. They exchange civilities. He tells her what the weather has been like in London, mentions that he has seen Elise socially on one or two occasions. *La pluie et le beau temps.* Makara says she is glad to hear that, and observes that Cambodia has had a good harvest this year. Things are going alright; as well as can be expected. There has been some violence with the garment factory workers. Their pay went up from 90 dollars a month to 120, but the landlords immediately put their rents up by the same amount. Do you call that fair?

Out of the blue, Lucas springs a serious question at her: in her younger days, did she have a special relationship with Ang? Makara remains silent, looking at him intently. She fills her teacup.

"Of course."

"Of course?"

"Of course." She turns her gaze to the window, then returns it to his face. "Ang was never satisfied by that sickly European woman. Of course we were together. In secret. For years. Why do you ask this?"

"It was an intuition. I wanted to check if my intuitions are sometimes right."

"Well you scored a point there, Mr Lucas. I will thank you not to pass this information on to Elise." There is a harder edge to her voice now. He is prying where he shouldn't be. But Lucas knows that sometimes it works best to destabilise a witness right from the start. A disingenuous wag of the tail, a gruff bark, and in you go.

"It must have been hard to marry after that."

"I was married forcibly. I had no choice."

"Interesting. When I was working at the tribunal, Makara, I heard testimony about forced marriages. I heard that people were gathered in a room, males at one end, females at the other, and the lights were turned out. You had to walk across the room and you had to marry whoever you stumbled into. The trick was to avoid bumping into a war amputee. Nobody wanted them."

"Go on."

"After the group had been married *en masse*, the purpose was to procreate, to produce clean minds and hearts for the revolution. Sex was stripped of any intimacy. Love was against the law. The Khmer Rouge cadres carefully watched the new couples having sex to make sure that that they copulated properly. Rape was commonplace."

"Continue."

"The village spies, the *schlopp*, would stand beneath the wooden floorboards of the raised houses and check that the copulation was free of love. Any sounds of pleasurable intimacy were punished by torture and death. Or to put it more simply, by having your brains beaten out with a hoe."

"And...?"

"Er, well, I just wanted to say that you will not upset me by saying how it was as I have already heard some of the accounts..."

"Mr Lucas, would it be very presumptuous of me to assume that you were working for the prosecution side?"

"I was. Yes."

"You don't surprise me. Well I am sure everything you say about the sex lives of Khmers in Democratic Kampuchea is true. It just doesn't tally with my experience, that's all." The look in her eye was stone hard. "I did not choose my husband. The regime chose him for me. So far so good for the prosecution. But Mr Lucas, he did not rape me. As a matter of fact he respected me. And I

[198]

respected him. We were both in our early thirties, young and strong. As far as I am aware nobody spied on us while we were sleeping. It was obvious to us that we had to accept the situation, or face very harsh consequences. So we did. It was a matter of common sense. We worked hard for the revolution, and we survived. From the respect we held for each other, our love grew. It was quite tentative at first, but we discovered that we were attracted to each other. By the time the regime was ended, we were completely inseparable. You see, you can't call everybody to testify in your tribunal. I have no doubt that you have heard some very traumatic things there, but if you want the full range of views and experiences and theories, you will have to interview all fifteen million people in the population. Then you might have a more balanced opinion."

"I see. I still don't think that respect was the defining characteristic of the regime."

"No. Clearly. But don't forget that most marriages today in Cambodia are still arranged. Not among the urban sophisticates perhaps, but everywhere else, including inside the government elite, people are matched up. It's not such a bad system. In your countries I believe you start with the infatuation and hope that the respect will follow. I read an article the other day that said that the chance of marriages failing in Europe was 42%. So your chances of success are just more than half. In this part of the world we try to begin with more distance. It doesn't always work either but the chances are higher. I know my husband would say the same thing if you had asked him the question."

"If you don't mind me asking, how long did your husband live after the end of the regime?"

"A long time, Mr Lucas. A long time. You can ask him yourself when he has finished watering the flowers."

The blue of the morning has turned into a rough midday glare. The light picks out objects on the kitchen shelf. The curved ribs of an egg whisk; a group of tea cups that do not belong to the same set. Not for the first time, Lucas is aware of his blundering insensitivity. Now that he understands that Makara is not alone, the evidence is suddenly everywhere. Two plates on the dish-rack, not one. An old electric drill. A heavily framed pair of glasses. And, talk of the devil, when the old man has finished hosing the plants he enters the apartment, nods casually in Lucas' direction, and suggests, in French, that he stay for lunch. He says his name is Chen. He has a round face, the jaw a few days short of a shave, circular glasses to match the round face, walks with a slight stoop and carries an air of good humour, as if anything is a fine reason to smile. Makara prepares rice in the rice-cooker and fries small fish on the range that is situated to the rear of the sofa. The man asks if Lucas likes Kampot pepper. Lucas replies in the affirmative. For the moment the conversation is going nowhere at all, but Chen seems to think there is enough to smile about. The plates have that slightly translucent sheen that you get with the cheapest kinds of crockery and the table is covered with a plastic cloth with pictures of olives and lavender on it. Here and there it has worn through. Offering the most banal conversation he can muster, Lucas asks if the cloth is a Provencal design and the man says it is fake Provencal and laughs. Makara heaps rice on to the plates with a blue plastic paddle and invites the two men to sit down. Chen tells Lucas to take some fish. Lucas passes the plate to Makara first, who bounces her head coquettishly to one side and forks herself a little deep-fried piece. They eat in silence. Then Chen breaks the quiet.

"It was a different time, don't you think? One of the faults of our age is that we judge past times by the standards of the present." He guffaws, as if he has just described Laurel and Hardy falling into a vat of flour. He raises the round glasses from his nose and wipes his face with a cloth.

"It was a different time. We wanted to change everything. In that, we were not mistaken Mr Lucas. We were right to want to change everything. You need to accept that we were right to want change. The colonial power walked off, leaving behind a puddle which they had shat in. Not a functioning country, just a festering puddle of shit. The king was quite happy with that. For him it was still the dark ages. Everybody believed the rain only fell from the skies because he told it to. We wanted to step into the twentieth century and bring about change through politics. We tried to take the democratic route you know, Mr er... Bellwether." He giggled again.

"Remember. March 1955. Sihanouk abdicated. He put his father Suramarit on the throne. You remember Suramarit? Of course not, you are far too young. Out of his golden cage, Sihanouk built a new political party, the *Sangkum Reastr Niyum*. So he drained away the support for the other new political parties. Sihanouk proposed — the man pauses to help himself to another fish — Sihanouk proposed — he giggles — that the Democrats fuse their party with his to establish a government of national unity. We said no. We *said no*. We, I mean my people, my brothers and sisters, my parents, all our people. I was still only a schoolboy at that time. Sihanouk was offended and he came down very hard on us. He sent his hit-men to break up our meetings. I mean to shoot people. They arrested hundreds of political activists. Closed all the newspapers. On polling day, the intimidation was completely brazen, the soldiers bullying us everywhere and surprise surprise Sihanouk won by a landslide."

Makara asks if her husband is going to tell the entire history of Cambodia from the 1950s. Chen chuckles, says no, of course not, but the point is important, very important. If a true election had been allowed to happen, in those early days of independence, it could have been the beginnings of parliamentary democracy. "But Sihanouk killed it in the egg. Revolution was our only choice. It was us and them. Them, all those wealthy corrupt people like in the movie you went to see last time you were here, and us..."

"How do you know I went to see that film?"

"We know where you go Mr Bellwether. Don't imagine we don't know. Ha ha."

This is when Lucas realises that he is not sitting with friends.

"Tell me about Vann" he blurts.

"Vann? Your friend Dermott? We had to be very careful with Vann. We made a mistake. Nary should never have done what he did with the father and the son. That was stupid. We had the son as an enemy after that. Normally he would have been killed as well but he slipped through the net. Then he got his pardon and we sent him to Vietnam for re-education and training. He was a bright spark you know."

He laughs, then stops abruptly, then takes a cloth and wipes his eyes. Makara has lowered her eyes. She is looking fixedly at one of the holes in the Provencal pattern.

"I was told to keep an eye on him. So I did. He seemed to be turning out alright. He worked hard. He was a good bureaucrat. I relaxed. I told my superiors that he was not going to make any trouble. Then, just when I had let down my guard, he disappeared overnight. Overnight! That was when I got it in the neck. Ha ha ha. They were furious with me. I was downgraded three levels!"

"And then?"

"And then he cropped up in France. No great mystery there. He had gone to join his family in France. Obviously we couldn't follow people around in Paris quite so easily as we can do it here. I had him watched in Paris and we had reports of him being sighted from time to time, but we couldn't monitor the entire Khmer community in Paris. And then his family exploded all over the place, the mother went to hospital, the daughters and the brothers just disappeared."

There is a pause. "What do you think happened to the daughters?"

"One of them may have died. Somebody claimed she was dead from some illness. The other, we found her much later in London. She was teaching in a university. She had ceased to matter by then."

"And the brother?"

"Vann Tepp? He went off the map. We lost touch. But then Nary was assassinated in Long Beach. Decapitated. We knew it had to be Vann. It had Vann's revenge written all over it. He had been sighted in Long Beach; the description was right. When Vann murdered Nary the shit hit the fan. It was my job to find him. I had six months. Get him, and I would be rewarded. Lose him, and I would lose my pension too. We must have talked to everyone who had been anywhere near Long Beach. Half of California. We didn't find Vann."

"Not until very much later, I believe."

"Not until recently. But by then the whole business was out of my hands. I was retired off. No pension of course." Chen giggles. He perspires heavily down his greying jowls. Makara shakes her head.

"So they finished Vann off in the end."

"Vann is no longer with us, from what I hear."

"Who did it?"

"That you will have to guess for yourself, I am afraid."

"Help me Chen."

"I helped you enough. I tried to warn you off."

"That was you? The seeds?"

"It was a joke. You know you English like jokes!" He guffaws with forced laughter. Asks his wife to make some tea. "It's an old fashioned Khmer warning code from days gone by. Strychnine seeds from the Cardamoms. Equals danger. Equals get away while you can. Equals fuck off and go home!"

The heat is pressing through the window panes and Lucas is perspiring down his back.

"Sorry Chen. But how the hell was I supposed to know the meaning of your little strychnine joke?"

"I knew you would work it out sooner or later. You spend your time reading Cambodian history don't you? Intelligent person like you, it was only a matter of time. The seeds were a way of giving you a fighting chance."

[203]

"I worked it out thanks to a Burmese botanist if you want to know."

"Indeed."

"But I didn't fuck off Chen. I'm still here. Please confirm what I already suspect."

Makara speaks. Lucas sees that her eyes are moist. "Lucas. You don't know the danger you are in. This has nothing to do with you at all. It's a Khmer story from start to finish. Just go away and please don't come back. Please, please go." She begins to weep.

Lucas says he understands. He will leave. He will go. But Chen must tell him who killed Vann.

Makara interjects again. "They saw his name. It was Nary's daughter who saw his name on a list. The people going to that big conference in Myanmar."

"And she told her brother."

Chen stares at the window.

"She told her brother Sambath" repeats Lucas.

Chen concedes. "Yes. She told Sambath."

There is a long silence, and Lucas rises to leave. He thanks his hosts for their hospitality. At the doorway, Makara is uncharacteristically affectionate. She does not embrace him, but holds his two hands tight in hers. Then she brings herself closer to him, and murmurs: "Thank you for caring. It means more than you realise. He was such a beautiful boy." She wipes her eyes with her sleeve.

III

Sovany thrashed the cottons against the stones. Thrashing washing was not her favourite pastime; far from it. Washing was meant to be washed in washing machines, but they did not have enough electricity in the village for that and even if they did the water supply was unreliable. There was no harm in hand washing, you could say, but there was little good in it either. Her sister said it was an improving occupation to be doing things with your hands, but Ka *would* say that and Sovany differed with Ka on a number of subjects.

Lucas had been in Phnom Penh. Thida had seen him once and Srey Pau had seen him twice. At no point had he contacted her. It seemed safe to say that he had no further interest in her. His love was a story, a fiction. Nothing more. Sovany knew about stories. She had grown up on stories. Stories told by her grandmother; stories told by her sisters, stories told by the travelling story tellers. In fact, there were some story tellers coming to the village in a few days' time. One of the stories that people told in the village was the great providential white man story. It was a deceptively simple story, which began with *Cross the river and go to Phnom Penh*. The central part of the story was *Meet a man from Australia*, and the end was *Have money and comfort, enough for the entire family*. Sovany had always suspected it was an old wives' tale, without being completely sure that she was right, and in the end, if only to settle her doubts, she had decided she would test it out. It was only fair to give it a go, because herding the buffaloes past the old bomb craters then bringing them back when the sun went down did not amount to doing something with your life. It did not. Every TV programme you ever saw was a different version of the same story about somebody leaving home to find their fortune in the big city. So one day, a good few years ago, she climbed on a truck bound for the ferry at Neak Luong, and eventually she got to Phnom Penh. It was a bit rough, and she was only twenty-two back then, but she was a tough young woman who expected little of life, and after the usual travails cleaning in bars and restaurants and even shovelling cement on a building site, Sovany found her way. The correct way. She knew very well that there were short cuts to money if you offered yourself to foreign men from China and Korea who prowled around the entertainment palaces on the fringes of the city, ready to consume the flesh of Khmer women as if they were eating pigs at New Year, but like most of her friends she was determined to avoid that path. She found her way by enrolling on a six-month waitress course run by a charity organization from France called *L'enfant Khmère*. The course was almost free of charge. She was taught the rudiments of what was expected in restaurants and how to tot up the bills and supervise the meals from kitchen to table and take an order without getting all muddled up and not get upset when the foreigners thought you were a brainless idiot and not respond when they flirted with you and all the while not seem cold of heart. It was mostly common sense. Just a matter of holding your head high, but not so high as to be the nearest target when the geckos started shitting from the ceiling. The training course was attached to a restaurant which used the trainees as free labour, and the place was right in the part of town the foreigners favoured the most, so she got to see a lot of the international people. By observing the foreigners and listening to them she began to comprehend their strange perversity. How they came to Cambodia wanting to understand it; desiring to help it; yearning to feel a deeper sympathy for it; needing to believe that they had a special insight into the Khmer soul as if Cambodia was a woman and they were gynaecologists staring into its most intimate parts. What sort of empty lives did these people have before, that they felt such strange needs? Some of them started organizations to care for children, some set up orphanages in villages they had never been to before, some brought rice to the poor or offered books in schools or opened surgeries so they could disinfect people. Because pity did not come naturally to her (why should it, Prey Veng was never a place of pity) it was understandable that Sovany should look down on these defeated people, but that only made the story of finding an Australian man harder because you could not be with a husband to whom you felt utterly superior — it just would not make sense. So when an Australian started coming to the NGO training restaurant more than once or twice and always tried to chat with her whenever he came, she knew she had found her man, but she did not know if she wanted him. His name was Kildark and he was from Brisbane and he had a head like a melon. A lot of the *barang* who hooked up with Cambodian girls looked like melons. Absence of beauty was just something you had to accept. They liked watching sport on TV and drinking a lot of Angkor beer and talking about beer as if it was a subject of importance. Kildark would often ask her about her favourite beers when he came to *L'enfant Khmère*.

The inflammation of her mother's lungs got worse during the monsoon and she gritted her teeth and decided to ditch her reservations and give it a go with Kildark. Underneath, he was okay, as she discovered. You needed to push him into the shower before you lay with him in bed, but once he was naked like that you could see he was soft and vulnerable and he would tell long stories about generations of Kildarks and big family problems and she saw that he belonged to the type looking for tenderness from her and all her Cambodian sisters. Well, okay, why not. Who was she to be all picky about her boyfriends? She let him enjoy her sweetness for a while, but then one day he declared he was moving on. It was as if she had put him back on the road like a mended truck and set him on his way. He was determined to go to Laos, it was part of his cosmic plan which was tattooed across his back in blue and pink, and he would remember her always.

After that Sovany decided to give the Australians a wide berth and to concentrate on the job. She graduated from the restaurant school and a lady with dyed orange hair came all the way from France to award the certificates and say what clever girls they all were and they could always count on her when they wanted a mother. Sovany was very relieved to be out of that madhouse of charity and she quickly found a job serving in one of the restaurants at the very top of Street 21. She worked hard, made a name as a diligent waitress, and duly caught the eye of the owner who promoted her to deputy manager and then, a year later, to full catering manager. When she was full manager her salary went up to 142 dollars a month, which meant that if she was careful, she could save about 50 to send home. It wasn't a lot, of course it wasn't, but it went a long way in Prey Veng. Her friends were all in the same position, all watching their every last *riel*, and they found inexpensive ways of having fun together — just strolling in Hun Sen Park or laughing together on Riverside as the Mekong flowed by, and money was not a big preoccupation. Not for them anyway, even if it was for their families.

Then the day came when a foreigner walked in and she knew without even thinking twice that this man was not going to ignore her. You could tell, often long before he knew it himself, just in the manner of a man's glance, if he was going to be distracted by you. He ate his beef and the beer girls went towards him like metal filings to a magnet. She instructed them to attend to their Angkor jugs and leave the customer alone. He was reading his Phnom Penh Post and obviously wanted some peace and quiet. But he put his eyes on her in that way, so eventually they said a few words and he was very forward with her and invited her to sit with him, which obviously she could not do. The next night he came again and ordered the beef with morning glory a second time. The advantage to this man was that he did not look like a melon. He had a fine look about him in fact — golden hair and a curious smile. You almost wanted to go up and stroke him. He surveyed everything, never stopped observing and looking, and you could feel him looking at you and when you caught him glancing at you he would smile as if to say what am I doing wrong when well he knew what he was doing wrong.

Sitting with the girls on Riverside, cracking dried seeds on their teeth and watching the mamas doing their syncopated fitness dances, she spoke about the *barang* man who had begun to stare at her and make her feel uneasy. Dany said there was no harm in trying and it had been a long time since she had cast her net and she did not want to dry up like a dehydrated papaya. Srey Pau chuckled a lot and said we are all dried papayas, all three of us, and we all need a good slice of beef in our morning glory. Srey Pau was like that. Always wanting a bit of you-know-what. Anyway the upshot was that the two girls agreed they would come to the restaurant if Sovany texted them to say that the man was dining there, and they would pose as innocent customers and deliver their verdict afterwards. So that is what they did. Srey Pau nearly ruined the plan by giggling so much into her beer, but the next day they met up and announced that this man was *extremely* acceptable. Verdict: 1) he did not look like a melon, 2) he was young and strong without a big belly on him, 3) although there was a match on TV he was not watching, so he did not live for sport and 4) you could tell by his suede loafers and his button-up shirt that he was not short of a dollar or two. Sovany was filled with dread at the verdict. It seemed to suggest that this man was meant for her.

He eventually invited Sovany to meet him in a bar of her choice after work. That was not possible. Quite impossible in fact, to sidle into a bar with a foreigner without setting tongues wagging all over the town. He was not upset at her refusal. He disappeared for a week, and returned with a proposal for lunch, so she accepted to eat at a French place a long way up along the river towards the north of the city where she knew nobody.

Dany and Srey Pau were entranced, watching in the wings as the drama slowly came to the boil, and they were delighted for Sovany that she should once again be swayed in the arms of sweet passion. Passion that was reciprocated by laughing Lu-Ka, as they called him (he seemed to laugh a lot, he seemed to be happy by nature). Lucas also scored high marks with Sovany for not seeming to want too much parenting. He said he had two good parents, including a very temperamental mother. Better still, he did not seem to need to be dispensing excruciating kindnesses every time he saw an unwashed Cambodian child. True, he worked for that foreign tribunal, but they paid him a huge salary, so let's not complain.

They married in the village. The parents came all the way from their country. Lucas' papa chatted a lot with Srey Pau. His mama was in a bit of a sulk. But his brother was a man with a very good heart. You could sense that straight away. His brother's wife also had a good heart. Sovany was very reassured by meeting Duncan and Rowena.

Thrash that washing.

Thrash that washing. Her sister brought Sovany's thoughts back to the present, back here to the flat lands of Prey Veng, where a brown-bodied boy had just jumped into the reservoir where they were doing the laundry. The bed sheets were all rinsed now. Ka clutched the ends of the first sheet while Sovany twisted the water out of it. Ka could always tell exactly what her elder sister was thinking. They shook the sheet, whacking it in the wind to get the wetness out, then they folded it together, their raised hands barely touching, their faces in close proximity if they were performing an old-fashioned dance.

"If he turned up here, today, would you go with him again, big sister?"

Ka had plaited her hair in one long shiny tassel falling down her back. Sovany hesitated, pensive. "I might you know. I might. Not just like that. Not on any condition. He would have to put a good case. I admit I loved him. I suppose to be honest I still do. Why deny it? If he could account for himself, if he could talk to me, if I felt he was sorry for the past, then I might take him back."

"What did he do to make you leave him?"

"That was the silly thing. He did not do anything, little sister. We left each other because we argued too much. We agreed about nothing. He wanted me to be a different person, maybe. He is a dreamer Ka, that's his problem. Don't marry a dreamer, little sister."

"I don't understand."

"I don't really understand either. But he did not really love me enough to adapt to our ways. That was the problem. He was not prepared to adapt to our ways."

Ka laughed and pinched her nostrils. "He didn't eat *prahoc*!"

Sovany was wistful. "He didn't want me to be a mother."

"Uy!"

A second bed sheet. Twist, shake, fold. Backward, forward. The same delicate minuet. The sisters' faces met.

"Did he have a problem with his ... his.... *thing*, that he gave you no babies?" But this was more than the younger woman was able to ask without erupting in a snotty guffaw. They had to re-wash a part of the cotton sheet.

They approached; withdrew. "No his thing was fine, little sister. No problem there. He was not one of those old *barang* who watch TV all day because they have no power. It was something else. He just felt different from our traditions. I think he was afraid of being sucked in to the family."

The younger woman took a deep breath. "What is it like big sister when you do it with a man?"

Sovany hesitated. "It is full of sweetness. Love is sweet. Then it can be bitter. Then it grows sweet again. I cannot explain. In that beautiful song of Ros Sereysothea, she asks if love is bitter or sweet. The answer is that it is both."

Ka composed herself. The two women stepped gently together, their bodies almost touching, their breath mingled.

"Give him one more chance, big sister. Just one more."

They are selling grilled crickets at the wharf in Neak Luong. Dented coaches and grimy trucks wait in line for the ferry across the Mekong. Women carry baskets of insect snacks on their heads, shielded from the hard light by masks and mittens. Children tap on the car windows, offering quail and duck eggs in transparent bags. A face so wrapped up that only the eyes are visible sells him a can of beer for three thousand riel. When his turn comes he drives the car on to the flat-bottom ferry that traverses the big, brown river. On the eastern bank, he finds a restaurant where he buys a dish of pork and rice, with a brace of prawns. There are also refreshing towels straight out of the freezer. Bliss, on this hot, heavy day. He eats slowly, descending into a beery trance. *Ch'long tonlé*. To cross the river, in the Khmer language. Traditionally, the term also means to deliver a child. Cross the Mekong, and your life will never be the same again.

His thoughts return to the previous day. He had decided that once he was suitably showered, shaven and after-shaven, he would walk down two streets and go and say a very quick hello to Makara. But saying hello to Makara was clearly problematic: he had said both hello and goodbye more than once to this dear old lady and she might not be inclined to see him yet again. But Makara was Makara, and there was no visit to Makara from which one did not emerge a little wiser. The extra dose of wisdom, he told himself, justified the risk. That of the husband, in particular. Everything should be done to avoid that husband. Come on, be sensible Lucas, forget Makara. You went the previous day anyway. Look. Let's toss for it. No coins in this country. With a ball-point he gouged M for Makara on a flat disc of hotel soap and flung it upwards. The soap came down and broke on the floor but it was clear on which side it had landed. M it was.

That was therefore the plan that Lucas followed. He put his clothes on the floor of the shower and stamped shampoo into them to wash away the airline odours. Then he hanged them on the frame of the shower, just like... Jesus, don't go there. He shaved with care. Off down the street, a new man.

Knock knock. *Bonjour Makara. Ah Monsieur Lucas, encore vous, quel bon vent vous amène?*

Nothing in particular, really, I just had the urge to say hello. This is some tea from London, I thought you might like to give it a try.

Earl Grey. And what a pretty tin it is in. I shall treasure this. Let me heat some water. We got rather caught up in history yesterday. I never asked how Elise is doing.

Elise, he said, was doing well. She was now a respected member of the Oriental Languages faculty and had a nice little place to live south of the river. Everything was going fine, all in all.

"Do tell me what her apartment is like, so I can imagine her there."

"Oh, I've never actually been inside."

"Oh. I see." Makara seemed disappointed. "Well. I do hope she is alright. She hasn't had it easy, poor child. But eventually you just have to pick up the pieces and move on. We all make mistakes. We have all made some dreadful mistakes, you might say. But life doesn't wait for you while you stop and ponder it all. None of us are getting any younger. I do so hope she finds some happiness of her own. You know what I mean. She is a lovely person, but she is far too strong for her own good."

"I'm sure you are right."

Makara poured tea. She hoped he was not an Englishman who took his tea with milk, because she did not happen to have any. She could send her husband off to Thai Huot supermarket to get some of course. It would be no trouble for him. Do him good actually. Don't be foolish said Lucas. It's just right as it is. They had run out of conversation, so he fussed around with his tea cup and looked around the room at the diverse objects in it. The draining board, the pink plastic colander, the soft coconut palm broom. His gaze came to rest on the family photograph he first saw on his initial visit. The family photo. Down at the beach on a hot summer's day. This, in Kep, meant nearly every day of the year, of course. Ang. Odette. Elise. Tepp. And gorgeous little Vuthy standing in the front. Odette bug-eyed in large sun-glasses to protect herself from the glare radiating off the Gulf of Thailand, her complexion paler than the others. Elise, skinny — a young teenager. A flowery one-piece stretched tight over the bony shoulders. Broad if ever-so-slightly dutiful smile. Tepp, precociously taciturn, puffing out his chest, a fishing net in one hand. Very laddish, very proud. Vuthy, stunning at ten, a smile to fall down for and worship. And the paterfamilias, strongly built, a man in baggy '60s swimming costume who looked honourably served by life, well contented with his lot, the left arm raised, the hand smoothing back his hair.

"That would have been in '67 I think. I remember because I took it on the same day as they killed Che Guevara. We heard about it on the radio. Ang was quite upset."

"Che?"

"Yes. Che. They killed him in Bolivia. They took him to an airport somewhere and they showed his body in the morgue for everyone to see. The military people there wanted to cut his head off as a trophy, but the CIA said that was going too far, so they only cut off his hands."

"You have a good memory for history."

"I don't know. Ang talked about it a lot. He was interested in all that Cuban stuff."

"Really? I wouldn't have guessed."

"Chen? There is some tea!" Her voice was shrill. "We have another visit from our British friend. He has brought the very same tea as they serve to her Majesty the Queen."

Lucas' confidence collapsed like mercury on a chilly day. In walked Chen. He was rubbing the sleep from his eyes.

"Well, well. The Englishman. I must say I really had not expected to see you here again quite so soon."

"Don't be difficult dear. It's very kind of him to think of us."

"You have a thick skin, Mr Bellwether."

"You know what? I do. I should not be here at all. You are absolutely right. I think ought to leave straight away. I hope you will excuse me."

"Finish your tea."

Lucas gulped the Earl Gey. What the hell had he been thinking of, to drop in here again? Had he become a complete and total idiot? His forehead started to perspire. He got up.

"I said, finish your tea."

Makara was silent.

That was the moment when Chen yawned. It was a long yawn and it was accompanied by a gesture, the left arm raised, the hand smoothing down his scalp. Lucas turned to the photograph, in which Ang was performing precisely the same gesture. He looked back at Chen, back at the photograph, swigged the remainder of his tea, tried to stand, discovered his legs would not hold him. He tried again, took a deep breath, hobbled to his feet, gave a ridiculous little bow and said he must be going, opened the door without waiting to be asked, and ran down the stair, stumbled on the landing, and continued running until he was lost in the twilight crowds on Norodom Boulevard.

*

In his Neak Luong daydream, Lucas imagines he is standing before a class of young Americans, giving them a lecture on the Vietnam War.

Neak Luong has always been a ferry town. Its sad place in history was assured on August 6, 1973, when a B-52 Stratofortress dropped a stick of bombs straight up the main street. It was a navigation error. The B-52 payload removed a large part of the town from the map and hundreds perished. There was a strong reaction in the US Congress which helped to end the Cambodia bombing. The Americans had begun bombing Cambodia to try and hit Vietcong troops that were taking shelter across the

[215]

border. The Vietnamese had moved further and further inland, and the raids had followed. The US Air Force term for the area of destruction created by a B-52 payload is a *box*. That's right, a box. The box is half a mile wide and two miles long. Anything inside the box is not merely destroyed but pulverised, as if it had never existed in the first place. The experience of B-52 bombing was so profoundly traumatising for the Cambodian peasants that many survivors never recovered their mental equilibrium. Some historians see it as a factor in the genocidal insanity that was to follow. The Neak Luong episode goes back to a time when it was not possible for the US to bomb Vietnam because peace talks were under way in Paris. As CIA director William Colby famously said, Cambodia was "the only game in town". Mortally wounded in Vietnam, his long range bombers sitting idly in Guam and Thailand, Nixon decided he might as well hammer Cambodia. He did.

In his dream, Lucas's students are appreciative. Instead of provoking them, as he had wished, he finds he has made new friends. They tell him it was awesomely interesting. One of them offers to play a digital warcraft game with him that is based on the Tet offensive in the Vietnam War. The past is just too far away, he realises. Nobody cares about it at all. Nobody gives a tinker's cuss. Unless of course they have a tie with it, a cabled bond that twists brown and bloody like an uncut umbilical cord. *Ch'long tonlé.* Cross over to the other side.

Truth to tell, it is unlikely that many people in the ferry town remember that August day in 1973 either. Like every other town in Cambodia, Neak Luong is packed with young people eager to make a living, busily thinking about their future, not their parents' past. Lucas stirs, orders coffee to wake himself up, pays the bill, moves on.

Yesterday was unproductive in other ways. A couple of cafés and restaurants are all it takes to discover that Sovany is not in town. What did you expect? He went to talk to his old mate Nol in Drive-Away-Hire 2000. Well, a business friend; a garage friend. He picked up a gutsy old Mitsubishi from the 1990s with wide fenders and a gear stick located by the steering shaft. It had fat tyres and made a good gargling noise as he drove away. Nol put a call through on his cell phone as soon as Lucas had gone.

*

"It's Nol. He's here. He hired a car."

"Where's he going?"

"Heading for the ferry at Neak Luong."

"He'll be going to find the woman." The man Nol is calling holds his phone to his right ear. The left side of his face is still too painful. There is an angry trench across his cheekbone. The stitches have not yet been removed — black criss-cross lacing the skin together. He asks:

"Who do we have down there? Reliable?"

"There's a guy in Kampong Trabek. Done jobs for us before."

"Can he put together a team?"

"Sure. Why not? Usual gratuities."

"Ok. And Nol, ..." Thirty seconds later the conversation is over.

*

After his lunch in Neak Luong, he drives back on to the main road. He passes through Kampong Trabek before turning left-wards down a dusty village track. Almost immediately a colossal sow steps into his path, not intimidated by the diesel-gargling Mitsubishi. He inches forward. The sow is a huge creature, dappled grey and pink, and she does not want to move. He gets out of the car, slams the door, approaches the animal, which grunts and turns on him. He hops back in to the vehicle and drives around it.

The big car slaloms through the dust. The path is rutted: hard beneath, with a sprinkling of powder mud on top. It is much drier than when he was last here. After almost two kilometres he reaches a cluster of monastic buildings gathered around a dusty square. The centre of the square is a mango tree. He applies the breaks and looks around. The tree is carrying heavy fruit, green

[217]

flushed with mauve. He switches off the engine and the car shudders as the engine dies. The monastery has a pink façade and roof curlicues, and another building with wooden shutters serves as the monks' residential quarters.

It is not good that Elise has got him back into the habit of occasional smoking. However, there seems to be something so prescripted about arriving in a one-horse village in a bashed-up four-wheel drive that he needs to respect the cliché. He taps the box of Marlboros before lighting up. Adjacent to the little temple, the wat, the fields stretch away, dried-out paddies scratched by bony cattle and black poultry. The horizon is pocked with sugar palms. It is this magical tranquillity of rural Cambodia that is often confused with beauty, but the two things, he concludes, are not the same. He breathes smoke. Children are leading their cows to graze, tugging at the ropes they have threaded through the beasts' noses. The glowering sky threatens. Don't let it rain. That's not in the script.

He decides he will walk the remaining distance that separates the monastery from the village. He kills the cigarette and parks the Mitsubishi discretely under a tree. He finds a stone to press under the back tyre, as people do here when their car brakes have seen better days. He weighs the heavy stone in his palm, then discards it. The old car is not rolling anywhere. He strides down the path. As he approaches the houses, he hears sounds and voices, increasing in volume as he gets nearer. When he arrives at the clearing, there are young men, stripped to the waist, busy building something. Swaying their torsos, these men are aware that their every move is watched by a gathering crowd of children. The men have assembled a wooden stage and now they are sawing wood to make a stand. When the wooden stand is ready they place a large amplifier on top of it, and start making a second stand. One man has climbed a big banyan tree and is threading cables through tree branches. The excitement among the children mounts. The sun is not ready to go down and yet it is almost twilight in the tall trees. Dry-footed boys gather round him, disperse, return, giggle, try out a few words of English, *what you name*, clutching their sides with the hilariousness of it all. Then the sound system explodes, convulsing the silence of the fields with a Cambodian 1970s rock-and-roll. The cows ignore it; the cockerels quicken their strut. The travelling theatre has come to town.

Here are the actresses, seated on plastic chairs beneath the acacia. They begin their make-up well in advance, using compact mirrors, taking advantage of what light there is. Over there the leading lady is seated in the lotus position in a purple underdress, studying her false eyelashes in a tiny mirror while a younger girl fans her with a wide brimmed hat. Three village boys watch, transfixed, as a painted female divinity, standing upright in yellow knickerbockers, is wrapped in shot-silk taffeta. More and more children gather to watch as the women don bracelets, tassels, tiaras, armbands and all the bling of their trade. The male actors have slung hammocks from the branches, where they lie slumped, reciting their lines. There are mothers now, with small children in their arms. Their eyes cannot devour enough of the scene. To their village, which is on nobody's map, the theatre has come. The actresses carry on, unperturbed; bangles, bracelets and pendants, they are entirely at ease dressing in front of such an avid audience, behaving as if they were quite alone.

Lucas lights another cigarette and continues to study the scene. This is a display of supreme patience. If you cannot dress in private, you just have to dress in public. Gradually, however, he comes to see that this is actually part of the performance. For many, perhaps, it is the most compelling part, the display that will stay in their dazzled memories as they walk home through the night. Never will they dress in gold, emerald and purple, but to see others doing so is — perhaps — almost as good.

The sky continues to grumble. Families of buffaloes walk unguided towards the village, skirting cavities in the earth. The rattle of the sugar palm fronds has the patter of rain, but it's only the breeze. Is the flat landscape not also a stage-set? An uncertain firmament above, a glow on the periphery. An egret travels diagonally across the sky, its flight course undecided. The music switches to a soupy Khmer ballad with a lot of electric organ, languid and unhurried.

Lucas walks into the adjacent field. He stops at a large cavity in the ground, perhaps one hundred metres across. B-52 crater. No doubt about that. There are several similarly large holes on the other side of the paddy flats. The sides of the crater are steep, with tufts of grass clinging to the flanks. The bottom of the hollow is inundated with stagnant black water, and lotus flowers are growing from the swamp, with pink bulb-shaped heads and long green stems.

Night falls. He returns to the clearing.

In the open air, beneath a large canvas awning, the players take their dinner. A stage has been built for the orchestra, which bongs into action; drums, xylophone and strings. The dressing continues, layer by layer. The men paint each other with ruddy cheeks and villainous moustaches. The women finally reach the moment where the silky hairpieces are pinned to their own buns. The age of the spectators increases as adolescents arrive, some on motorcycles. The innocence of the scene gives way to something more fraught. Motorcycle exhaust drowns the smell of grease paint. The crowd grows, running now, jumping over hammock strings, losing control. Then it rains. Somebody rushes to cover the electrical console in plastic sheeting. There is a head technician who is everywhere, issuing orders, tugging at his cigarette. Separate torrents of rainwater are sloshing from the roof of the makeshift theatre. The players lose their readiness but the crowd becomes more energetic and restless. Fortunately, the tempest is short-lived. After half an hour, the sky is voided. Suddenly cloudless, it is illuminated by a huge orange moon, and standing on her own beneath that orange moon, as if it were the brim of her hat, is Sovany.

He makes no move to approach her. The mere sight of her is enough for him. Around her, a hundred people crouch in expectation as the silhouette puppetry begins. The *Reamker* stories begin to unfold, well-known tales peopled with vengeful gods, comically knock-kneed peasants and characterful animals. When the two shadows start a punch-up, the children scream with glee. Now Sovany has crouched down among the children, and she laughs when they do. She is wearing a cotton printed dress which outlines her small figure. In due course the leather silhouettes are put away, and the lights go down with a buzz and a fizz. The generator is working to full capacity. It is time for the high point of the evening, the costume drama. Lucas is transfixed. He is watching her watching and she cannot see him. Every time she joins the burst of laughter, his heart warms to her. That smile.

The story tells how the god Chandra grants his daughter permission to visit the realm of the humans. Strolling in the terrestrial realm, the daughter is smitten with passion for a labourer who is bonded in debt to a heartless landowner and whose mother is sick. She picks a flower that he has grown, and there her troubles begin, for the denizens of heaven must never touch the things of the earth.

The play is well received. Lucas reads every moment and mood as it illuminates Sovany's face. She is one of hundreds. All around the crowd, the faces bathed by the stage lights, there are nods of approval and complicit smiles, and from the back there is heckling when the landlord steps on to the stage. The old Buddhist tale — callous landlords, crippling debt and sickness; an untouchable elite dressed in gold — all of this resonates with clarity in a farming community in Prey Veng. Alarm, relief, merriment, distress. Sovany is gripped. There is a comical subplot which gets roars of laughter from the children. Towards the back of the gathering, the ambience is convivial. People hail their friends, cluster around the stall that sells skewered meat-balls for 500 riel, and catch up on the news. A handful of adults have come to join her now, swinging infants in their arms, laughing at the funny scenes and looking wistful at the tragic ones. One of them places an arm across her back and whispers in her ear. Sovany is shocked, disturbed, and starts to look over her shoulder.

After the final tear has been shed on stage, there are no curtain calls, merely a revving of scooter engines as the crowd shifts towards the village path. The soirée is quickly over. The troupe dismantles, unplugs, cleans up. Lucas steps slowly towards Sovany. A sour smell is rising from the area of the crater. Crickets are screaming at the night. His shirt is wet with perspiration and drizzled with rain. He holds out his hands and moves towards her. She has seen him by now. She does not move from where she stands but looks at him, puzzled, different emotions crossing her face as if she were still watching the play. She is surprised, indignant, delighted, angry.

"Lucas. What are you doing here?"

"I came to find you Sovany."

"Why?"

Now they are face to face. Her face, Sovany's face, a face that is gentle, a face that cares.

"I miss you. I have plans for us. I want us to be together again."

"Why?"

"Walk with me."

The crickets have gone insane and the moon has moved stage left. As she walks, the damp dust clings to her plastic sandals and settles between her toes. She glances at the moon, angrily, then at him, and allows a smile to cross her lips.

"You always were a crazy man Lucas."

"Sovany it is time for us to be together."

"So last time you came to Phnom Penh it was not the right time for you?" Accusing now. "You were in Phnom Penh Lucas and you did not call me. So I knew you did not care about me. Why do you come now if you did not come then? You know you have forgotten me."

"I had a lot of complicated things to settle there. I was not ready." She shoots him a glance of steel. "No not that sort of thing Sovany. Stuff with my work, the government, all to do with history, with a long time ago…"

"Ah. *Khmai Krahamm* work." She grabs his arm to stop her foot sliding into a rut.

"Do you know where Portugal is Sovany?"

"I am too old for your questions now Lucas."

"Do you?"

"Yes. Expensive wine that *barang* drink. Not good wine."

"It's a small country in Europe. A quiet country, smaller than Cambodia but calm like Cambodia. There is a town called Oporto where they make the wine for us foreigners. It is very pretty. I will buy an apartment there and we will live there together and start a family and you will be happy. We will be happy."

"You're crazy."

"Think about it. Come with me to the car. We will drive to a nice hotel and you can spend the night thinking about it."

"Nice hotel? No nice hotels here. Hotels are on the other side, and the ferry is closed now. Here we have only guest houses. Bad places."

"I know I have not been good to you Sovany. I want to make it better for you now."

"You want me to talk in Portugal language? Kralococu cocu cocu? Like this?" She starts giggling. He laughs with her. Retrieves her fallen hand. God it was so small that hand, the wrist so slight, you could bid for it in a porcelain auction in Christie's. There are little hardened places on the palms that were not there before, but it is still her hand, the hand that lay dark against the sheet on those translucent morning awakenings.

"So does it have to be a guest house?"

"I don't want one. No guest house. I am not a bad woman."

"Well let's just talk in the car perhaps. I want you now Sovany. Our future is together."

They walk on. The path grows dark. No more street lights, only the febrile moon and the empty orange sky. She grips more firmly to his arm to prevent herself slipping in the slime. The buildings of the monastery come into view, and the few illuminated windows lend a feeble glow to the scene. He recognises where he has put the car from the configuration of the trees, and there it is, parked and waiting. There seems to be some movement around it, a reflection of light on the rear window that is momentarily blocked by a figure moving swiftly. A monk perhaps, or the monastery guardian. Sovany freezes, both hands suddenly gripping his left arm. She has seen something he has not, sensed a malevolent presence. Then a torch is on, a pencil beam tunnelling to his face. A second torch is switched on, a standard lamp that lights the scene with less precision and more light. Now he can see what is waiting for them.

Bugs. Little men. Ordinary men in sandals and dirty trousers. Six of them. T-shirts or denim tops, except for one, who has a leather jacket and a handgun stuffed in his crotch. All of them in full-face crash helmets, visors down. All carrying sticks. Not farm sticks, not random shafts of wood with a nail through the end, but shiny black truncheons. Government-issue truncheons.

Sovany is paralysed. She stands behind his back, still holding one arm, soundlessly trembling. Lucas does nothing, makes no move. His eyes dart from one figure to another, to the car, to the ground.

The stone.

Still nobody makes a move. Each side waiting for the other.

With his left hand, Lucas releases Sovany's grasp. Fists instantly tighten on truncheons. Sweeping his arm low, Lucas hunkers to the left and grabs the stone. He closes his left hand around it, then the other, advances three paces and brings his two hands, stone first, straight into the visor of the leather jacket man. As hard as he can. There is a satisfying crackle of broken plastic. Leather jacket goes down, his truncheon tumbles. Lucas collects it up then thumps it down with all his bullock force behind the man's head where the helmet no longer covers his neck. Momentary confusion among the rest when the leader is down. Lucas pulls Sovany's arm with a yank that can dislocate it, heaps her body over his broad shoulder and runs for it. Gets the fuck out of there.

But running for it with someone on your shoulder, even a little someone like Sovany, is no option at all with five people chasing you. His knees want to give way. He can't breathe. Only the darkness will save them. Torch beams slice the paddies. Put the woman down. They weave, holding hands, follow a path along the dyke, then double back, traverse the little earthen squares. They can move faster now Sovany is running too. A dry crack and a fizz as a bullet shaves the tree bark. Another shot.

"Lucas. They are shooting me! Stop!"

"No! Don't stop!"

He tugs her again. She doesn't want to come but he is giving her no choice. Head down, back bent, over another dried-up irrigation dyke, cross another prickly field and yes! A chance! A crater. Jesus fuck almighty, hold tight he tells her as they tumble and bump down the steep banks of the hollow, blind as bats, hold tight Sovany. Don't make any noise. Wham. A hard lump of turf strikes his rump and knocks his spine. Kicks the wind out of his lungs. Water. They are in water. Going down, but slowly now, softly, up to their shoulders in putrid lotus swamp. They hold each other. She is trembling violently. So is he, he realises. He holds her tighter. There is something wonderful in this B-52 sludge, in the embrace of these leaves and flowers. Clench her. Torchlight flickers above. Head down. Voices. Angry voices, all nasal and high-pitched like truly angry Cambodians. The light explores the crater but it is the weak torch, not the strong one. A random shot in the swamp, a spit of water. The people go away. The voices recede.

"Remember Portugal" he whispers.

"Fuck your Portugal" she whispers back.

They lie in the stench for a long time. A very long time. He knows it is a long time because dawn has begun to break when they start to move. They pull themselves out and start to scale the steep bank. He slips back down and she loses her footing because she is below him and now they are back in the ooze again. She looks about her. This way, she says, and they work their way to the other side of the pool. She points out a little path, barely cut in the flanks of the earth but better than just scaling it like an idiot. People come down here she says, they need a path. And what in fuck's name would they come down here for, he asks. He is spent, exhausted, can take no more. They come down here to gather lotus of course. Follow me. She leads him, step by step, out of the bomb crater.

When they push their heads over the rim, they see the six people waiting for them. The men have their helmets pitched backwards on their heads like Grecian heroes after a battle, visors up, but there is nothing noble in their faces. One glance shows Lucas that they are ordinary people, as ordinary as they come, hired hands who are paid to slaughter a sow or beat down a man or maim a woman, whatever pays. They are smoking together. One of the men has gashes on his cheek where Lucas splintered his visor. The plastic has torn his flesh. When Lucas registers that the group is still there, it is if his courage has fallen from his chest and sunk in the mud below. He has no more attack in him. None at all. This is where the brave story ends. The head down, shoulders in, close your eyes and brave it for England — it's all spent. Done. Real life has caught up.

The men have seen their two victims and they rise slowly. They are tired, fed up that all this has taken quite so long. They are angered in a smouldering, self-indulgent way. This has taken all night, and now they deserve some kind of reward. The foreigner has wasted their time and the time has come to hurt him badly. How? Well, we will see how won't we, Sovany?

One of them walks across slowly, still smoking, in his direction. The man flicks the cigarette on to the dry ground. He stands above Lucas. Is this the number two, Lucas wonders, the master-sergeant who does the doing at splinterface's bidding? Come on then. Do it. There is no fight in Lucas. No fight at all. The master-sergeant makes a little trot like a rugby player executing a quick conversion and boots Lucas hard in the liver. Lucas tumbles, and gets another much harder kick that feels as if it has cracked a couple of ribs. Torn every strand of muscle down one side. Then a shove in the face with the sandal sole that turns him into a cascading sack of potatoes. He is rolling down the crater bank, and falls deep in the black water, kicking lotus stalk and reed mesh, coming up for air with a spit and a burst of lung. He knows he is out of the way now; he is an afterthought. It's Sovany they want to hurt.

Sovany. Sovany. Lucas knows this is going to be bad. Not the kind of thing you want to watch. You get a good idea anyway from the screaming, that pig-being-killed kind of screaming, but something pushes him to be there in the slaughter with Sovany. So he levers himself up, like the kind of sinister insect a child wants to drown but which fights back, insists on staying alive and the child lets it live for the sheer entertainment. He falls; the pain in his side is too great. Ten minutes later he claws his way up the bank and falls down again and all the while the yelling and screaming continue. She is howling like the fowls do when the badger has gnawed its way into the roost and is starting to chew the first hen. Out of control. Crawl up the B-52 hole, slowly, inch by inch, and maybe in thirty minutes you will be there, in time to do something for this girl and take her to Europe and make her a home with nice pillows and Egyptian cotton sheets. Some hope.

He scrambles, upwards, inch by inch. Yard by yard. The others can't be bothered with him. Sovany is occupying their attention. She's more fun, let's face it. She's a lot more fun. He makes progress, slow and stupid progress, but progress anyway, but before he finally gets to the top there is silence. No more screaming. The dawn is so silent that he thinks the men have gone. Gone? Gone. We are going to be alright then?

For a while he thinks that it really might be all alright after all. We can all go home and forget about it. Lesson learnt. He rises to the top of the rim.

There is nothing there. The sugar palm trunk, and that is all. Lucas hauls himself from the crater and crawls to the tree, and using the trunk to support himself, stands up. He sees the nearby mound of a termite nest, grey and crumbly. Beside the termite mound a dash of colour catches his eye, and he hobbles over to inspect. Rags: the shredded remains of Sovany's cotton dress.

Oh God. Are there any more discoveries to be made? Further down the path a bra has been strapped around a palm trunk, as if this was all merely some nutty student party. A chance for a really good laugh.

He vomits. There are houses down the road. People are already rising from sleep. If he can get to the houses he can ask. But his ribs are fractured and he is almost unable to walk. The pain of retching almost makes him faint. And when he does get to the first house, which like all the others is built on stilts, the woman sitting beneath it trots up her wooden staircase and locks the door behind her. Doors slam at the neighbouring houses. Shutters bang shut. A mother hastily herds her children upstairs. He is not wanted here. He is not wanted at all. There is nothing for it. Sovany has gone.

As long as he can find the strength to get to the car. He throws up again, his insides straining, and he yelps with the pain. The keys are still in his pocket and though the remote button is drowned the manual lock clunks open. Lucas revs up the car, and sets off slowly. The dust path is agony with the car lurching to left and right. Once on the main road he guns the Mitsubishi straight towards the river and catches the first ferry of the morning over to the other side, in the direction of Phnom Penh.

He gets to the hotel room and stands for an eternity in the shower, while his own digestive system voids itself as best it can. He sits afterwards on his bed, pale, trembling and dizzy. He needs to feel emptied, it helps with the trembling and the waves of cold that sweep through him, and he returns to the bathroom to vomit and shit again.

The best he can do, the greatest act of kindness, is to leave well alone. Go away. Never come back. That is what he is still trying to tell himself when he boards his flight at Pochentong, never to return.

V

Mission a failure. Returning as scheduled.

That gauntlet they make you run at Terminal 4. Faces alive with expectation as the passengers come through, the tour guides and the cab drivers holding up name cards like priests raising the host, Costa's coffee behind the multitude clunking out lattes and double mochas. Poised at the end, leaning gently on the rail, too superior to join the throng, she waits. Consciously retro, she wears sunglasses and a silk scarf swept back over her neck as women used to in Italian films.

What a surprise. What a very nice surprise. That is not entirely dishonest. True, he had made sure she knew the time of arrival, which was not the subtlest of invitations, but for Elise to actually take the step of deciding to come (after all Lewisham to Heathrow is quite a trot, isn't it?) well, that took ... something. Oh, screw it Lucas, she has brought the car which you didn't know she owned and you don't have to take the Piccadilly Line and she is a star in her firmament, a rather distant galaxy that doesn't — clearly doesn't — obey the rules of our own, but thank the Lord for the small mercies he dispenses, including the fact that she got her tenner in to the car park machine before he did, fumbling with all the wrong currencies.

"I got your message."

"Elise. I can't tell you what this means to me. It was an exhausting flight." As flights tend to be when you hit the liqueur trolley at 35,000 feet. But if anybody knows any other way to sleep away the pain of cattle class with two cracked ribs, dysfunctional intestines and a face that looks like a punctured football, they are welcome to make suggestions.

"My God, Lucas, what on earth did they do to you? We need to get you to a hospital."

"Not today. Please."

Elise is a confident driver, it turns out, and they are soon on the

M4 and heading into the city, and by the time the road has turned into Marylebone, Lucas is only half way through his story. By the time they are clogged in central London, he has told her what happened and she has to pull in by someone's front garden while he throws up in their lavender bushes. Retching and straining on an empty stomach, he studies the dark brown mulch in the flower bed which reminds him of the Cambodian seed he still has in his living room. Long before they reach the bit in Fulham where you have the Blue Moon dry cleaners and the Edwardian pub, he has finished his narrative and has locked himself into silence. It is all too unspeakable. Nightmares with no words belong to illiterate Cambodians and not to English people with flats in Fulham and unsalted butter in the fridge.

"If what you are telling me is true" she concludes "you are going to need to stay away from that part of the world for a very long time. Unless you want them to do Sovany's sister as well."

They park in one of the side lanes and he humps his luggage on his shoulder, drops it, and she picks it up for him. He tells her to come up for a drink. She dumps his bags down while he clonks about in the fridge for a bottle of wine, apologises that he won't be joining her on the white, he is aching for a cup of coffee. They relax, finally, on the sofa. Lucas weeps quietly, then gets up to attend to his bowels.

Elise, he senses, is feeling almost victorious. She sits legs crossed (she is in jeans and flats today) and radiates a kind of pride. She has a victim on her hands, a victim of Democratic Kampuchea, and she is comfortable with that because the territory is familiar. She is a close friend by now; they have shared thoughts on things that matter deeply. He feels a far greater need for her than he ever has before. It is true that she is proprietorial about her suffering, has worded her deeds of entitlement in a way that allows her to shuffle the facts around as she pleases. Instead of picking holes in her arguments, as he has been trained to do, all he wants to do is join her in her deeper pain, as if victimhood will protect him from the evil he has seen done. And abetted.

"Cheers." Coffee cup chinks with glass of Sainsbury's Sauvignon.

The coffee is actually helping. You wouldn't think so, but it is. As his belly quietens, so the pictures fade by one degree in his mind. That degree of comfort is what it takes to claw his way back to the place he belongs, the place of prosecutorial inquisition. Something tells him that if he can find Elise guilty in some way, then he will be less in need of her, less a party culpable by association with her country, whatever it is called. He knows what to find Elise guilty of. Dishonesty. Fabulating. Concealing the facts. If he can catch her out on that count he will step back and maybe feel cleaner.

He knows he likes Elise, a hundred years too old though she may be. Her face is drawn with a light touch, she is exquisitely brittle while actually being as strong as a fire-iron; she has refined hands; her eyes are full of knowledge. If he kissed her he would taste the wine which would be much nicer than this sour taste of coffee. He gets up from the sofa, runs a hand through his thick hair. His face is grey, the flesh of a sick man. He really doesn't want to do this, but it has to be done.

"By the way, Elise, I didn't tell you. I dropped in on Makara again."

"Oh. Good. How is she? I hope you didn't meet that husband. He's best avoided."

"He came in at the end. Actually I skedaddled pretty quick after he made an appearance."

"Wise man. Yes, sure. One more drop won't do any harm."

He tops her up and poses the bottle carefully on the oak table. Studies the label — bright green. New Zealand.

"She has a photo up on a ledge. It's of you all. The family; no Makara, I guess she was the one taking the picture. She said it was taken on the day that Che Guevara was killed in Bolivia. Sometime in 1967."

"Makara. She always did have a memory for those things."

"It's a lovely photo actually. A beautiful beach holiday in the sunshine."

[231]

"Happy days. We were all very innocent then."

"Elise, your father in the photograph is running his left hand through his hair. A bit like this. It's not that the hair is untidy or anything, it's obviously a kind of mannerism he has adopted."

"I don't remember. It's too long ago. Do you have a cigarette by any chance?"

In we go. Hold tight everybody.

"Chen, Makara's husband, stroked his head in exactly the same way. A head that was precisely the same shape as your father's. Older, but the same head. Eyes that stared in the same way. The same pivoting of the shoulders."

Elise is extracting the cigarette from the packet. She stops what she is doing while the cigarette is only half out. She gazes at the box and pushes the papery tube back in again, very slowly. She closes the pack. She turns her face to Lucas, a face marked by despair and, for a brief moment, by entreaty as well.

"I have outstayed my welcome Lucas."

She rises, turns towards the front door.

"You haven't finished your wine."

She rotates her head towards the glass on the table, then shakes it as if denying a charge, looks back at him.

"No I haven't, have I?" She grabs the glass, gulps, splashes her cashmere pullover. "Can I go now?"

"No you can't."

He lays his hands across her shoulders. She comes slowly towards him and lets him take her in his arms. He holds her for a short time before a knife of pain cuts his ribs. After that she sits back down on the sofa and returns to the cigarette packet.

"What is it you want to know, Lucas?"

"Am I right? Am I wrong?"

She laughs a dry, un-amused laugh. It is a while before she speaks again. There is a lot of work with the cigarette lighter, meticulous studying of the fingernails.

"Of course you are right. You know you are right."

Wait. Then a new cigarette. Then a speech.

"Not everything over there is quite the same as here. In Asia our way with families is, you know, rather freer. You have your nuclear families here, mother, father, two children, but it's more amorphous with us. People come and people go, the shape of things changes. People, aunts and uncles, cousins, bring up children who are not their own. The load is shared in a, a bigger kind of basket. In the beginning we, we... started off as that western kind of family, then Cambodia stepped in and asserted its traditional rights to do things its own way. Cambodia was Makara you might say."

She is coming at it from quite a distance, he thinks. But he is giving no prompting this time. Besides, she is talking as if she has prepared for this. As if she had been waiting for a long time to tell him this.

"I don't know if you guessed, Lucas. Father was terribly taken with Makara. It wasn't that he was tired of mother, I think he cared for her deeply, very deeply, but he was quite helpless when Makara was there. And mother sort of came to realise that the family had silently changed. Nobody said anything. People kept quiet. As children we were not even aware of what was going on. When Makara was pregnant, we were told she was going away for a while to look after her sick father in Battambang, and off she went to Battambang, and then mother went to Phnom Penh and we all stayed at the beach with father. We were both just children then. So when father said there was going to be another baby we thought it was the most natural thing in the world, and when it was Makara who spent most of her time looking after Vuthy instead of mother, well why not, she was there to help us wasn't she? Vuthy was one of the family. More than that. We adored Vuthy, she was such a lovely child. We forgave her anything, and I can tell you she could be very naughty that girl. She smiled her way through her days, and she never complained or cried. So we just carried on like that. Vuthy was just Vuthy. A bit more Khmer than us but nobody gave a toss. And the family got more loose — cousins from Siem Riep who came to study in Phnom Penh and who became part of the household for one or two years, you know, there was not a sense of privacy or ownership of our parents because they belonged to a wider family. It was a happy thing really. Father would always lecture us about sharing things, the fruits of the earth were given to all mortals to enjoy, don't be a dog in the manger, if Han or Rithy or Lucien don't have enough money for schoolbooks then give them yours, and I admired him for that, it was different. I looked up to him. He had a very definite attitude towards private property, he didn't really appreciate it. I don't know where he derived his philosophy from."

She takes a contemplative pull on the cigarette, lowers her voice to a smoky whisper. "Darling little Vuthy...what a wicked girl you were." She continues, more assertive.

"Tepp on the other hand was not so sure about all of this. He liked the traditional side of father, he liked the soldier in him, he wasn't convinced about love your neighbour. He was much more into bomb your neighbour. He was in seventh heaven when father would dress up in his uniform, teach him about the rifles and all that, show him his medals. I remember once they went to an air show together in Pochentong. It was a boy's outing, and after that he would talk of nothing but the Dassault fighters and weapons systems and all that stuff that boys like. He was more conservative than his parents in a way. He wanted a mother and a father and at a pinch a sister, but he felt threatened by the liberal approach, with Makara as mother number two. But they kept up appearances, mind you, she never slept with father in the home, the place in the marital bed was always mother's. I honestly didn't realise how much mother was sacrificing, how much she was suffering, until I was quite a bit older. Until things were really starting to get dangerous in Phnom Penh and we were being shelled and shot from the other side of the river. And then with mother we would go on our errands, helping those refugees, and it was dangerous you know, there were mutilated bodies in the street, people broken in pieces, and that was when she told me that whatever her marriage was, it didn't add up to happiness and if I did one thing in life it was never to let myself become dominated by a husband."

"Advice you have wisely followed" comments Lucas.

"I damn well hope so" she replies.

The telephone rings. An intermission.

"Mr Lucas Bellwether?"

"Becky. What can I do for you?"

She has an engagement for him. He turns it down.

Elise has gone to stand by the window while he is on the phone. He takes up position beside her and they look down on the roofs of the red buses lining up alongside the common. It is calming, in a gently hypnotic way, to watch the traffic go by. People whose lives look empty, an emptiness that he envies. There is a woman sitting at the bus stop but she does not seem to want to catch a bus. She is content just to be seated at the stop. When another woman places herself at the opposite end of the bench, the first one engages her in conversation. It has rained a bit, but not much. The road shines as if it is made of new tyre rubber. Further down the street to their left, there is a high-end vegetable shop where everything is organic, the butter is from France, and the bread is baked daily round the clock. The lady who runs it is piling some purple cabbages on her pavement stall. Elise asks him if he shops there and he says yes, more than he cares to admit, it's dreadfully pricy but it's dead convenient.

Dead convenient, she repeats.

He feels a rise of prosecutorial prowess. "Can you explain something to me Elise? I am quite muddled by all the things you have told me so let me just get one thing clear. Are you trying to tell me that Vann Ang, your father, was some kind of Marxist?"

"He read a lot of books."

"What do you mean by that?" Better now. He is getting back into his stride.

"He read a lot. It wasn't exactly common in those days to be an army officer and enjoy reading books. I don't know what he was reading. I was too young to remember. But he had been brought up by his family to think. His father was an old Issarak warrior who fought against the French back in the 40s and 50s. Anyone who thought in those days, who looked at what they saw around them after one hundred years of being a colony could only come to one conclusion really. Which was that the entire system needed turning upside down and reinventing."

"These were not views that endeared him to the military establishment he served."

"No doubt. But people are complicated Lucas. They also need to make a living. You can't expect everybody's lives to follow easy patterns. It was more in his head than his heart, perhaps."

"And that is where these ideas stayed?"

"No. Remember 1967. There was an uprising in Samlaut, a peasant rebellion, and father was involved in repressing it. The peasants attacked a few army depots, killed a few people, stole the rifles, that sort of thing, and the punishment they got was savage. Father's infantry were paid a sum of money for each enemy head they brought in, so some of his soldiers would go out and find farmers working the rice fields and hack off their heads for the price of a bowl of rice. He told us, Tepp and I, of peasants' heads stacked up like coconuts. He was disgusted by that. It was a turning point for him. At the same time as he told us about Guevara, who was wandering around the jungle in Bolivia and dodging the CIA. And then killed. But it was only a lot later, a great deal later, that Tepp told me that father was acting as an informer for the rebellion. Actually spying for the Khmer Rouge machine."

"Wow. Different story altogether."

"Yes. Different story altogether. And one that Tepp could never accept. He told me he nursed a terrible grudge against his father for spying for the enemy. He was deeply disappointed in him. It went against all his conservative, straightforward principles which he said he had inherited from father and which father was betraying."

"And, fast forward if you don't mind — he tops up the Sauvignon, pours himself one too — Tepp must have been a very confused man, or boy, when he was forced to…, to execute your father (he pauses, in case the memory makes her weep, but it does not) and, afterwards, I don't know, a complete wreck."

Elise lights a cigarette. She smokes it, indifferent to any impulse to continue the discussion. She even opens the heavy art book on the table, which falls open on a 13th century sandstone torso.

"Look at her" she murmurs, entranced. "Lakshmi. She is stunning isn't she? The stone is so gorgeous, grey, but with that ochre layering below the surface. Look at those eyebrows, meeting in the middle, sort of Frida Kahlo, but without that Mexican battiness, more like an archer's bow. This is human flesh that invites your caress, Lucas. This plummeting torso, it's what the French call *la chute des reins*."

Lucas gets up and fetches a clean ashtray. He goes into the kitchen. His fatigue has moved to a higher plane of wakefulness where the mind has interdicted the body's plea for sleep. He shuffles the frozen bricks stacked in his freezer, selects one of Ro's home-made lasagnes and without even consulting Elise he puts the oven on to pre-heat. This woman doesn't want to be rushed; fine by me. He returns to the living room and asks Elise if she wants to check the news. It is eight o'clock. She declines; says she prefers the radio to the TV. Television gives her headaches. Then she returns to her tale.

"He told me it was as if he had hit his head with an axe. He said that to me and I believed him. That he had killed him. But the truth was that Tepp did not kill his father. It was one of their tests. There was no bullet in the pistol. The gun just clicked and father was alive. They believed in smashing all family bonds, you know. A true revolutionary had no feelings for his siblings. His only love was for the revolution. It was quite common for them to get children to shoot their parents. Sometimes for real, sometimes not. Families were anathema. They were to be expunged from history."

"When did he tell you he did not kill his father?"

"Later. In Paris."

"And Nary?"

"Oh Tepp killed Nary all right. Nary had humiliated him to the core by forcing him to go through the mock execution. I didn't need to persuade my brother to kill Nary. He went straight and did it. Blew his head off right there in the US of A."

"So you never said you wanted Nary's head on a silver platter."

"No. Sorry. I didn't actually." She meditates, seated upright. The oven is hot so Lucas puts in the lasagne. Forty minutes. Boils water for the frozen beans. He remarks that truth seems to be a tradeable commodity in Asia. She gives him a cramped smile.

"You see Lucas, I think Tepp did kill his father. In his mind he was finished with him. He just blew him away, got rid of him. A philanderer and a spy. Which was worse in Tepp's estimation? Who knows. But after that awful moment in his life, he decided to forget his father had ever existed. It was too complicated. Don't underestimate the exhaustion of simply surviving a regime like Democratic Kampuchea. You are physically spent, but mentally and spiritually drained as well. The mind has no time for complications, dual loyalties, cover stories, anything like that. Tepp was absolutely spent. He simply cut off all relations with his father after that."

"And so did you."

"Yes. I had my own reasons. To do with mother."

"Explain."

"You can work it out for yourself."

She turns the pages of the book to a new photo. A bronze female deity, with wings and a tail curled in an S shape. The tail has a sharp spike at the end. Delight registers in her eyes.

"But Ang kept an eye on his son" adds Lucas. "After 1975 I assume he worked openly for the regime."

"Yes. I accept that. Tepp would certainly have been worked to death and tossed in a pit somewhere if father hadn't moved him to Kampong Chhnang and then, I assume at least, had him included in the pardon list. His father did not desert him."

"Didn't he help have him killed in Myanmar?"

"Father? No Lucas, he did not. That was Nary's children. Sambath, and Thirith pulling strings."

He pauses. "I notice you still call him father."

"He is my father. I have only one father. It is simply that I do not wish him to be included in my life. That's all."

"Don't you miss him? Don't you ever want to go and see him?"

"Lucas there are people in this life who are born with what is called a good heart. You have to understand that I am not one of them. I am not able to wish for the sentimental end that you have in mind."

"No. Clearly not. But there is one thing that intrigues me."

"Really? Only one?"

He ignores the rebuff. "Yes. The fact is, you led me to him."

"Perhaps. Yes, yes, perhaps I did. Father... I do hope he is contented with Makara. I admit to that." She pauses, looks towards the window, before abruptly resuming. "But now you must understand that you can never go back to that country again. Ever. I am sorry you had to learn all these things the hard way."

In the kitchen, he thuds the lasagne into two pieces with a plastic spade and serves it with the beans which he butters and peppers. It looks rather meagre fare so he uncorks a bottle of Montepulciano and changes the glasses.

"Oh my. The maestro does it again."

"It qualifies more as a snack than a meal."

"I don't think so." She eats with relish. The conversation ceases.

All of a sudden, he is no longer interested to pry into Elise's life. The wine is taking hold of him, flesh and spirit, washing over him that grandiose sensation of simply being back in his home. He is no longer planning anything. He pours himself another glass. Does he want her? She can go; she can stay. She can do what she wants. She can hold her peace or she can confess to telling him lies. She can say she was a Vietnamese camp commandant for all it matters to him at this stage. Suddenly, he has had enough. Other people's itineraries, the botched weft of that messy rag that we all make of our lives, all those tatty bits hanging off and none of the patterns properly aligned: he no longer cares. What point is there in making any effort at all? He will never return to Cambodia, they have made quite sure of that, so why care about any of its histories anymore?

Elise takes the plates and he hears her washing them in the sink. There is an exultant look about the woman now, as if months of planning have somehow reached fruition. He asks her if she wants something to wash down the dinner, an Armagnac or a Laphroaig, and she says no, let's not bother. All I really need is a bit of good company Lucas, and she leads him towards the bedroom like a dog on a lead and undoes his shirt for him.

When he stirs in the morning, he sees her black hair falling all around the pillow in swirls and cascades. For a long time he watches an artery vibrating through the whiteness of her neck. Without waking her, he rises from the duvet and walks naked into the living room. That is where, in the morning light, he sees something that he had not noticed the previous evening. The seed in the glass has sprouted. Curling across the little table is a vigorous green tendril of Cambodian strychnine.